WHAT WAS TRUE

WHAT WAS TRUE

UNDENIABLE TRILOGY - BOOK THREE

JOLIE MOORE

MOORE DIGITAL
MEDIA INC

This edition published by
Moore Digital Media Inc
1125 N Fairfax Ave, Unit 46071
West Hollywood, California 90046

Cover: Najla Qamber Designs
Photo: Jenn LeBlanc Studio Smexy
eISBN: 978-1-64414-017-8
ISBN: 978-1-64414-034-5

CHAPTER ONE
ISABELLA

THE FLIGHT to Rome had been long. Eleven hours from Los Angeles. Even in first class, it hadn't been the best experience of my life. The lay-flat bed and free pajamas had helped. But fine (airplane) food and alcohol had done nothing for the jet lag.

Sleep couldn't be bought.

I didn't want to miss Daniel's private jet, but I did. With him, there had been little jet lag. Though the hit to my circadian rhythm had probably been masked by the excitement of being a twenty-year-old rolling with a billionaire baller.

The flight from Rome to Bari had been on a smaller jet with tiny seats. Now that I was north of thirty, I noticed these kinds of things. I was happy to get off and get my bag after the second plane landed.

Once I was in the terminal, I took my first glimpse of Italy. Bari was a tiny airport. I ran to the ladies' room before women could form a line. The toilet had no seat. Just the ceramic bowl. I'd seen the same in Rome. Normally I'd care about that kind of thing, but my full bladder overcame my inner germaphobe.

When I emerged from the bathroom, passing the line of women I'd beaten to the facilities, I was surprised to see that the "Welcome to Puglia" sign on the wall had a hashtag.

Italy had come into the social media age, I guess. The way Mama had talked about the "old country," it was disconcerting to see that the old had become new, with Instagrammable spots and high-speed Wi-Fi.

After a few minutes, one of the baggage carousels started turning. My cases were the first out. I stacked them on a free cart and took myself toward the Nothing to Declare exit. I'd already done the customs and passport thing in Rome.

There were lots of men with dark hair, dark eyes, and olive skin holding up signs. I let out the breath I felt like I'd been holding since I'd boarded that flight at LAX. Even though it was achingly unfamiliar, I felt at home in a way I hadn't since I'd left Philadelphia. I'd fit right in here with people who looked like me. Squaring my tired shoulders, I walked up to the guy with the "Aconi" sign.

"*Buon pomeriggio*! You speak Italian?" he asked as he folded the sign and edged me away from the cart. His forearm muscles bunched as he squeezed the handle and wove through the crowd like a running back.

"No. Sorry," I answered. Even though I was in Adidas and not the kind of heels Daniel had preferred while flying, I didn't catch up to the driver until he paused at the crosswalk.

"Aconi is Italian, no?" He was on the move again, dodging cars. I had no idea if pedestrians had right of way here. Even if they did, I suspected I'd have to keep a close eye on traffic.

"Italian from Philly." At his blank look, I went on. "Philadelphia, in the United States."

"I don't speak much English," he said in heavily accented English. He paused at a small silver hatchback and opened the trunk lid and piled my luggage in. He closed the lift gate with a slam and opened the back door for me. I folded my big American myself into the tiny Italian backseat. It was a couple of minutes before he got into the driver's seat. He started the car, used a stick shift to get us moving. After he paid for parking, he turned back to me.

"You go to Gallipoli?"

"Yes." I nodded vigorously, the universal sign of affirmation when language was a barrier.

"*Strada Provinciale?*" he asked while taking a sharp turn. I took that as my opportunity to buckle myself in. I didn't want to die in a car accident before I finished what I'd come here to do.

"Sure. Yes. That's it," I said hoping indeed that *was* it, nodding again, meeting his warm brown eyes in the rearview mirror.

I'd lived with my Italian parents, one fresh off the boat. I'd lived in Philly's little Italy, but somehow this driver's Italian was so much more...Italian. If we were in Philly, I would have totally come back at him for messing with me with the over-the-top accent. Something told me this guy was not at all joking.

"About an hour. Okay," he said. Then he turned on music, which could have been any station in Philadelphia with its mixture of R&B and rock and roll.

"Thanks." I laid my head against the rest and watched

the scenery roll by. It was like California only with groves of olive instead of orange trees. Green plants against a dusty brown background. I don't know what I'd expected, but I closed my eyes against the familiar.

"'Scusi? Signora?"

My eyes snapped open with a start, zeroing in on the digital clock on his dash. I'd slept that hour away. The driver was looking back at me expectantly. I looked out of the windows and noticed we weren't moving. In fact, we were in front of a large driveway. The ten-foot-wide gates etched with "Masseria San Rocco" were closed.

I shuffled through my huge red plaid tote and fished out a picture I'd printed. I looked from it to the gates and back. This was it.

"Si, si," I said, nodding.

Satisfied, the driver turned off the car and came around to my door, pulling it open. My jet-lagged self practically spilled out onto the sandy driveway. I did my best to pick myself up and try to look perky. I hefted my bag and strode toward the gate beside the drive. Flicking through my phone, I found the six-digit code the property manager had messaged me. He'd promised someone would meet me in person within an hour or so of my arrival, so I texted to let him know I was here.

With a squeak, the gate gave way. I pushed it open and followed the grassy path to the door. Another code and that was open as well. The house was cool and deadly silent. Thick walls quieted the traffic and beach noise that had been noticeable in the drive.

"Signora? Where to put?" The driver shrugged, a hot-pink designer monogram bag in each hand. I tried not to cringe at the nearly neon suitcases. Daniel had bought them for me in college during a surprise trip to Paris. I'd been so thrilled to pick them out at the Louis Vuitton store on the Champs-Élysées. I'd felt so light walking out of the store with nothing heavier than a new wallet in my hands, only to have all four pieces hand delivered to our hotel suite at the Four Seasons just hours later. Money had felt like liberty back then, before it had become a prison.

I looked at the living room, its tile floor beige, the walls white, the ceilings natural wood beams. Self-doubt nearly choked off my reply. Either I was on a true path of self-exploration, or I was about to make the worst mistake of my life.

"Here is fine." I pushed out.

He lined all four pieces up against the wall. I fished in my bag for some euros, gave him a fifty, and nodded my thanks.

"*Grazie, signora.*" He held up the orange note, then tucked it into his shirt pocket with a smile. "Enjoy your time in Italia."

I followed the smiling driver to the front door and closed it behind him.

If there was one thing I could not stand, it was the sound of silence. I prowled around the rental house until I found a device I could plug my phone into. I fished through my bag, trying to unearth my cell from the change of clothes, makeup in several Ziploc bags, and the other electronics and cords I'd carried on. How it had sunk to the bottom within minutes was a mystery I'd save for another day.

When I couldn't lay hands on the slim, sturdy block of metal and glass, I tried not to panic, though my heart sped up. If I'd dropped it outside and it broke, I was sunk. It wasn't like

L.A., where I could walk a block to the Apple store and replace it in less than an hour.

I needed the pulse of a drumbeat, the thump of bass. Without it, I'd drown under the weight of my own thoughts, regrets, recriminations.

I only had thirty Xanax on hand. I wasn't ready to blow through those quite yet. I'd need to save that chemical balm for my first encounter with my half-brother, and the father who'd walked out on me because, without his blood, I hadn't been enough.

My stomach turned at that thought. The pill bottles were at the top of my bag. Klonopin in one. Xanax in another. Ambien in a third. It was the L.A. cocktail. What so many of us used to get through a day and night without being swallowed up by uncomfortable feelings.

I pushed the bottles aside. I didn't want them. Not yet. For now, music would help drown out the feelings. I'd save the pills for night, when the rushing thoughts made sleep nearly impossible.

For now, Nirvana.

I knelt on the floor and gently turned the bag on its side, spilling the contents on the travertine.

A wooden box was the first thing to hit the floor. The impact jimmied the little lock and the contents spilled out.

As it always did, this box stopped me dead in my tracks. I'd picked it up from one of those hippie shops on Melrose that sold crystals and incense. It looked so innocent on the outside, carved, painted wood. The contents, they got me every single time.

Even under pain of death, I'd never admit to anyone that

I had a sentimental side. That I'd ever had keepsakes of any kind. Those girls at Owen, copycats of the ones I'd met at Woodward Tillman, who'd scrapbooked every freaking event, had made me nauseous and practically given me hives.

There was one teeny-tiny part of me that had envied them, though. That had copied them. Hence this box.

One by one, I looked at the small pieces of my past that littered the floor.

Jake's eighth-grade schedule. The paper was soft at the creases, the blue ink nearly faded. I'd taken it when he hadn't been looking a few weeks into the school year. I'd felt comforted knowing where he was in the middle school, which had seemed huge to me at the time. I liked knowing that if I needed him, I could find him.

The EB at the top of a receipt threw me for a second. EB Games. Wow, that was a blast from the past. I wondered if they were even still in business. I assumed most people bought their games from big box stores these days.

The only letter I could read was "Z."

The Legend of Zelda. God, we'd played that for hours. That's when it had probably started, I think. My mom's affair. There was no other explanation for their permissiveness.

I pushed the paper aside and took out the ticket stubs from the Led Zeppelin concert.

I wanted to laugh and cry at the same time. Every good memory was tinged with bad.

Every single one.

The gas station receipts from Connecticut. The napkin from that restaurant we'd eaten at in Meriden. If other people's clouds had silver linings, mine had black ones.

I picked it all up and shoved it back into the box. I didn't even know why in the hell I was keeping any of it. I was in Italy to clean up my past, not wallow in it. Maybe I'd shove this pile of paper and cardboard into the little fire pit I'd seen in the pictures online.

I closed my eyes, opened them. I needed to get out of my head.

I needed to have a look at this place. Make sure it was like it looked online before any refund period passed. I nearly tripped on the phone that disappeared and reappeared like Houdini. I picked it up, tapped and scrolled until I found the Screaming Trees.

Fuck Nirvana.

It wasn't enough.

I seated it in place. I was running my fingers along the buttons when the sound of someone speaking stopped me in my tracks.

"Are you the new guest?" The question came from a voice that was American. A voice that sounded deadly familiar.

I turned away from the buttons and dials on the Bluetooth speaker and spun around as slowly as I could because I was afraid of who I was going to see.

It was him. I wasn't ready. I thought I'd have more time. I thought I'd be able to control our meeting. I'd chosen this place next door to his on purpose.

So he couldn't pretend I wasn't in Italy.

So he couldn't pretend I didn't exist.

So he couldn't ignore me.

"Isabella?" he asked when I'd turned enough that he could see my features.

"I...uh...Daddy?" I turned fully. I had no choice but to face the past—face the man I'd thought was my father for the first twelve years of my life—without the benefit of anti-anxiety medication. Rationing out Xanax suddenly felt like the world's stupidest decision, right behind the one to make this trip.

Damn.

"What are *you* doing here?" He looked like he'd seen a ghost. His normally olive skin was pale beneath a healthy tan. "I was doing a favor for the owner. I live next door," he explained. His hands, those big strong hands I remembered, were thrown wide in surprise, shock, awe. I felt like I was the bomb dropped onto an unsuspecting Middle East mosque.

"I know. The about-you-living-there part. Not about you being here now. Not that part." I faltered. My brain couldn't process the fact of him standing here. Not all at once. He was here, but he was in my memories, too. My very first one of him catching me when I nearly fell into one of the little lakes at Fairmount Park when I was only three.

Another when he rescued one of my favorite glitter sandals from the banks of the Schuylkill River by lowering himself over the railing to some huge, slippery black rocks. I'd been four that time.

The man here now was so much older than I remembered. I wasn't the only one who'd changed in all those years.

"You're. Wow. You're a grown woman," he started. "You look different and the same at the same time. I...wow...Arturo wouldn't recognize you."

I guess I'd changed as well.

"Where is he?" I asked. My father hadn't been the only one I'd missed. When my family had broken up, I'd lost my brother as well. It was probably the reason I'd leaned on Jake so hard. I'd substituted one boy for another. Only Jake hadn't been a brother. My feelings had changed from fraternal to romantic in the space of a year.

"Who?" he asked. For a moment, it was like he'd read my thoughts. That Jake had somehow materialized. My eyes scanned the room, but I was pretty sure we were still alone.

"Arturo?" My voice did a definite uptalk thing Daniel would have hated. But sheer panic welled up for a long second. I'd always assumed Arturo was alive, well, and kicking here in Italy. If something had happened or changed, I'd always thought Mama would have broken her silence to at least tell me that. But maybe not. We hadn't spoken more than a handful of times in the last few years.

She'd made her choices.

I'd made mine.

Most of those choices had been bad.

"He works in Bari," my...father...step-father...Francis answered.

"The place where I landed. That town?" I asked. It was easier than addressing even the simple question of who we were to each other.

My brother's dad. Maybe that was it. Maybe that's all he was to me.

The only person who knew Francis Aconi wasn't my real dad, besides my mother of course, was Jake. I'd never told anyone else about my origins or the humiliating way

I'd discovered them. Wasn't exactly first-date conversation. Not that I'd had a lot of dates. Either Daniel or Jake had occupied my thoughts, if not my time, for far too many years.

"Yes. Bari," Francis answered, snapping me back to the present.

He didn't say another word.

Neither did I.

I openly stared. He looked like the man I'd lived with until he'd gone away. The only difference was that his hair was gray. Not the only difference, but the one that stood out the most. The one that made him look the least like the father of my childhood. The rest was so achingly familiar it made my heart hurt in a way it hadn't in so very long.

Even his cologne hadn't changed. It was a spicy, earthy scent that had lingered in his chair long after he'd gone. I'd sat in only that chair until I came home one day and the smell was gone. Mama had shampooed it, obliterating him in a single afternoon.

"How have your last twenty-two years and three months been?" Not that I'd been counting. But of course I'd been counting.

"Was it that long?" He shrugged as if we were talking about not having seen each other in a week or a month.

"How could you just leave like that?" I'd wanted to ask the question later. After I'd slept, gotten over my jet lag, had a chance to get a lay of the land. Not today of all days, when I wasn't the least bit mentally prepared for the answer.

"It wasn't about you."

I wanted to believe him, but the way his voice faltered at

the end led me to believe that it was exactly about me, as I'd always thought.

"Because you weren't my biological father? I know that now. But I didn't know it then. I just thought you must not have loved me. That I must have done something wrong. Somehow *been* wrong, broken, not enough."

"I loved you."

His words hit me like a freight train. In three words, he confirmed my greatest fear. That the moment he'd found out we didn't share blood, his love for me had died like a leaf withering on a vine.

"Past tense." That came out through clenched teeth. My jaw was aching from holding it together.

"No. Not that. It was a shock." His backpedal wasn't convincing. Especially when it wasn't followed by a contrite and immediate correction.

"I was shocked, too. When I found out. But I didn't stop loving you. I wrote you letters when I found your mother, Nona's address in Mom's dresser. I waited for you for years. I used to think you'd show up one day with Arturo and take me to Disneyworld."

"Disneyworld. We were supposed to go for your eleventh birthday." He snapped his fingers like I'd reminded him of a missed grocery item. "God, I forgot that promise."

"This is...wow...I can't believe that I lived for something you forgot." I kind of wanted to throw up, but I hadn't eaten anything for hours. I'd do nothing but dry heave macerated nuts over a strange toilet.

"It's just that with the divorce, and Arturo, and moving back to Italy... It wasn't easy."

Defeated, I leaned against the cold stucco wall. I'd forgotten I'd had the damned box in my hands. It slipped, and the contents went fluttering to the tile floor for the second time that day.

"What is all this stuff?"

"Nothing." I scrambled to pick everything up and jam it all back in the box. Unfortunately, I didn't move fast enough. He bent down and took the two stubs into his broad hands. Hands that I'd long thought were like mine. Now we were genetic strangers.

"Are these stubs? You saw Led Zeppelin at Madison Square Garden?"

"I went because it was the kind of show you'd have taken us to. At least, that's what I thought." I didn't know what was true now. In fact I hadn't had much truth in my life for years.

"Was it good?"

"That was the night Maria Sofia told me you weren't my father, my real father."

"I'm sorry. I didn't want you to find out that way."

"What way? What way was I supposed to find out? You left and everyone in Philadelphia was tight-lipped. And tight-fisted with money, apparently. After we moved out of the house, we moved to Camden."

He tried to hide his wince of disgust, but he couldn't.

"It was exactly what you were thinking. Rats, charity food, roaches."

"You look fine now. Expensive clothes. That keepsake box is Louboutin."

"Is that it? I look fine. So you're off the hook."

"I...have to welcome other guests. He pulled out a

computer printout of a spreadsheet. "I've got six more properties to go." On cue, his cell bleated some kind of Android ringtone. "I'll see you around." He thrust a set of keys toward me, along with a stapled stack of papers. "Keys. Instructions on heat, air, appliances. Emergency numbers. Gotta go."

He lifted the first two fingers of his right hand in a kind of salute and had disappeared before I could get in any more words, any more questions, could seek an explanation.

Francis Aconi hadn't even hugged me.

CHAPTER TWO

JAKE

NOW

MARCELLA CLARK STOOD in my office. Her e-mail signature had identified her as Vice President of Legal Affairs. I still wasn't one hundred percent sure what her department did. They seemed to have a finger in about a thousand different pies, from clearing music on television shows to talent contracts.

"Do you maybe want to sit down?" I asked. She was casually dressed in black jeans, motorcycle boots, a simple sweater, but she was a tiny bit intimidating nonetheless.

"Huh?" She paused for a long moment, sizing me up. "You sound different than I thought."

"Less Chinese. More New Jersey." I said it for her. It was what everyone thought, but wouldn't say. Not after middle school, anyway.

"So yeah. I wouldn't have said that out loud."

I had to smile. Her honesty was refreshing. Most people wouldn't have said what *she* had out loud. There would have been a lot of blinking and pretending that they hadn't noticed the differences between us.

"Went back and forth between China and the US," I explained.

"Right. I, uh, met the other men on the board."

That last was a little cagey, but I knew what she was getting at. I was Americanized, probably an obvious choice to interface with the staff. My father's investors—star-struck Chinese billionaires who could buy their way into anything they wanted—didn't even have to learn a lick of English to waltz into almost any room in the world.

"They're my father's cronies. He had to get the money from somewhere to float this entire operation. The first rule of investing is to diversify, spread the risk."

I was probably talking way too much, but I wanted her to know that I understood much of the staff felt like new owner-ship was some kind of foreign invasion.

From the beginning, I'd wanted to reassure everyone that us coming in was the best move to revitalize a company that was still operating as if it were 1950 and it was one of only a few choices on the air.

"Right. So that's the reason I'm here to talk to you," Marcella said. Though she presented herself confidently, there was an underlying hesitancy about her.

"Investing? Diversification? Your e-mail was vague, but I thought it was something network related."

"So. This is awkward. You've heard of Me Too and Time's Up, right?" She'd made the hashtag symbol with the first two fingers of both hands when she'd been speaking.

"I've taken in the work of Ronan Farrow. He did a hell of

a piece on Harvey Weinstein; ex-Mossad agents was over the top. Skimmed the Les Moonves one. After the first, they all seem like repeats of the same. Lock a woman in your office or hotel room. Feel her up. Derail her career if she puts up a fight. Rinse. Repeat."

"That's about the gist of it."

"CBT's in the clear, right? We specifically asked about this during the due diligence phase. Nothing popped up. Dana Berry ran a tight ship. It's one of the reasons we paid a premium price for the network. Please tell me we don't need to issue a memo about having some kind of under-the-desk remote door lock like Matt Lauer. No one here has that, right?"

"About that..."

"Kevin Manning? *Buzz* host Claude Crossley? I've had some weird feelings about those guys. Or is it worse? Is it a woman? Please don't tell me that equal opportunity sexual harassment will be CBT's ticket to the front cover of the *New Yorker*."

"Jake. Can I call you Jake? You mentioned that during the tour. Us calling you by your first name..."

"Jake's fine."

Marcella cleared her throat. Pushed her hair back behind her ears. Leaned forward a little. I leaned in response. Bracing myself for the bad news because no one did this much preamble with good news.

"It's your father. He's the problem. You and 'his cronies,' is that what you called them? All of you need to do some triangulation."

I didn't want to look weak. I was trained not to look weak.

But Marcella's words were like a swift kick to the solar plexus. I huffed out a painful breath. Sat back in my chair. Swiveled so the back was to her, and I could take in the sound stages outside the window. Settled myself. Turned back around.

I leaned forward again, this time bracing my head on my hands and my elbows on the desk, the posture of the damned. "What happened?"

"Have you heard of *Brothers Kim*?"

"Of course. Highest-rated new show this year. Sitcom with that half-Korean guy who won the comedian reality show *Heir to the Throne*." I was proud of my hard-won knowledge. I'd been a quick study of CBT's lineup under Connor Quinlan.

"Right. So the woman who plays his mom is Kiki Yun. Your father summoned her up to his office. He'd said something about asking her to help him raise money for some Asian-American charity. Once she was in his office, he locked the door..."

I leaned back in the chair. Covered my face with my right hand. Spoke through my fingers. "Felt her up? Threatened to derail her career? I think we just did this dance a few minutes ago."

"More or less."

"And..." My hand wiped down my face. I felt around my desk for a pen. Found a retractable one. Clicked it a few minutes, satisfying my temporary urge to run out of this office and take my own father by the throat.

There hadn't been a single thing in my life that hadn't been messed up by my father's proclivities, although I did have to cut him slack because without them, I wouldn't have been born. I wished he'd stopped there some thirty-plus years ago. Would have saved me, Min Li, Maria Aconi and Bella a lot of heartache.

"I thought you'd seem more surprised."

"You don't know my father." I clicked the pen a few more times. "And...?" She didn't seem done. I wanted the other shoe to drop.

"The other...the other is a much bigger problem."

"Go on."

"*Screenplayed* has been CBT's highest-rated reality show for three years."

I nodded. *Cash Cow* would have been a much better name. "The one with the actors who all live in a house with writers trying to put together sitcom and drama pitches," I confirmed.

"We've managed to get two successful shows out of that. The audience being invested in the process has made the show's ratings successes."

Whoever had thought up the idea had been ingenious. Viewers who had voted on the ideas were also avid viewers when their shows came to life a few months later.

"How many viewers for *Screenplayed*?"

"Six point seven on Sunday. Six point four on Wednesday."

"So about thirteen million eyeballs."

"For network TV in a world where streaming and binge watching has taken over. Those are super solid numbers."

"My dad?" I'd gotten the lecture on streaming versus cable versus network more times than I could count on my fingers and toes. I needed to get back to the big problem I was going to be somehow left to address alone.

"He said he wanted to visit the house. Connor Quinlan—"

"New VP of Program Practices."

"Right. Okay. I guess you got an introduction to them with Blue's penis." Marcella was referring to the incident months back where a rock star, high on cannabis, had dropped his bass guitar and played his private parts instead. CBT would have been drowning in fines if I hadn't personally guaranteed payment to the FCC.

"So, Connor explained to Mr. Wu...your dad...that he could drive up to the house in Malibu. Even tour. But he couldn't talk to the guests because he was in a position of power. Like he could ultimately green light a show or not. Or he could cancel it."

"And..."

"So he somehow got into the bedroom of Tara Stewart— she's one of the actresses this go-round. And he told her that if she would be his mistress—his California mistress, I guess— then he'd make sure she was on another network show if she didn't win a role on this one."

"I'll handle him."

"Right. Okay. I get that. But it's not the biggest problem. He's breached the integrity of the show. That promise has compromised the entire production. Unless we can find a way around the contest rules—and it's not looking good— we'll have to scrap the entire season or face some kind of *Quiz Show* type scandal."

"Shit. What will you substitute in its place?"

"Don't know. There's always something on deck. Couple of sitcoms one night. Drama another. Or some second-tier reality show. That will be cheaper. Programming will work that out. Not my circus."

"So, you're here…"

"To deliver the bad news. To get assurance from the top brass that your father will be out."

"He'll be out."

"Yesterday would be good."

"Don't worry about that. I'll handle it."

"Thanks. This is a relief. I thought this would be harder. That you'd insist he stay. That we'd have to scrap two and a half hours of television a week on the schedule."

"I'll have a talk with your boss, Connor, and our outside law firm. Even with my father gone, we may have to scrap two and a half hours of television."

"I'm sorry."

"Not sorrier than I am. If we can't fix this, our profits may evaporate overnight. We'll be no better off than the other terrestrial networks. My speech on investment and diversification sounds stupid now."

"Maybe not. You still have the car business to fall back on, right?"

I wasn't ready to return to Nanjing or New Jersey. Even without Bella to inspire me, I was determined to make this work.

"Thank you for being the brave one," I said, looking Marcella in the eye. "I imagine you picked the short straw."

"It was coffee stirrers, but I volunteered anyway."

"Maybe you won. If there's an opening for something

you'd like to step into, let me know. I'll make it happen. CBT needs someone with your guts in leadership."

"Thank you. I think."

I stood. Buttoned my suit jacket. "If you'll excuse me. I need to have a talk with my father."

"Right. Yes. Sorry." She scrunched her nose. "Good luck?"

"Thanks." I didn't wait to see her out. Alexandra could do that. I'd hired her the minute Isabella had left. My instincts had been right about Bella's former assistant. She'd made the last few weeks the smoothest of my short entertainment career.

"Alexandra."

She pulled ear buds from her ears. "Yes, Mr. Wu?"

"I told you that you could call me Jake."

"Right, Mr. Wu. I'll consider that. What do you need?"

"Can you show Marcella Clark out. After she leaves, get whatever info you can find on her in a memo to me. I want to promote her and need to know where her skill set would be best served.

"In the meantime, I'm going upstairs to see my father. Please let his assistant know that I'm on my way over and that we are not to be disturbed unless there's a fire or earthquake, and maybe not even then."

"Gotcha. DND."

The short walk to my father's office was what I imagined it would be like taking my last steps on a hostile ship's gangplank. My steps were slow and deliberate as I tried and failed to think of a way to avoid the inevitable. I didn't hold back my anger when I strode past his assistant, stormed into his office and slammed the door behind me, causing several papers to flutter from his desk to his floor.

"What are you doing? Don't slam the door. That's rude," he said without even looking up. The disapproval rolled off his lips like I was thirteen again and I'd tracked Toms River mud into the house after Maria had cleaned.

"Rude? I apologize for my bad manners. Door slamming is the least of my problems today."

"What problems do you have today?" He looked up at me then. He lifted a hand and snapped his fingers. "Oh, yes, I know. I heard that your precious Isabella left. Her mother says that she's in Italy."

That caught me up short. It shouldn't have. The man had a knack for pressing people's buttons.

"You talked to Maria Aconi?" I asked, my patience already razor thin.

"She's been our housekeeper for twenty years. Of course I've spoken with her," he said so innocently, as if butter wouldn't melt in his mouth.

"Are you fucking kidding me with this? Housekeeper? That's rich." I shook my head. I sounded like Isabella during one of her rebellious phases. This talking back had never been my style, but it was right now. I suddenly got it—Bella's frustration with the whole damn thing. It had taken me some years, but I think I was finally where she'd been during her Owen years.

"What is wrong with you today, Wu Jian?" For a second, my father faltered. I knew because he dropped the fountain pen he'd been holding. It was not like my father to make a single move that wasn't planned and deliberate.

"Call me Jake," I said. Jake Wu was going to be the one who had to fire his father. Wu Jian was a little too obedient for that task.

"I've never called you by that American name," he spat.

"What's wrong with me?" I asked rhetorically, throwing back my head and taking in the ceiling. "Let's see. I just had a visit from Legal Affairs. I've been tasked with the job of firing you, my own father, because you're jeopardizing the network."

"What? I came in here and saved this network. We've put in more cash than they've had in years."

"The two shows that are the true cash cows are in trouble."

"And that's my fault how?"

"Kiki Yun and Tara Stewart."

"Beautiful women."

"Whom you hit on."

"Since when is telling a beautiful woman that you appreciate her a crime?"

"When the network has to cancel its highest-rated show because they can't assure contest integrity."

"All those big words from my Harvard graduate. I'm just a peasant boy from Qingdao. What are you saying?"

"That you can't fucking touch the merchandise. Even though you've always fucking touched the merchandise. First my mother, then Isabella's. But it stops *now*. At least at CBT. You can't shit where you eat, and you've shit all over this damned place."

Carefully, my father capped his pen. Inserted it into a gold-toned cup on his desk. He stood, lifted the few papers that had fluttered to the floor after I came in and stacked them carefully. He pushed his hands together, squaring piles of papers and manila folders. He pushed in his chair. Buttoned his jacket then smiled at me like the cat who'd eaten the canary.

"Then you need to take over."

"Take over what?"

"Entertainment. You've been in America a long time. You went to high school and college here. I'm putting this in your hands. I have to get back to Nanjing. I need to put some things in place at the factory there, then do the same in New Jersey."

Just like that, Feng Wu had slipped through my fingers like he'd probably slipped through my mother's and Min Li's and maybe even Maria Aconi's. He was going, yes, but still wasn't being held accountable for the many lives he ran through like a bull in a china shop.

I was in charge. He was going home. It was my mess to clean up.

THE KNOCK on the door startled me. Not awake exactly, but made my heart beat a little faster and my eyes open all the way. I'd tried to go down to the beach and soak in the sun that was supposed to reset my circadian rhythm and cure my jet lag, but it hadn't worked.

I'd been hot, and sweaty, and itchy with sand grains in all the wrong places. Eventually, I'd come back to the villa, its air conditioning a crutch—for the last four days.

The banging continued. I looked at the clock. What in the hell could ever be so urgent at eleven o'clock on a Saturday? Up until now, I couldn't have pointed out a single thing the Italians got excited about. Everyone seemed to have time to chat. Time to close up shops for two or three hours in the afternoon. Time to amble down the town's streets at a pace that could be generously called slow.

"Hold on. Just a minute," I yelled as I pulled some tights over my underwear and straightened my tank top. I'd said that twice, but of course, the person with the noisy fists probably didn't understand English. After my first and last trip to the market, I realized that my Italian was limited to food and parental commands. Not enough for fluency.

I swung open the thick wood door while simultaneously trying to swipe to Google Translate on my phone so I could answer whatever question or respond to an emergency.

When I met the visitor's eyes, when my brain registered who it was, the phone clattered to the floor, though I'd been unaware of even letting it go.

"Arturo? Jesus fucking Christ. You could have called. I don't think my heart can take this surprise shit," I nearly shouted. "How in the hell are you?"

I punched him in the arm for emphasis. His flinch was unexpected. I'm pretty sure I'd hit him harder when I was eight. Deep down I knew it wasn't the right greeting, the yelling, the punching. But anything else would make me cry. I did not cry.

"Has Italy made you soft? No birthday beats?"

When he didn't answer, I closed my mouth and took him in. Kind of in the same way I had to acclimate to Francis. Arturo was both who I remembered and someone new entirely.

He wasn't fourteen anymore, on the cusp of manhood. He was a full-grown man. He had a moustache and beard, close-cropped, as was the style everywhere in the world now. Not just Brooklyn and Los Angeles, I guess. He was in a suit, on a Saturday. Maybe it was work clothes, though I couldn't think of anyone else I'd seen in a black suit since I'd been here. Not with these temperatures. Nobody had mentioned Italy was so freaking hot.

"Isabella. It's...um...well. It's good to see you. Can I come in?"

I retrieved my phone from the tile floor, glad to see that I hadn't broken the damned thing. The way I was going, it wouldn't survive my time here. I jammed it in the tank's bra strap, then threw the door open wide enough for him to come through, along with a wave of Italian spring heat.

"Sure, I guess," I said while I stepped back. "Do you want to go out? Do you have a car? Maybe we can have some kind of late seafood lunch. There has to be a restaurant that's open during these siesta hours between lunch and dinner."

"We need to talk."

There was no warmth or humor in his voice. What in the hell happened, I wanted to ask, to all that Italian warmth and hospitality I'd heard so much about? Even with my shit Italian, the shopkeepers and restaurant owners had been nicer than my own relatives. Although the word "relative" was relative.

"I know," I said, trying to match his solemn tone. "I don't have anything here, though. Other than wine and some olives and cheese. It's why I thought going out was a good idea. I could change into something better to match you. It would only take me about ten minutes."

"Can you stop talking for a second?"

"Um...so-sorry. I'm just kind of excited to see you. It's been so long. I mean, Mama talked about you sometimes. But not a lot. I think it hurt too much. At least I hope that's what it was."

"Isabella," he said, nearly shouting my name, stopping my

mouth in its tracks. Arturo grabbed my biceps in his hands. Jerked me forward a bit. "Dad died."

"Wait. Who? What? *Your* dad? The guy who's not my dad?" Arturo looked so confused that I finally laid it out as best I could. "Francis Aconi? He died?"

"He took my Vespa out on Tuesday but didn't come home. *La polizia* found him and the scooter Wednesday in Lecce."

"Your dad died. Wow."

For a wild moment, I felt relief. Relief that Francis Aconi hadn't just ignored me. Hadn't abandoned me a second time like the first. I'd given him one day to get over the shock. Then a second to get used to the idea of me being here. I had planned to knock on his door on Wednesday, but I'd chickened out, binge watching Netflix on the tiny European-sized flat screen instead. Then the last two days had been even harder, thinking he'd completely ignored me, our need to hash out the past once and for all.

The longer I'd put it off, the more difficult it had become to rouse myself, get dressed, and face down my past.

Shame flooded me for that relief—and the relief over not having to confront Francis and have a series of hard conversations. My history of confrontation had always turned out badly. With Mama. With Mr. Wu. With Jake...

"He was your dad too," Arturo said, barging into my thoughts.

"No, that's just the thing, Arturo." I squinted at him, wondering what he'd been told. If Francis Aconi had spun a tale different from the truth that had landed on me from my mother's mouth. I looked at him fully this time, my eyes wide open.

The one thing that hadn't changed on either Francis or Arturo was the eyes. His brown eyes, lighter than mine, flecked with green specks, were the same as they'd always been. The same that had teased me. The same that had bickered with me over who got the front seat when only Mama or Daddy was in the car. The same that I'd looked up to with equal parts fierce adoration and envy. I'd always thought he knew more than me. Knew all the secrets the adults kept.

"The thing is that...he wasn't. They got divorced because..." I couldn't bring myself to say *our dad*. "...when he found out."

The shock on my brother's face, I was sure was a mirror of my own that horrible night of the Led Zeppelin concert.

I couldn't look at him for a moment longer.

No longer self-conscious about being barefoot or in the wrong clothes or tired or not Italian enough, I walked from the vestibule to the living room and sat heavily on the couch. Neither the weird smell nor scratchy texture of the Ikea furniture bothered me this time.

He hitched up the legs of his pants, then sat next to me. "The funeral will be this afternoon."

"Funeral?"

Arturo passed me what looked a lot like a flyer for a missing person or animal. Instead of where to return a lost Francis, it had funeral information below a smiling picture that was at least a decade old. More like the father I remembered and less like the man who'd turned up on my doorstep not six days prior. His name was in huge bold letters. The rest was information about what I assumed was a funeral mass to be held at four o'clock at *Sacro Cuore di Gesu*.

"The Sacred Heart of Jesus?" I translated. Funny, the words I knew.

"It's a modern church. He liked the priest there."

My not-father went to church? Had a favorite priest? Was dead? None of it made sense. Oh, it made a lot of sense on the surface. I suspected many Italians still went to Mass, loved their churches, loved their priests.

The father I remembered had been irreverent and agnostic, if not atheist. Barely went to church unless it was a holiday or wedding or funeral. Had made lots of jokes about how over the top Catholics were. Maybe he'd been there repenting for the sin of forsaking his daughter. I nodded. I liked that idea. Made me feel a whole lot better. But I guess I'd never know.

I turned toward Arturo, ready to process the information.

"Okay...what happened?" I wanted to rule out shock of long-lost *not* daughter turning up and causing heart attack. I knew my mind was spinning out. Creating its own story with me at the center. I swallowed to keep the tears back. I was never going to get to know my father. He was never going to get to know me. When my brother didn't answer, I wondered if I'd committed a cultural faux pas. "Is that a thing you can ask?"

"He was supposed to check someone in or out at a hilltop house in Lecce. The police think that some asshole in an Audi came around the curve a little too fast and clipped him. Maybe Papa overcorrected. Either way, he probably was

forced down into some bushes at the bottom of a ravine."
Arturo paused.

I stopped looking at my hands and turned to him. But it
was the same as looking at Francis Aconi. It hurt to see him
there. He took in a huge breath that may have also been a sob.

"I thought he was maybe with a woman friend, so I didn't
call him. Didn't even *think* to call him. Then the police
knocked on my door."

His fist came up to his face. He pushed it into his mouth
as if that could single-handedly keep the tears at bay. His
sadness was contagious, and suddenly, my throat closed up
and I wanted to do anything to keep my own tears from
leaking out.

"It's two. How far away is the church?"

"Get dressed. I'll take you there."

I nodded, then stood and walked back to the bedroom I'd
claimed. If there was one thing I'd learned from so many
years with Daniel, it was that I should always pack something
in my suitcase that was appropriate for most occasions. I dug
through the mostly unpacked bags and pulled out a Free
People maxi dress. It was long, black, and covered up the
important parts. The fact that it was shapeless or that I'd paid
a couple of hundred dollars for something with an intentionally frayed hem would have to be overlooked for now.

I slipped it over my tank, shoehorned my feet into
sandals, wondering if the Pope would curse me for having
open toes, and then went back to the living room, figuring the
Catholic church had survived worse.

Arturo was standing, pacing, while he talked to—or
maybe more accurately, argued with—someone in rapid Ital-

ian. I fiddled with my own phone so it didn't look like I was rudely watching him, even though that was exactly what was happening.

I couldn't figure which was more disconcerting. His adult self or the fact that he spoke an entirely different language even though we'd started out in the same place. If Daddy had taken me here, rescued me from Mama, I wondered how my life would have turned out.

I wouldn't have met Jake, that's for sure. Nor Daniel, probably. Would I even have gone to Owen? Maybe I'd have attended some university in Europe for all four years instead of doing my JYA for Daniel's convenience. Maybe I'd have even met a nice guy and done the now unthinkable, gotten married.

"Everything okay?" I asked after he disconnected and shoved the Samsung into his pocket.

"Fine. Let's go."

I locked up per the instructions from Francis and followed Arturo outside. I tried not to be sad that the last encounter with him was about rental logistics.

The brown Fiat was the only car in the drive. When Arturo turned the key in the lock, I opened the passenger door and got in. European cars always reminded me of clown cars from bad black and white television comedies. I kind of expected there to be fifteen Ronald McDonalds in the tiny backseats, but I kept my eyes forward and my thoughts to myself.

"We have to pick up Nonna," he said.

The Gallipoli Grandma is how I thought of her. There had been no love lost between Francis' mother and my own. I only had a vague memory of meeting Carmela Aconi when I was about ten and she'd come to Philadelphia. She'd been at our house for maybe two or three days before Mama and her had a screaming argument and Francis' mother had packed her bags and stalked out.

In my child brain, she'd walked herself to the Philly airport and gotten on the first plane to Italy. My adult brain realized that was highly unlikely. I shifted in the passenger seat, moving the seat belt so it wasn't cutting into my neck.

"Do you remember when Mama and Grandma Carmela got into that fight?"

Eyes firmly on the road, Arturo nodded.

"Do you think she came right back here or did she stay at a hotel or something?"

"You don't remember?"

I shook my head. There had been the fight. I'd gone to gymnastics and dance that day, then life had gone on as normal...until it hadn't.

"She stayed with Uncle Benito. Nonna didn't like Aunt Orla's Irish cooking. That's why she'd come to stay with us in the first place."

"How come I never saw her after that?"

Arturo wrestled the car around a hairpin turn, but remained silent for a long moment before he finally answered.

"I never thought about it. Papa and I went to a couple of huge dinners she made at Benito's house with Aunt Orla and their boys and stuff."

"Mama and I weren't invited, and you never thought about it?"

"Dad said Mama and Nonna had a fight."

"Mama had the fight. What about me?"

"You were always so busy with gymnastics."

It didn't compute. My grandmother gets on a plane from the old country to visit her two sons, her only children in the world, and her only grandchildren, but doesn't want to see her only granddaughter before she turns around and flies back?

"You know what I think they were arguing about?"

Arturo sighed as he pulled up to a squat tan house. "What, Isabella?"

"Maybe it was about Paolo Leoni."

He turned his eyes toward me, and I tried to integrate his child self with his adult self in my head.

"Who's that?"

"My real father. Maybe Grandma Carmela knew something Daddy didn't. Nothing was exactly the same after Grandma left."

"Can we talk about this later? This really isn't the time. Please don't bring it up while Nonna is in the car. She's taking this especially hard. She's not a young woman by any means, and her youngest son just died."

Like a suitably chastised child, I closed my mouth. Resisted the urge to mime twisting a lock and tossing away an invisible key. I didn't have to match their antipathy.

"Is that her?" The woman who opened the front door, lace curtains billowing out around her, was tiny compared to my memory of the woman shouting down my mother in the kitchen.

Arturo didn't answer. Instead, he opened the driver's

door and came around to my side. "You'll have to sit in the back." Without ceremony, he gestured for me to get out.

I unfolded myself, got out, flipped the latch moving the seat forward, then squeezed myself into the back. I was sweating by then. Lifting my hair from my neck, I tried to get some of the rapidly heating air against my skin.

I looked out of my small backseat window to see Arturo, his arm around Nonna's waist, escorting her to the car. He helped her sit, then lifted her legs into the foot well, before buckling her in like a child.

The minute Arturo was in and the car started, Nonna turned to him.

"*Chi è lei?*" she asked. I had enough Italian to know she'd asked who I was. I'm not sure if it stung or if I was relieved that she had no idea about my identity.

"*Figlia di Maria,*" Arturo answered. That one *did* sting. Not his sister, but Maria's daughter.

"*La illegittima?*"

Nonna's question needed no translation. I felt like I'd walked into some nineteenth-century costume drama, where my parentage with the most salacious thing to happen since the end of the Victorian era.

Arturo, at least, didn't pretend to misunderstand. Instead, he changed the subject to something about the church and funeral.

I got lost after those words. I was grateful that the church was no more than a mile from Nonna's house and we were parking at the edge of a large piazza within minutes. Arturo helped Nonna from the car and I jumped out of the backseat right after.

"Do you..." Arturo started. His eyes swung between his grandmother and me, *Maria's daughter*.

"I'll figure it out. Seat myself. Thanks for the ride," I said, then stalked off toward the steps. At least I had that on the old woman—youth and agility. I followed the other gray-haired people and entered the church. Its cool darkness was welcome.

I picked up a program, the hands of God huge on the front, then found a space in the second-row pew. The first had a small cordon meant to reserve it for family. I didn't want to shock anyone by sitting myself in the front. I could observe, mourn, whatever, safely from this vantage point.

I'd been so busy trying not to be seen that when I lifted my head, my father's body took me by surprise. There he was in a crisply pressed gray suit, hands primly folded, eyes closed.

And...dead.

Unmoving.

At rest.

The coffin was plain wood except for his name affixed on the side. Francis Aconi was spelled out in wood letters nailed to it.

Tears smarted, not so much for his death, but for the loss of my father all those years ago, and not the loss of closure. I ducked my head again and recited the rosary, not for its supposed redemptive power, but as a kind of familiar meditation.

It was four thirty before the funeral started. Though the mass was in Italian, it was little different from the masses I'd attended in Latin. I stood, prayed, responded and knelt on cue.

Eventually the priest stepped aside and a couple of gray-haired men, who I assume were his friends, came forward and spoke about Francis. The third, when he started in English, got my full attention.

"I want to thank you all for gathering today. Those of us who are Italian and those of us who are Italian-American. That was the thing I loved most about Francis, that he brought all of us together. Whether it was espresso in the piazza in the morning or grilled sausage at Macelleria Ta'Carne at night.

"Even more than that, he was an amazing father. When he moved back home, everyone wondered how a single man could raise a son, because we know Italian men need their mothers."

The crowd laughed as if on cue at this one.

"He did an amazing job. Got Arturo through some rough teenage years, into university, and now, even though he works in Bari, he still came home on weekends to help out Francis and Signora Aconi.

"Francis was a good man, Gallipoli was lucky to have had him as long as it did. May he rest in peace."

When the priest turned his eyes upon Nonna, she shook her head, a sob erupting.

"Arturo?" the priest asked.

Arturo stood, his walk to the podium as slow as a walk down the wedding aisle.

"*Grazie*. Thank you all for coming to honor my father. I won't repeat what you've all said here. He was a good man, a great father, and a wonderful son. I wouldn't be standing here before you if he hadn't pulled my head out of...you know where...when I was in my teens. I'd left the only home I'd known and was floundering.

"He put me on the task of renovating Nonna's house. For a year, I plastered and painted. Working with my hands helped heal me. I'll never forget the lessons I learned that first hard year."

He repeated his little speech in Italian, ending with a kiss of his hands against our father's cheek.

The priest looked expectantly at the crowd. It reminded me of that part of a wedding where the officiant said, "speak now or forever hold your peace."

Before I knew what was happening, I was standing and shifting my way from the pew into the aisle. I nearly tripped over the hem of my dress, but righted myself before I did anything embarrassing and walked to the podium. The priest's eyebrows rose a fraction of an inch, but he stepped aside anyway.

Arturo's watery eyes held a question. Nonna's daggers.

"Francis Aconi was my father too—for the first eleven years of my life, at least. He used to take me for Chinese food for my birthday. Hold dance parties in our living room when I was a kid. He would take me to gymnastics and ballet and never complain about being surrounded by rooms filled with giggling girls. I loved the father that he was for those years. I truly did.

"When he disappeared, I didn't know what to make of it. Eventually my mother—whom many of you know, Maria

Sofia Aconi—explained why the only father I'd ever known left us, took my brother, and came here to Gallipoli.

"I wanted nothing more than to talk to him one last time. Meet him again, reconcile what had happened. I saw him on Sunday when I landed here. We only talked briefly. I wish I'd had the opportunity to know the man you're talking about, but his life was cut short this week. I'll never get the answers I was seeking, I guess. I'm sorry. I won't take up any more of your time.

"Rest in peace, Papa, the only father I've ever known," I said when passing the coffin.

I did the sign of the cross. Bowed my head for a respectful second.

"*Riposare in pace,*" I said, repeating the phrase I'd heard so many utter in the church. Then I stepped down and went back to my seat.

The coffin closed, I watched as the pallbearers lifted it upon their shoulders, the funeral director quickly following with huge stands of white and orange flowers. Francis Aconi's remains disappeared into a hearse. Nonna and Arturo followed, as well as a beautifully turned out woman in her fifties who I assume was the friend Arturo had thought Francis had been visiting when he hadn't brought the scooter back home.

I turned away. I didn't need to see him buried. Francis Aconi had left me twelve years ago, and seeing soil and flowers dropped over his coffin wasn't going to change that fact.

It was like someone had turned off the movie halfway through or snatched a book out of my hands before I could get to the three-quarter mark. I wasn't sure there was any more resolution here in Italy than there had been in Los Angeles.

I strode out of the piazza to the main road. Found a cab and pointed him toward my rented villa. I had no idea what was next for me, but it probably wasn't here in Gallipoli.

THERE WAS no love lost in this room for Liling. I'd called an emergency meeting to fix the problem that my father had created.

It was me, Liling, newly added to the payroll as CBT's head of scheduling, the VP in charge of program planning; Jesse Gregory, the head of all entertainment; and Connor Quinlan, who had over the past year proved to be an ally in the way that Isabella, with all our shared baggage, never would have been.

I'd appointed myself head of prime time entertainment. A coveted spot that no one thought me qualified to have. They were probably right, but I was protecting the family investment, not climbing my way to the top of the Hollywood food chain. I did not have to question my own loyalty.

If there was one thing I loved about America, it was that it shared a very important trait with China. People did not publicly show their displeasure.

Here it was covered by smiles. In China, the faces would have been stoic. But the result was the same. Though no one wanted to be here, not one of them would say it out loud. Well-paying jobs in entertainment were too few and too precious to be squandered over a minor turf war.

Once everyone was seated, I turned to Connor.

"Can you quickly brief everyone on the issue?"

"Sure, Jake. There's been a breach of protocol on *Screenplayed*. We'll need to scrap this year's show. It was scheduled to air over the end of summer through September with twenty episodes remaining."

"What happened?" Gregory asked.

"It's an internal issue that's being handled. Due to potential liability or lawsuits, legal affairs has prohibited any discussion of the matter," Connor said. These executive faces were anything but inscrutable. They were wondering how he'd come to have access to knowledge denied them. He continued, "There's no reason the show won't be back next summer."

I interrupted before cross-examination could start. "In the meantime, however, we need a short- and long-term solution to replace the show. Preferably with one with ratings as high or higher and a cost as low."

"That's a tall order," Gregory said. "A ratings winner is like trying to capture light in a bottle."

"It is. But I'm sure you're up to the task," I said, trying not to be annoyed that he wasn't ready with a solution right out of the gate. "It's the reason I've brought Liling Jiang on board. We met in boarding school years ago, actually. In the meantime, she studied film at NYU and USC. Additionally, she's worked for the very successful Red Dragon Television in China. She has a background in storytelling and programming, so it's a perfect fit."

"Thanks, Jake, for the intro. You can call me Lily." No shrinking flower of any type, she sat forward in earnest. Her silk blouse over ripped jeans and thousand-dollar shoes was exactly the right approach. I'd doubted my decision to hire her for a second when we'd met this morning. Now I was assured I'd made the right choice.

"I know that I'm new here," she continued, "but I want to jump in and contribute. When I was at Red Dragon and the communist government would pull a show for one reason or another, we often had to step in with a quick replacement. So I've faced this before.

"The one thing that was true about our entertainment division there was that almost everyone had a pet project they'd kept in reserve. Kind of like the Black List but internal."

She'd explained to me this morning that the Black List was a fourteen-year-old passion project that served as a repository for the favorite but unproduced screenplays in town.

"I'd love to know what you guys have seen pitched or heard about that wasn't green-lighted, but maybe should be."

And this is why I'd hired Liling. Five minutes ago, they'd come into this room hating her, the outsider who'd somehow gotten a plum job. And now she'd turned the tables. Told them they could make their dreams come true or at least those for some friend or schoolmate or amazing unknown talent who'd pitched the network but had been turned down.

It was not so different from the premise for the gutted show. Tell people they can have what they want and they weren't your enemies any longer.

I pressed a button on the intercom in front of me and on cue, Alexandra appeared behind someone from the commissary, a tray of specialty coffees, muffins and pastries.

"What kind of coffee?" Gregory asked. "I have allergies."

Alexandra had warned me that I couldn't use food as a bribe in a city where everyone was on a fad diet, or intolerant of something, or vegan.

"I called your assistants and got your favorites. There should be a turmeric almond milk latte with an espresso shot, a skinny non-fat cappuccino, a standard macchiato, and a Diet Coke." She looked at each face. "Got it right?"

Everyone nodded in near unison, their hands outstretched.

"Perfect. Enjoy your meeting. Jake, you'll let me know if you need anything?"

I nodded. "Thanks, Alexandra."

She gave me a single-finger salute and followed the caterer, pushing a now-empty tray from the room.

With everyone suitably placated by caffeine and sugar, the rest of the meeting was far more amiable than it had been when it started.

Two hours later, we had a solid start. Liling had a list of proposed shows that she'd follow up on with various producers and their production companies. I had made at least a valiant start towards cleaning up the mess my father made.

I could even start addressing the letter to my successor, a

practice Alexandra had mentioned. Executives knowing their tenures were short-lived often left letters in their desk drawers with words of encouragement for whoever next occupied their chair. I wanted to hand over a successful schedule, no matter what it took.

"CAN YOU COME TO NEW YORK?" No hello or how are you. Just a question.

This. This is what I got for answering the phone without careful screening. A few weeks in Italy and I was getting soft, the hard city shell no longer burnished to a shine. I'd have to work on that when I made my next plan. I just wish I knew what was up next.

"Claire Harper?" I pulled the phone away and looked at the area code and number. It didn't have a name, but came up as a Manhattan 212 area code. So I didn't know the number, but the voice was familiar after living together for four years.

"Yes. It's me, Claire," she acknowledged.

"Where did you get my number?" I didn't mean to sound rude, but a call from her of all people took me by surprise. Claire's "love you but lose my number" nonvitation to her wedding years ago was the last communication I'd expected to receive for the rest of our lives. It had certainly seemed that final seven years ago.

"Owen alumni office. Is it okay to call you? Are you busy right now?" If the hesitancy in her voice was any indication, she *had* meant for her note to me to be her last.

"I'm in Italy right now." My answer was a non sequitur, but I couldn't think of anything to say to ease the awkwardness of this moment. I wasn't even sure if that was my job.

"Oh, on vacation? Visiting your dad?" The attempt at small talk was awkward. We'd once known everything about each other. Time and distance had put a lie to what was once true.

"Attended his funeral, actually," I admitted, not giving even a little on my end to make Claire more comfortable. That wasn't my job, from what I could see. Any apology would have to come from her end. I yearned for those words, though. I'd missed her. Fiercely at first, less so as time went on.

Nowadays, I think I missed the closeness of a woman friend the most. New friends were never the same as the old ones. I hadn't had many new friends over the years. Daniel had kept me busy. Getting ahead at work had taken up the rest of the time.

"Oh, I'm so sorry." She said the right words, but for the wrong reason. "Is this a bad time? I remember that you weren't close."

I rolled my neck, listening to the assortment of cracks that hadn't been there in my early twenties when we'd lived together.

"Let's just talk now. There will be no better time. What were you saying about New York?"

"I live here now."

"How is..." I reached into my memory for that aristocratic name that had been foil-embossed on the nonvitation she'd sent years ago. "Leland Phelps, the third?"

"Married to a new Missus Phelps." Her tone was matter-of-fact.

"Oh, Claire. I'm sorry." I was uttering the words of apology I'd wanted to hear. "Did you guys have kids?"

"One. Just one. He's five."

"What's his name?"

"Henry." Her voice softened.

"Claire..." Henry. Henri, short for Henrietta, had been the name of our...handler...madam...pimp, those many years ago.

"I know." Her sigh was long and filled with the weight of secrets, lies, and half-truths. "There's a long story there I'll tell you when I see you."

"We're on different continents." Having a long-overdue phone conversation and seeing each other seemed literally worlds apart.

"I heard you left CBT."

"Remind me not to update Owen anymore. There are no secrets in a digital world," I said. I'd sent info over to the university in the hopes of networking to my next job when I was ready to tackle a search for work.

"The alumni network isn't exactly the same as making an announcement on Facebook."

She was right about that. I had social media accounts, but rarely posted. I'd certainly stopped checking other people's accounts when that had left me with nothing but a sense of inadequacy at having a life that was anything but normal.

Them with their picket fences and kids and summers on the Cape or on some Midwest lake. Me with Daniel in Monaco or Ibiza had felt like I lived life on a different planet.

"What are you doing in New York?" I asked. "I thought you and Leland were in DC."

"We were. He still is. I think he's planning on running for the US Senate at least, or the top job at most."

"Wow." Not keeping up on social media did not mean I could ignore the news completely. Claire and Leland had been a great-looking couple that photographers and newspapers loved. Much like Gavin Newsom and his first wife, Claire and Leland had been compared to the Kennedys. Guess the days of Bill Clintons and John Edwardses sticking with the smart women who'd brought them to the dance were over.

"I was political collateral damage."

"Sorry." There was that word again in the wrong place and time.

"I was too," Claire said. "I'm not sure I am anymore. My therapist said I should do something for others rather than dwell on myself. That's what I want to talk to you about."

"Okay…" I said, ready to be hit up for a donation. Times must be hard if she was dialing my number.

"I'm starting a nonprofit. I just closed on a building in Clinton Hill. It's perfect. You have to see it."

"What's the nonprofit?" Had she somehow heard about my little send off from Daniel? Though I was sure there was no way she could have.

I was one hundred percent sure that's an update I hadn't shared with Owen. If I had, the development office would be chasing me down daily for donations, building funds, and prompting me to leave the school something in my will.

"Julie House."

My stomach cramped so hard, I nearly doubled over. I asked the next question even though I knew the answer.

"What's the mission of Julie House?"

"To give women who want to leave 'the life' a place to rehabilitate...make that transition."

I didn't pretend ignorance. I don't think we'd ever used the phrase "the life" between us, but it had hung out there nevertheless, one of the many euphemisms for the world's oldest profession.

"Aren't there a thousand of these already?" I assumed a horde of religious organizations existed to save the Mary Magdalenes of the world from themselves.

"Surprisingly not. The younger ones become wards of the county or state. The older ones are mostly sent to prison or drug rehab. Ours...mine will be different, though. My focus is on high-end escorts. Most from elite colleges who did it for the reasons we did."

I hadn't missed her use of the word "our." I'm not sure if it was a slip that was about me or if she had other partners.

"Why me, Claire?" I asked. Of all the offers I'd imagined coming my way after sending in my update to Owen, this... this had not been one.

"Are you looking to go back into entertainment?" she asked.

"I'm not sure what I'm looking for," I answered truthfully. I'd thought I was looking for my father. But he was dead. I'd thought I was looking for reconciliation with my brother, but I was thinking our relationship was dead as well. Maria Sofia and Arturo Aconi had put the final nails in that coffin.

Arturo had left me a brief note about keeping in touch and wishing me safe travels home. I had already exhausted my relationship with Jake and the Wus and my mother. Maybe I was looking for myself, but I didn't say that to Claire. I'd keep my late adolescent search for meaning to myself.

"Then come here. You know the restlessness you feel? The feeling like you don't fit in? Like you're not sure what to do next? I had that, too. It's not just some kind of existential crises, Isabella. It's the universe telling you it's time to heal the past."

That cramp in my stomach tightened just a tiny bit more. While she'd described how I'd been feeling almost to the letter, I'd have denied it to anyone who'd asked.

"Jesus. Did you just say 'the universe?' Are you sure you're not calling me from California?" I teased. It was the kind of banter we'd shared years ago.

"Fine. That was probably a little woo-woo."

"A little?"

"I've been reading a lot of self-help books, okay, and a lot of it is bullshit about manifesting and vision boards. But I believe the underlying part. That Julie House is the best way to move forward. For me at least. I was just making a guess about you."

"So...why did you call me?" If she was going to ask for money, I wanted to get there sooner rather than later, so I could cut her a check and go back to work on forgetting the mistakes I'd made over the last decade.

"I want you to come see this place. Read my business plan. Agree to become a co-executive director with me."

Of all the things I'd thought of when I'd picked up the phone, this hadn't been it. First, I'd thought it was some CBT number I didn't recognize, begging me to come back. Then I'd hoped that it was some new number from Daniel because, despite it all...I missed him. My mind hadn't had time to alight on a third possibility before I'd pressed the green phone icon.

In that moment, though, I made a decision. One that I hoped I wouldn't regret. If life was about moving forward as well as addressing the past, then there was no better way to do it than this. At least it was something. I was tired of standing still. I made a snap decision I hoped I wouldn't regret.

"I'll book a flight now. Give me the address."

Before I'd thought better of it, I'd booked a flight for the next day—and was in the hot, humid, and badly in-need-of-an-update Kennedy airport in Queens in less than twenty-four hours.

The thirty-minute drive from JFK to Clinton Street freaked me out. I hadn't been in the city for 9/11, but the empty streets gave me the feeling that something had just happened.

"Why isn't there traffic?" I asked the driver. "It's Wednesday."

"You're American?"

I nodded. My accent was East Coast. His, I couldn't quite place, but he wasn't born in the states.

"It's the Fourth of July. Independence Day."

I picked up my phone to see the date flash on the screen. He was right. I'd forgotten all about it. Before I could find Claire's number and dial, we were pulling up to a mansion on the corner of Clinton and Willoughby.

"This right?" the driver asked, looking between me and the tablet he had mounted to his dashboard. Mansions were probably not his usual drop-off spots. Those people had black cars and drivers. Daniel certainly hadn't taken a taxi that I'd ever seen. Someone who knew him by name was always at the private jet hangar to whisk us into whatever city we were visiting.

"Yes, I'm sure this is it." I nodded in confirmation at his unsure look.

He turned off the car and came around for my door. In another second, he had my hot-pink cases on the sidewalk.

"I thought it was you!" Claire exclaimed as she came down a set of side steps and pulled me into a hug. I let some of my anger and resentment seep away at the familiar touch. One that had comforted me many times after my mother had abandoned the role.

A little boy, who I hadn't noticed initially, pulled at her arm.

"Henry. This is Mommy's friend from college, Isabella. Izzie. We were roommates at Owen."

"Hi," he said in a small, sheepish voice before ducking behind his mother's slim white pencil capris.

"Hi," I returned. Kids weren't in my wheelhouse. The

executives at CBT had acted like children, but their vocabu-
laries had probably been more advanced, even if their
tantrums hadn't.

"Let's get your bags inside," Claire said, taking control of
my arrival.

The driver followed Claire's instructions and took the
bags through the door to a small vestibule. She was anything
but the country mouse from Maryland's eastern shore that I'd
met in college. She commanded the driver with a certain
sense of self that said she'd learned how to hold her own with
Leland Phelps, the third.

Once the cabbie was dismissed and we were all inside the
cool, but not cold open-plan kitchen and living room, a
woman emerged from some back room and took Henry with
her before any introductions could be made.

"Nanny?" I inquired. "Works on the Fourth?"

"Triple time." Money still greased a lot of wheels in the
world.

"I'm so sorry. I didn't think to check the date before." I
cursed myself for yet another apology. Something about
being with this woman who'd known me when I was Izzie,
and before I was ice-queen executive Isabella, set me back a
decade in self-composure.

"It's no problem. Let me get you set up in your room."

She took me to the back of the apartment. I'd hefted the
smallest of the bags to the guest bedroom. It was a fair size for
New York, this small bedroom in the ground-floor flat. Not
that the four-story mansion had been anything to sneeze at.
I'd have to ask more about why she was living downstairs, but
I told her I wanted to clean up first. I did need to wash the

smell of stale recirculated airplane air from me, but I wanted to get my bearings, as well.

I took a quick shower and came back to find Claire at the sleek white dining table with something golden and fizzy in hand.

"I'm probably dehydrated, but give me one of those anyway."

She handed over the flute. I drank deeply. Poured my own refill from the heavy green wine bottle.

"Let me get you some water." Claire stood and pulled out one of those filter pitchers from a sleek fridge I hadn't noticed it, blended in so well with the gloss-white cabinets.

"You live here?" I asked.

"It's a small apartment I'm taking so I can work in the same building. The whole thing was built in nineteen-oh-one. Not sure when this was pulled out. It's small, but it suits."

"Small?" It was as large as a classic six, albeit without a separate dining room. Lack of formal eating hardly seemed a hardship. My face belied my feelings. I'd done my level best at a resting bitch face for years, but it had been hard to maintain after that first flight from Los Angeles.

"Not for New York, no. Compared to before..."

"Life with Leland Phelps, the third."

"Fin," she corrected.

"Fin?"

"'Leland is my father and was my grandfather. Call me Fin. Short for Finley.' He must have said that a thousand times to a thousand different people." Claire paused. This time she was the one to drink down her entire flute. I poured her a refill.

"First, I need to apologize."

"For what?" I asked. But my question was completely disingenuous. From my count, this apology was about seven years overdue.

"The wedding invite. It was so completely callous and unnecessary, but Fin and his family scared me. I missed you so much that day. It was a cold winter wedding. His family was colder. The girls from Owen who stood up for me weren't my real friends, even if their pedigrees were perfect, and the picture I submitted to the Owen alumni magazine was flawlessly staged. I had my head up my ass. Fortunately, it didn't stay there long."

Eight years seemed like a long time by my count. I'd missed the picture because I'd thrown out every glossy Owen magazine that had arrived at my various addresses ever since that day. I knew if I'd seen that picture, I wouldn't have been able to maintain the careful façade I'd cultivated after that devastating night in Philadelphia when Claire, Jake, and even Daniel had disappointed me.

"You divorced?" I asked, because otherwise none of this made any sense. If Leland the third—excuse me, Fin—was still in the picture, I'd still be in Italy, and she'd be in Chanel or Lily Pulitzer or something equally pinky-beige, serving bourbon to southern politicians in some horse-filled field or drinks to wealthy donors on Long Island.

"Unfortunately for Fin's political prospects, yes. He'd have had it annulled if he could. Tried to. Said I'd married him under false pretense."

"How'd he find out about...the past? I'm assuming that was it. That he found out you were a Julie."

"Henri told him. Thought he already knew. She knew Leland Phelps the second. Had provided him with services..."

It was a stretch for me to believe that someone in the business of discretion could be so...indiscrete. Not for the first time did I wonder if Henri didn't suffer from some kind of envy or jealousy. She'd been a Julie once, but before the era of the multibillionaire, when wealthy men were well off, not mega rich. She was still working for a living while watching girls far younger than her doing a lot less for the same kind of lifestyle.

"You believe that?" I didn't think the words "inadvertent" and "disclosure" ever truly belonged in the same sentence.

"She was never out to hurt us, Izzie. Maybe she wasn't as...I don't know...nurturing as she could have been. But she was never vindictive. We were at a party on the Upper West Side. She said something. One thing led to another and next thing I know, I was out on my ass with the clothes on my back and my two-year-old on my hip."

"You went back to Maryland," I said, completing the picture. She'd always been the type whose family loved her, would take her in. "Saved some more cats." The last was in reference to a story she'd told me during our freshman year that had solidified in my head that she was fundamentally good. As opposed to the fundamentally flawed person I'd seen myself as back then.

"Until I could figure out what in the hell to do. Took me six months to realize that I needed to come back and fight." She waived a hand, taking in the roof over our heads. "This is the result. He paid me off. I signed a nondisclosure agreement. Our marriage was only three years. I was easily erased from his carefully crafted biography. At most, I was a youthful indiscretion." I could see from the pained look on her face that he wasn't so easily erased from her own personal history. "The first payment went into this house," she continued, her blasé tone no mask for the pain. "The second an annuity for us. The third will be seed money for Julie House."

It was a lot to take in. A lot. I ignored the money for a moment and started with the most basic of questions.

"Your last name?"

"Harper. Back to Harper. You can be sure I couldn't keep that, either. Poor Henry lost Phelps as well. Henry Harper sounds like a silly character in a Fitzgerald novel.

"He didn't want to keep your son?"

"He's convinced Henry isn't his."

"Really? Didn't you do DNA? It isn't the eighteen hundreds. Or even the nineteen hundreds."

She shook her head so vehemently that even I wondered whether Henry was a Phelps. I was starting to think maybe I should subject myself and Paolo Leoni—if he really did exist —to a cheek swab. What if there was some bigger truth out there that I didn't know? Maybe finding the answer to the puzzle of my origins would ease some of the restlessness in me.

"I don't know what he really believes. That's the story the family has decided upon. So it is thus."

I'd experienced firsthand, more than once, how fickle the rich could be. Maybe the truth didn't matter here. Either way,

I kept my opinions to myself. Instead, I commented on her language.

"Thus?"

"I did major in comparative religion at Owen. Gotta get some use out of that degree."

I think we'd both majored in how to please men. How to subvert our own desires. Had graduated magna cum laude in that major.

"Why Julie House? Why now? You didn't have a hard time getting out of 'the life,' as some call it. You did what you were supposed to do.

Got an Ivy League degree. Married up. Probably volunteered on boards for organizations like this one. It wasn't like Henri had you trapped in some room and wouldn't let you out until you made your daily dick quota."

"Was it that easy for you? There was a picture of you and Daniel on Page Six just last year."

I wanted to snatch that bottle of alcohol out of her hand and down the entire thing. Every so often, the bachelor billionaire and head of the world's largest staffing firm would step out to one formal event or another.

Inevitably, I was on his arm. Occasionally, someone would think we were some version of Bennifer or Brangelina and take a picture. On a slow news night, when Oprah or one of the Chrises—Hemsworth or Evans—weren't in attendance, some lowly researcher would look us up and print our names in tiny print below a picture of Daniel cutting a fine form in a European tux and me in the designer of the moment.

"Daniel and I aren't together," I announced. "That chapter of my life is firmly closed."

"How did you do it?" Claire's question seemed anything but innocuous.

"Made a decision. Stuck to it." I didn't tell her how that decision had taken nearly a decade to make.

"I never broke it off."

Her voice was a whisper. Henry and his nanny laughed, their voices like music from the back of the apartment.

"Wait, what?" I put down my glass and leaned in to make sure I'd heard what I thought I'd heard.

A much clearer picture of the Phelps family decision and Claire's possible betrayal was coming into focus.

"Is Henry...?"

"I don't know."

I searched my brain for the guy. The guy that Henrietta had set her up with. I think I'd seen him in a Bentley a single time, slowly navigating the winding campus roads, looking for our dorm.

"I remember you having designer luggage. I remember you going to Maine or something to look at leaves that Thanksgiving you didn't go home. But that was years ago. Wasn't he married?"

"Still is."

"Jesus. Are you the center's first client?" Sounded like she needed Julie House more than anyone she'd sign up as a client.

"Not funny. Seriously. Tell me how you let go of Daniel."

"It was time. That was all. It was time. It was making my life too complicated. I needed to simplify. I went to dinner and broke it off."

"That simple?"

"No. Not that simple," I said. But I wasn't going to go into the decade plus of hemming and hawing I'd done. His proposal. All the strings that he'd used to bind us, my job, my car, my apartment. "It's just that a guy...kind of helped it along."

"So you have a boyfriend? One who understands... accepts your past?" She asked it like I'd found a unicorn, centaur or some other mythical creature, and not just an open-minded guy.

"It was Jake."

"Oh, Jesus, Lord in heaven."

"You're not even Catholic. Calm the fuck down. The coast is clear. There's no boyfriend. There's no Daniel. There's no Jake."

"I'm sorry."

"I'm not. You know what? This is a good idea, this Julie House. I don't have a single reason to go back to L.A. I'll do it. I'll help you. Whatever it takes."

It wasn't the first rash decision I'd made, but probably the best. The thought of another girl getting caught up in a billionaire's web like I had been filled me with empathy I didn't even know I had.

"Thank you." Claire held her hands in front of her heart in prayer position. I expected the next words out of her mouth to be Namaste. I cut off any further show of gratitude.

"One condition."

"You name it. Is it salary? I'll pay you what you were earning. You can stay here, too. You can have the guest room. As long as you don't mind Henry."

"It isn't a single one of those."

"What then?"

"Do you still want to be with..."

"Rolland Nielsen."

"The...CEO of..." It took only a moment before I latched on to who he was. The company's blue and yellow logo popped into my head.

"The largest department store in the world. Yes, that one."

"Jesus. Fuck. You should fundraise straight out of Henrietta's Rolodex."

"To answer your question. No. I don't want to be with him. Not anymore. I want to help other girls...women...make the change. I want to raise my son to treat women with respect."

"Then you need to start with you, first. Let's call him. Set up a meeting before the alcohol bravado wears off. Deal?"

"Deal."

"LOLA, why is it that you're having a hard time severing your link?" The woman asking the question was Dr. Thelma Banks. The psychologist had been our first hire last year. Neither Claire nor I bought into the abuse/sex worker myth, exactly.

It was too pat an explanation that allowed a sex-negative culture to flourish at the same time that same society failed to protect girls' and women's bodies.

But if a girl wanted to leave, for whatever reason, she'd need some pretty hefty support. I'd had ten million reasons. Dr. Banks was the first pillar for the clients. As I watched today's session unfold, I tried not to second-guess that hiring decision.

"I don't want to be homeless," Lola said, tears brimming. "It's beautiful here in Clinton Hill. Brooklyn has cleaned up. But it's different up in Spanish Harlem. People are still living by the skin of their teeth. Especially since gentrification has taken over the city."

"Do you honestly think that with a degree in chemistry from an Ivy with a strong reputation for placing alumni at pharmaceutical companies that you're just a step away from homelessness?"

"The barista around the corner has a degree in engineering from Fordham." A single tear slid down her perfect cheek. She was tall, lithe, beautiful. I could see why she'd succeeded as a Julie. Rich men had probably gone crazy for her "exotic" look paired with a perfect pedigree. "I didn't come from a rich family. I don't have anyone who's gonna make a call and get me in somewhere. I did all the internships. I took out all the loans. And you know what? I'm still a half Puerto Rican girl raised above East Ninety-Sixth Street.

"If you give me my old phone, I'll just call him this one last time. He said that he'd pay off my debt if I stay with him another year. If he does that, then I can look for a job. Maybe even get a place to live with some roommates."

"Lola. You have a perfectly good iPhone there in your hand. You know the policy."

This is where I'd lent my experience to Julie House. The phone that he'd given you, your sugar daddy, had to be the first link in the chain to be broken. We took those phones the minute they walked in the door. Before they had a chance to second-guess their decision to come here. If I'd thrown any of Daniel's Blackberries into the ocean like I'd envisioned so many times in my head, then I'd have been freer to make good decisions for myself instead of turning to him anytime something got hard.

Those expensive smartphones/tethers were locked tight in a safe in Claire's apartment. We gave them a brand-new iPhone, helped them program in friends and family, then confiscated the other. The first few days, most of them walked around like we'd severed a limb.

"I don't know what I was thinking. Sex work isn't shameful," Lola said. "Wanting money isn't shameful. I just want the things my other friends from school got. That's only fair."

"Our time is up, ladies," Dr. Banks announced. "Let's talk about this again tomorrow. You all are fierce women more than capable of taking care of yourselves. You have to believe in yourselves though to make truth of that statement."

The therapist stood, gathered the notepad she'd had on her lap and nodded at me as she strode to her office.

Honestly, I thought therapy was a crock at worst or maybe just a crutch at best.

Why in the heck eight strong, smart women needed it was beyond me. They needed to quit the sugar daddies, get a job, and figure it the fuck out. There was only so much talking and crying. Doing couldn't come soon enough. More than half a year in, and I wasn't at all sure what more we could give them than this.

I shook my head clear of that uncharitable thought. It wasn't fair of me. I expected them to fast track something that had taken me nearly a decade.

Before we'd opened, with Dr. Banks' help, we'd laid out a treatment plan/plan of attack. First was getting them here. Turns out that was the easy part.

Second was severing contact with their Henri stand-in, be it a pimp, madam, or good friend. Then we got them into therapy and set them up with a career coach in their desired field.

The last thing Claire and I'd decided was that there wasn't a time limit. We budgeted for each woman to be there about nine months, the time to birth a new person, but didn't place a hard limit.

Out of the first ten women we'd taken in, just two had "graduated." While I was fiercely proud of those first two, they'd had what Lola wanted, outside support. They'd had middle-class families who were there to help once the women had the guts to ask for it.

The current crop were more like Claire and I, who'd only had ourselves to rely upon. That wasn't proving to be quite enough. We'd been brainstorming about what else we could do. Right now, the number-one option on the table was hiring a life coach. Someone to pull together all the elements, therapy, career counseling, and make Julie House into a more powerful launching pad.

As the women filed past on their way to their rooms for a break before lunch, I didn't express my disappointment with any of them. It had taken me too far long to figure it out. Longer than nine months.

But if someone had plucked me from Philadelphia or even Olde Haven, installed me in a Brooklyn mansion with my expenses covered, a chef, therapy, and career guidance, I'd have left Daniel the hell alone a whole lot earlier.

I think.

My own phone buzzed and I looked down. It was a text from Claire. She wanted to discuss Julie House. Maybe she had a line on a good life coach who wasn't turned off by our mission and clientele or middling salary.

Instead of answering her text, I walked the ten feet to her

office, closed the door and sat down in one of the comfy chairs she'd installed. It was more sunroom than office. She'd left the bigger rooms for Dr. Banks and the career counselor.

I'd declined office space at the house. I mostly worked at my new Bond Street apartment, in my second bedroom, and my space was much more functional. Cabinets, dual monitors, and stacks of applications to review. Word of mouth had put us more in demand than I'd expected.

"What's up? I was just poking my head into group therapy. I don't know if we need Dr. Banks or a surgeon."

"Surgeon?"

"To install a spine in these girls. For fuck's sake. They have degrees and more resources than most people on Earth. Or maybe to separate them from their sugar daddies like the one they perform on conjoined twins."

"Not a lot of sympathy?"

"I do have it. Sympathy, I mean." I softened my voice. "I really do. It's just that it's a hell of a leg up they have here. I'd happily have left Daniel earlier if my very existence hadn't depended on it. They still have families that love them, maybe can't financially back them like half the kids slumming it in Bushwick, but they have that extra, I don't know, support they need to launch. Kids with less do it every day."

"Maybe Henrietta wasn't so great. I've been thinking a lot about that lately. Maybe she's able to read people better than most. Look, she plucked us like ripe fruit. We were vulnerable because we wanted one kind of life even though we had another. You wanted to be like the family your mom worked for."

"I never wanted to be like them," I protested. I didn't

want to *be* like them. Not exactly. I'd felt then I deserved to have what they did, though.

Daniel had given it to me.

For a price.

"You know what I mean. You got used to a certain lifestyle. I'm sure living with ten girls in a Bronx walkup eating ramen wasn't appealing."

I looked away from Claire and turned toward the window. Brooklynites were going about their business as usual, none the wiser about the women who lived in Julie House. The placard was small and nondescript, like the signs I remembered from Woodward Tillman. I wanted the memory of my last years to be as innocuous.

I didn't want to think about the very complicated circumstances that had led me down the long Daniel path.

"You buzzed," I said when I turned back to her. I hadn't realized how much Julie House would trigger memories of my time with Daniel.

"I got a proposal that I think we should consider."

"All ears." I flicked my phone to silent and pushed it to the far side of the gray-washed farmhouse table Claire used in place of a traditional desk. She folded her hands. Took a deep breath. I braced myself.

"I'm not trying to be pessimistic. And I don't want you to consider anything I'm saying as suggesting I'm giving up on Julie House."

I tried not to squirm as that feeling of a leaden weight in my stomach grew. In the last year, Julie House had become important to me. It had given me a new lease on life. Something to care about. A mission.

"Someone has approached us. Suggested that we would do well to add a life coach to our group."

"We're looking. We can't afford the top people right now. We decided that the therapist was essential, as was the career counselor. The other people became kind of esoteric as we couldn't necessarily see their immediate worth. I'm sure if we keep plugging and networking, we'll find some wife of a rich Ivy alum who will consider our salary purse money, but do it for the love of the job."

It's what I was doing. The entire salary I took went to rent and food. The interest from the money Daniel had given me paid for everything else. Though in the first year, that hadn't been much. I didn't need the designer clothes. I'd made a decision to ditch a lot of them so the girls could see that a woman could live a full life without them.

"They'd work for free," Claire offered

"Jesus. Is it someone just out of school looking for an internship? I don't think our women are hardy enough to be guinea pigs."

"It's Olga Simon."

"*Her*? She's one of most well-known coaches in the country. On par with Mel Robbins and Eckhart Tolle. Why would she work for free? Did she get cast out of Oprah's inner circle or something?" I paused for a long moment, trying to work it all out in my head. "There's a catch. There's always a string. What am I missing?"

Claire extended her arms across her desk as if we were going to hold hands. She took a very deep breath, then spoke.

"Century Film Productions has approached us."

"That's the in-house production arm of CBT," I fired back.

"So Google tells me. Anyway, they're pitching a show."

"Are you acting on the side or something to pay for a life coach? I thought we were going to seek out strategic donors for this specific purpose if our search didn't pan out." I was so very confused. One of the things I loved about Julie House was that it was one hundred eighty degrees from the cutthroat world of entertainment. No competition. No ratings. No censors. No confusion.

"They want to feature Julie House in a show that will give the viewers the stories of girls getting out of the life."

"Are you serious?" She couldn't be serious. It took me a long second, but even then I couldn't wrap my brain around what she'd just said. "Don't you think this is just a tiny bit exploitative?" I matched the words "tiny bit" with my hands as wide as they would go. "For women who have maybe, just maybe, already been exploited?"

"Normally, yes. I'd agree with you. But I had lunch with Lily Jiang, and she promises that it won't be splashy or over the top. No Housewives. No girls from the shore. *Heir to the Throne* was kind of silly, but it was comedians. *Screenplayed* was really good, though."

I only half listened as she rambled through a reality show checklist.

"Did you say Lily Jiang?"

"Do you know her?"

"She was once Jake Wu's fiancée. May be his wife by now. I don't know." Although in my heart, I did know. That would be too big a coup for the Wus to keep a secret. I'd probably be the first one on the invitation list. My second wedding nonvitation. It was amazing the number of people who didn't want me someplace.

"Oh."

That "oh" made me shift in my seat. That "oh" made it sound like my life as a single woman was a tragedy. That "oh" made it sound like I was pining for a man to come save me. None of that was the least bit true.

I sat up and cleared my throat and took hold of my dignity. "She's a shill for Jake."

"A shill?"

"They had to have had a look at the website. Once they knew I was involved, she was sent to target you. If Jake had so much as texted me, I'd have given him a hard no." I picked up my phone, then put it down again. I only had Julie House and personal e-mails synced. My professional Isabella e-mail was solely on my laptop. There was little cause to use it these days. I'd set it up for when I'd need to look for a real job. But I'd left it for CBT...Connor, Bronwyn, and a few others. If any of them reached out, I hadn't seen it yet.

"I wonder what in the hell is going on at CBT. I never looked at any of the e-mails that weren't from HR."

"From what Lily said, they've put together a new team..."

"Code for someone was fired."

"Really? It sounded so upbeat."

"The word 'no' doesn't exist in entertainment. God forbid you offend anybody who may climb the ladder faster than you."

"Anyway, this new team wants to do a different kind of

reality show. One that's more like the new Oprah. Uplifting. Showing personal improvement."

That's what they'd said to Claire. I imagine in the meeting the adjectives had been more along the lines of "gritty'" appealing to "urban viewers" and "Christian conservative" viewers alike. I had to admit it was kind of brilliant. The people on the coasts would love the subversive nature of the subject matter. The rest in the middle would love a story of redemption. There was a rare show where all the viewers went away satisfied.

"How do you think this would work?" I asked. I had to admit I was a little intrigued. With the proliferation of cable, there were a lot more shows that were doing good things for people. And a lot less Jerry Springer and Maury Povich.

"We've been at this about nine months and it's slow going. The biggest issue, according to you, is that there's nothing pressing to make them jumpstart their new lives. I think that maybe this could be it. You've been frustrated by their inability to move forward, and Dr. Banks' seeming ineffectiveness. I mean, I get it."

I was proud of Claire. She'd really made an effort to keep her own sugar daddy at bay, standing in as kind of a role model. On top of it, she'd launched Julie House. Not that we expected them to all start a nonprofit. But we did expect them to take that first step. It was looking like that first was the hardest for women who hadn't stood on their own as adults.

"What's something as public as a network show going to do that Julie House and Dr. Banks can't?"

"Dare them to fail in public. These girls did not just go to prestigious schools for the education. They more or less did it as a 'fuck you' to all the people who said they couldn't or wouldn't succeed. I think a show could harness that. Use their shame—not of sex...but of public failure and humiliation—to get them to make the final break and take control of their futures."

It made so much damned sense, but I still hated it nonetheless.

"Do you still think Henri exploited us? Our youth? Our naiveté?" I asked. "I'd always thought I was making all the decisions." Now, I wasn't so sure.

"I'm not sure. We made a decision to trade one asset we had, our bodies, for money. It's a decision women make the world over. It was more lucrative than working as a barista. Starbucks could not have covered tuition."

"I don't want to be like Henri, Claire. But Julie House was your idea. This should be your decision."

With Jake involved in any way, I recognized my bias. My head wanted to say no, but my gut was telling me something different. It was telling me that I had to do whatever was in my power to give these girls a chance. One neither Claire nor and I had ever had.

It was only fair that I leave a final decision up to Claire.

"THIS IS A GREAT OPPORTUNITY. We can help you do this work that you find important—rescuing women from prostitution."

"Did you say rescue?" Did he say prostitution? In my mind, there was a difference between a hooker and an escort. I would never say that out loud, though. It wasn't feminist of me. And maybe, it was possible that Claire and I weren't all that different. Although I'd always have the knowledge that Daniel had truly loved me. Had offered to marry me before God and everyone else.

Jake looked like he was trying to be earnest. Trying to keep that judgment off his own face. I looked away from him. Validating his unspoken thoughts would only make me feel worse about myself than I already did.

I couldn't believe I'd agreed to this meeting. What had I been thinking? Here I was in Jake's hotel suite, listening to his personalized pitch for the show. Claire was still on the fence, so she'd set up this meeting to get me on board, I think to make the decision easier on herself.

Then I shook my head just the tiniest bit, so that Jake didn't notice. I knew exactly why I'd agreed to this. A mixture of curiosity and nostalgia.

My head didn't want anything to do with Jake because it had a wonderful understanding that dealing with him always led to heartache if not heartbreak.

But my heart?

My heart just wanted to see him one more time. There was no rational reason for that feeling. One more time when I was sixteen. One more time in Los Angeles. This time, I vowed silently, would be the last. For once and for all, this thing had to be done between us. I had to get him out of my system. I thought I'd been doing a bang-up job until this reality show proposal had come along.

"What's wrong with that?" Jake was asking.

"Hmm?" I couldn't quite follow his train of thought. I'd been too busy trying to push him out of my head.

"I was asking you what was wrong with my terminology. That's what you're objecting to, right? Not just the idea of me being involved."

I wasn't going to touch that last part with a ten-foot pole.

"Rescuing makes them victims. Which they're not. These are women who need help making a lifestyle change, like a diet show."

"Going from selling their bodies for sex to working a legitimate job?" Jake asked. I looked at his eyes, his hands...to assess his motives, his true feelings about this work. All of a sudden it was vitally important that he not judge the Julie House residents harshly. That he not put that pox on them that so many people did when it came to women and sex work.

"You've got all of this the wrong way around," I insisted.

"What? Not politically correct enough? Sometimes I miss China. We don't have to tiptoe around every goddamn subject."

"Except how your communism makes some people billionaires and leaves huge swaths in grinding poverty. That's a far cry from 'each according to his ability, to each according to his needs.'"

A deep furrow appeared in his brow. "You're quoting Marx."

"I'm quoting Karl Marx because I don't think you understand one damned thing about the Julie House mission."

"So explain it to me."

The weird thing about having known someone for twenty-plus years was that I could read him like a book—eighty percent of the time. I didn't think he was being deliberately obtuse. That would make him too much of an asshole. The Jake I'd known had redeeming qualities that had kept him from being a carbon copy of his father. I leaned forward, tried again.

"These aren't crack whores giving ten-dollar blow jobs on the corner of Forty-Second Street. No offense to those women." And I meant that. Whenever I passed someone like that on the street or in a park, I had a "but for the grace of God go I" moment.

"They have a completely different set of motivations, and I hope for them they get out if they want or at least aren't suffering criminal penalties at a rate greater than the men they service."

"What's the difference? From where I sit, your girls are working a few hours a week for a full-time salary and don't want to work full time for the same money."

"Is that how you saw me? Some lazy woman who wanted to lay on her back rather than sit in a leather executive chair?" I didn't like that it mattered what Jake thought about me, my past with Daniel, but it did—more than I wanted it to.

"Um...no. You're different," stumbled from his lips. I wanted to agree with him. Bolster his argument about how he was right. But that would sell the same girls short that I wanted to help.

"Different how?" I pestered. We were practically knee to knee now.

He blinked once before he responded as if the answer was obvious. "I knew you before."

"You could have known them. Two went to your vaunted prep school in Connecticut. One Owen. A sprinkling of Ivies, Seven Sisters schools, the other elites in Massachusetts and Pennsylvania." For the most part, rich and accomplished men didn't want dumb girls on their arms. They wanted arm candy that not only looked good but could also discuss the North Korean and Iranian nuclear crises at the same time. I'd stopped ignoring world politics when I met Daniel, and then took up subscriptions to *The Economist* and *The Wall Street Journal.*

"The issue is," I spelled out, "giving up the lifestyle. It's not something I think you'd get because you've always been rich. Do you know what it's like to live on the other side?"

I pushed against his knee, used the leverage to stand up and move toward the window, where I could watch the poor walking down the sidewalk in the awful heat, and the rich getting out of one air-conditioned limo or another.

"You live alongside rich people, but you're not *among* them. It's not obvious every moment of every day, but some days the differences are stark." I beckoned to him. "Come look."

He stood next to me. I closed my nose against his familiar smell before I could get carried away by sense memory. I pointed down from the window toward Church Street.

"You see that girl in the blue slacks, light blue blouse? That outfit says Ann Taylor. Not cheap, but not designer, either. Her bag, a Louis Vuitton. Probably the only expensive thing she owns. Makes her feel like she belongs. See the woman about to cross her path into that doorman building? She looks about the same, right?"

Jake nodded.

"Her suit? Carolina Herrera. More expensive by a factor of ten. Same for that bag. Burberry. Casual, but four times the price of that girl's bag. It's not that woman's only one. She's wearing a pink designer suit and her bag matches. That pink plaid isn't an everyday bag.

"And that's just the clothes. The apartment will be three times bigger and a million times more expensive. The Hampton's beach house will be hers, not a shared rental. They'll both fly to Paris. One coach, one first class. I could go on. But the differences are stark from that young woman's point of view, probably. Especially for our Julie House women. Like me, they've seen both sides up close and personal."

Jake's hand on my arm caused a shudder deep within me. I hid it with a pretend cough, then cleared my throat. He didn't let go, but gently turned me toward him.

"Is it the same for you? We practically grew up in the same house."

I looked for signs he was being disingenuous. The Chinese weren't different from the British in this way. Servants practically lived with their employers. Mama and I certainly had. But no one, master nor servant, forgot their station.

America pretended to blur those lines with its staunch belief, if not practice, of meritocracy. For the first time, I wondered if we'd remembered all of the last twenty-plus years completely differently. After a long moment where I considered my words, I spoke.

"I had Christmas with Mama in the house. You had New York City, or Shanghai, or Europe. Spring break, I was with Mama. Maybe a trip to the Jersey Shore if the weather had warmed up enough. One year you went to Egypt to see the pyramids because Mrs. Li wanted to see the world wonders and ride a camel. I was home helping Mama make and freeze your dad's favorite pasta."

At least he had the good grace to look almost pained at that last. Because that's how it had been. We'd lived and shaped our lives around the Wus.

"Our situation was...unique."

"Not really. Claire gets accepted to Owen. Her family is thrilled. Nowhere in the brochure do you see her shoving down her dinner in less than five minutes so she can get into the kitchen and begin her shift spraying down dishes and running them through the washer while the chef is surprising the other kids with cream puffs he made that night for fun."

"Where does..." I could practically see him sorting through his English language words for the right one, the politically correct one. "...escorting come in?"

"This conversation is off the record, right?"

"I'm not a journalist."

"This is a crime we're talking about. A low-level, not often prosecuted one, but still a violation of the law, nonetheless. I don't want you turning anyone in."

"I'm not a tattle. If I learned only one thing in China, it was how to keep my mouth shut."

Maybe I'd judged those communists far too harshly. I let out a sigh I feel like I'd been holding for more than a decade. I'd had no idea how much this work would bring up old stuff. Stuff I'd thought I'd put away years ago, if not last year, when I'd severed ties with Daniel once and for all.

"Henri. Henrietta Mosier was our...handler." Not Madame, never Madame. "When your dad cut me off, I had to make tuition or I was going to be 'separated from the university,' to use Owen's term."

"I still can't believe he—"

"It's done. It was done years ago. She gave me a way to earn enough to pay tuition. Tuition. Not coffee and beer money that work study would have provided."

"Why didn't you just transfer to Rutgers or community college."

"Because those were good enough for you? Because I'm

some kind of second-class citizen? The rich kids get the elite schools and the poor kids get something else that's good enough, but not good enough for you?"

"Because you wouldn't have to give up your dignity."

"What dignity? The kind that had Claire serving drinks to grad school students and her own professors?"

"It's honest work."

"Sex work is honest work. In fact, it's probably the most honest work out there."

"How could you do it, though? Have sex with that man...Daniel?"

I flashed back to the one time they'd met. The one time my two worlds had collided. That night in Philadelphia when Jake's former bully and now friend, Cole Lehman, had insulted me, and Jake had come to my apartment to apologize. The apartment subsidized by Daniel.

"Maybe you don't remember, but when you first met him, you were there to make up for the fact that your friend had so easily defined me by who I'd slept with."

"Sometimes I wonder if there are enough sorries in the world to make up for what my family, my friends, said and did to you," Jake mused.

"The first thing we tell Julie House clients is that there's no changing the past." I'd finally taken that to heart. I couldn't go back and make Mrs. Li approve of me. Or Mr. Wu keep his promises. Or make the Jake of the past love me like I'd loved him. Or make my mother more loyal or either of my fathers love me. The past was just that—long gone and immutable. My goal was to put the past in a lockbox for the

Julie House women so they could begin their futures much more quickly.

"But Daniel? He was like sixty or something," Jake said, sounding like a bad song on repeat.

"Isn't that always the question? The one the sex positive *and* sex negative focus on. The sex is the least of it. It's just an act."

"Just an act?" Jake's face pulled into another frown. I wanted to say what Mama had warned, about it freezing that way, but I resisted. For a fleeting second, I wondered if he was thinking about one of the two times we'd been together, nearly fourteen years apart. That first time it had felt like he was performing an act. The second time, I think I'd been the one performing. Neither had been built on genuine emotion for the both of us.

"That's what I'm trying to tell you. The part that makes it hard to leave is traveling first class, enjoying the finest in dining, fashion, hotels."

"It's not..."

"It's not what? What if I told you, you had to travel coach? Give up your custom suits. That you had to stay in New Jersey or New York or even China, but you couldn't travel between them. Where are you staying now?" I took a turn around the room like a game show model.

"Four Seasons," he mumbled.

"That's not on CBT's dime." If our per diem hadn't even allowed for taxis in L.A. city limits, surely it didn't cover luxury hotels in one of the world's most expensive cities.

"I upgraded myself," he admitted.

"Where's Lily staying? No, fuck it, she's one of you. Where's *Alexandra* staying?"

"The Marriott." He winced like he'd left my former assistant, now his, in a cardboard box under the Brooklyn Bridge. He leaned forward, earnest again, thrusting out his arms in a way that I knew meant he was about to give an unnecessary explanation, like the rich did when they got caught employing a double standard. "CBT has a deal with—"

"But not good enough for *you*. You see the double standard, right? And it's not as if these women have to work fifteen johns a night in a roadside motel. It's a single man. A long-term relationship...agreement, per se."

He walked toward his floor-to-ceiling windows and practically pressed his beautiful nose against the glass. Jake thrust his hands into the pockets of his flawlessly fitted pants and closed his eyes for a long moment. In the reflection, I could see them open again. He turned to me; the full force of his gaze practically penetrated me.

"Claire isn't going to say yes to the show unless you do. You know that, right? You hold all the cards here, Isabella."

"I think this is a bad idea." I paused for a few seconds. "A very, very bad idea." I knew my hesitation was a moment too long.

"But..."

"What we're doing isn't working for everyone. They don't want to change even though they know what they're doing can't go on forever. That their bodies have an expiration date."

"Is that a yes?"

"That's a yes with a long list of conditions." I wanted to go to bat for the girls. Do whatever I needed to make sure they weren't left in the predatory hands of television producers.

"I always did love a negotiation. Can we discuss it over dinner?"

CHAPTER EIGHT
JAKE

NOW

"WHERE DO YOU WANT TO GO?" Isabella asked as she picked up her phone, tuning me out. I was so surprised by her quick and easy acquiescence that I stumbled over my response.

"I thought we'd stay here. Order room service. Easier for me to take notes that way."

"Sure, whatever," she said. I was ninety-nine percent sure she didn't know what she'd just agreed to. Last year, she'd said that she and Daniel were over, but watching Isabella with her nose in her phone made me uncertain.

I wasn't sure why I cared. No, I was exactly sure why I cared, and the fact that the flame between us flickered but never died was hard to take. But she'd said no to us more than a year ago. I was still on the fence as to whether I'd accepted her rejection as her last and final answer. There was something inside my head. A little seed of doubt that said we had unfinished business.

I left the living room and walked through the short hall

back to the suite's bedroom and picked up the phone next to the bed. I flipped through the too-long room service menu before I placed an order for salad, seared tuna and New York cheesecake. I hesitated for a second, but decided against their signature tagliatelle.

Isabella had always been particular about her Italian food. Her mother Maria's being the standard against which all others were judged. Before I hung up, my last request was to get to the top of the queue. I wanted the food here before she could change her mind. Bella seemed as skittish as a cat.

When I came out, she hadn't moved, her head was still buried in the phone like it had the secret to the Holy Grail. I stood and watched her, unobserved. I'd rarely done this as an adult, but had a million times when we'd lived together in Toms River. When I was supposed to be studying, I'd turn my head and see her through the window. She'd be running or laughing or playing. I'd never decided which had been stronger, my envy of her ease at happiness or my longing to share it with her.

"Work?" I tried to make my voice light. But light wasn't my forte. The weight of more than two decades of our history laid heavily in that single word.

"Stuff about my dad," she said. Isabella turned the phone over in her hand. Rhinestones on the back of the case caught the light, sending sparks across the wall and ceiling. She lifted her chin. Met my gaze. "My...uh...the dad I had in Philadelphia."

We were both quiet for a long moment before I acknowledged that painful moment we'd shared. "I remember."

She put the phone face down on the couch cushion and

looked at me. I pretended not to notice that her eyes were almost brimming with tears...almost. I think she learned, probably starting at my father's knee, how to keep her feelings in check. I know I certainly did.

My "what happened?" corresponded exactly with a knock on the door. Suddenly, I regretted that push to get the food right away.

"Who's that?" she asked as she glanced toward the door.

"Dinner."

"Oh." I could see the confusion replace sadness in her eyes.

"I mentioned room service. Easier to continue our conversation. The tables at New York restaurants are so tiny the meals barely fit, much less paper for notes."

Her "Oh. Okay," was more resigned than enthusiastic. I took it.

That routine where the room service guy unfurls a table cloth on a table he rolled in, plops silver trays down, then lifts each with a flourish was all of a sudden far too long.

When I'd placed the order, I'd imagined Isabella being wowed by the spectacle of high-end service. But I could see in her world-weary eyes, it wasn't the kind of thing that impressed her anymore. I pushed a large cash tip toward the attendant, stopping him mid-display, signed the bill in his leather pouch and all but shoved him out the door.

Isabella unwound her long legs from under her and took a chair at the small dining table. She didn't say anything about it being nearly as small as a New York restaurant table. There was no room for more than the dishes before us. I followed suit and sat across from her, laying the heavy linen napkin in my lap.

"This looks good for hotel food. Wonder what Alexandra is having?" Isabella arched an eyebrow, whether in humor or condemnation, I couldn't tell. I leaned toward the former as it made feel a lot better.

"I'll give her a raise. Buy her a steak or send her to Nobu for her birthday. But we're most definitely not talking about CBT's travel budget right now." I turned my head to the phone abandoned on the couch. "What happened?"

"Happened?" She look at the nearly perfect place setting, the heavy weight of the utensils keeping the tablecloth firmly in place.

"With your dad, Bella," I said. We'd been intimate in more ways than most. I didn't have the energy to pretend that we were just work colleagues taking a meeting about a potential project. "With your dad."

"He wasn't my dad." Looking me directly in the eyes, she did nothing to shield the pain radiating from them. "That's the crux of it, isn't it?"

In that one moment, I loved Bella more fiercely than I ever had. The urge to protect her overwhelmed my senses, protect her from a future of hurts and slights like this one that said she didn't belong.

In my mind, I whispered the words, "you'll always belong to me, with me," because it was true. Truer than anything I'd ever understood before or since.

I didn't say anything out loud, though. Scooted my seat in. Passed the butter, bread basket, and salad dressing. I excused myself and pulled a bottle of Viognier from the fridge. I poured each of us a generous amount. Isabella drank the first glass as if it were water.

I didn't comment. Something told me that she wasn't normally a heavy drinker. Probably needed something to calm the jumble of feelings swirling inside. I merely refilled before sitting the bottle in the silver ice bucket that had come up with dinner.

"I guess he never sold the house in Philly," she started, after she'd taken a few bites of food. She set her heavy fork on the china. "Mama said he'd sold it. But I guess that's just what he'd told her when he kicked us out. It's been a rental all these years. Long paid off. He died without a will. In the eyes of the Pennsylvania probate court, I'm still his daughter. He never disclaimed me during the divorce process. Legally, I'm Francis Aconi's daughter. So much irony in that."

She looked toward the window. It didn't take a psychic to read her thoughts. I knew then she was reliving her life. Recasting herself in the role of a Philly girl with a single mom with autonomy. Replacing the image of what had instead been true, her mom willingly beholden to my dad in a home where Isabella had to come in second place.

"I had a friend from college, who's now a lawyer, look up the old divorce papers. Mama agreed to no support and some generic visitation schedule—which never happened, obviously. Nowhere was there any mention that he wasn't my father. He didn't ask for any kind of test. Didn't make any formal claim. Anyway, the house is worth something like nine hundred thousand dollars. Which, if sold, would have to be split between Arturo and I. My brother wants me to give my portion to his grandmother—Francis' mother."

That money, probably four hundred thousand after all the various fees and taxes, would probably make a huge difference in Bella's life. I kind of wanted to wire her that amount to set her free from this dilemma. That kind of gesture wouldn't go over well at all, so I didn't even suggest it. Instead I topped up her wine, then my own.

"What are you going to do?"

"I don't know. Honestly, I really don't know. I mean, I guess it's not really my money. But Nonna hates me so much. I'm just the offspring of some slut who trapped her son."

"Hey there with the language," I admonished. I hated the idea of Bella thinking of herself that way. No matter her beginnings, she'd become an amazing, wonderful woman.

It was so crystal clear to me now that I'd made too many mistakes. Almost, but not quite, messed things up beyond fixing.

"Seriously. Tell me you haven't thought those same words about me, or if not me, then Claire or the women at Julie House."

"Other people may think like that, but I don't." I'm glad she didn't reference my own stepmother. Those words would not have been misplaced in Min Li's mouth.

"How could that be? Almost ninety-nine percent of the population thinks like that."

"Do you remember the time that Father sent me to China?"

"Which time? My punishment was to be sent to my room. Yours was to be sidelined to China like it was one big reeducation camp."

She was right about that. I'd stopped being so wildly

disobedient after that first time. Father had held on to my American visa like it was a hostage. I hadn't felt truly liberated until I'd gotten permanent US residency a few years back. That, coupled with a generous salary and perks, had finally given me the independence to do my own thing. The latest sexual harassment allegations against Father had only made it all the more easy for me to forge my own path. Step out of his locus of control.

"Anyway, he took me to a..." Whorehouse wasn't the word I'd use, not now with the show about Julie House on the line. She wouldn't understand the Chinese word. I hedged. "A house where you could visit a woman. I...I couldn't go in."

"Why not? That seems like most guys' dream. You didn't even have to do it yourself, get up the courage. Your dad did all that for you. Delivered you."

"The way he was talking in the car on the way over. I think...I think that my mother could have maybe worked there at one time."

It was the first time I'd ever admitted that out loud. But I think Bella was the only person in the world who would understand what that meant. To find out the parent you'd thought was yours...wasn't.

Food forgotten, she stared at me, mouth agape. It took five long seconds before she closed her lips. Pursed them. Then her face softened in what I hoped was sympathy more than pity. Starving African children were to be pitied. Begging Indian ones that you saw in Mysore. Stray dogs in Greece. With all my advantages, I did not deserve pity.

"Your mother? Min Li? I thought she was from a rich family your father married into. Then took over her father's business, turning him from upper middle class to million-aire." She recited the same story that everyone believed. The one that was buried at the end of magazine articles glorifying my father's business acumen.

"That. All that is true. The last part, at least. Min Li isn't my mother." I let silence fill the pause in conversation. "We have more in common than you think." The last I said quietly. I think it's one reason I'd always felt an unbreakable connection to her after that night when we'd walked in on my father and her mother, and Maria had revealed the truth about Isabella's own parentage.

Though now I see Maria Aconi's revelation for what it was—the biggest deflection ever to keep Bella from questioning the inappropriate scene we'd walked in on.

My father's own deflection had been to send me for "reeducation" in China, then to boarding school.

They'd punished us for their transgressions.

"Really?" Isabella's "really" wasn't the excited utterance of someone who'd just learned she had something in common with a friend, but instead the defeated utterance of someone who'd been lied to one time too many.

After a prolonged sigh, her voice came out whispered, "Oh my God. Really. When...? How...? I don't know what to say."

"The when and how doesn't really matter. There's no time that kind of information isn't a shock and surprise. I'm telling you because I get it. How you feel like you're in between two different worlds. The public one where people think someone is your parent and the private one where everyone knows the truth."

Isabella pushed away the half-eaten food and retreated to the couch. Her shoes came off and she tucked her long legs under her. I threw a large cloth napkin over the leftovers and pushed the rolling table by the door. I wasn't any hungrier than she was.

I should have sat across from her a safe five feet away in the swiveling office chair or even in the side chair. Anywhere that wasn't within touching distance. I couldn't help myself though, taking up the space right next to her. Not so close as to be inappropriate, but close enough that I could feel the heat, smell the perfume coming from her skin.

"You keep the money, though, right?" she asked.

"Me?" I didn't follow

"The money from Min Li's family." She said it like it was an indictment.

"It's twice removed. Father built DynoAppliances, then automotive, now CBT. It's not the same as the money you have coming to you."

"Maybe not. Then. I don't want the house. I don't want the money. But giving it to a woman who denies my very existence because of something I had zero control over makes me crazy."

Against my better judgment, I took her hands in mine, silently urging her to turn toward me. She did, then she lifted her eyes. They met mine. That pull was there in an instant. That thing that had always been between us blazed bright.

"Don't make a decision now," I said. I folded her fingers tighter within mine.

"I have to disclaim within some number of days. That's what my lawyer friend says."

"That's just it." I pulled her hands closer, against my chest. "You don't. You can take the property and decide later. Disclaim later or whatever. The one thing I've learned with all the Dyno iterations is not to be pressured into a decision that's not life or death. It never benefits you, just the person pushing their agenda."

Maybe I'd learned that lesson best from the Liling fiasco. There'd been no hurry to get engaged except to forward everyone's agenda but my own.

I'd let them push me around one time too many. Now I took my time with every decision, whether it needed it or not. But my suspicion hadn't dialed back in all these years.

Instead of pulling back, Bella leaned forward. I was quickly enveloped in her unique fragrance of vanilla and lemon and something distinctly her. I fought the urge to pull her even closer.

"Oh my God. You're right. I don't know why I was caving to that. I would never have allowed anyone at CBT to push me around like that. Thank you. Thank you. Thank you."

She punctured that third thanks with a kiss that was meant for my cheek, but when I turned toward her, landed instead on my lips. I'm sure that wasn't at all what she meant to do, but I didn't pull away. In fact, I did a Sheryl Sandberg and leaned in.

Most of my sense memories involved food. Noodles in Shanghai. Dumplings in Nanjing. My first fresh pasta in New Jersey. But Bella's kiss was the most potent memory of them all. In less than the time it took for me to close my eyes, I was back on that Greyhound bus, her hand in mine, my lips on hers.

Unlike that first time, this time my kiss was unhurried. I explored her lips with mine. When she opened to gasp or take a breath, I didn't pull back. I leaned in even more, tracing first her lips with my tongue, then caressed her tongue. It was the wine that was making me heady. At least, that's what I wanted to believe, because this had been the furthest thing from my mind when I'd invited her here to convince her to do the show.

I pulled away to take my own breath, hoping to slow the heaving of my chest. Isabella's look was not that of a confused sixteen-year-old or the calculated one from last year. It was like that first kiss on the New York, New Jersey state line. Bella eyes were open, her expression one of vulnerability. That alone was the biggest aphrodisiac ever.

I fitted my fingers in her hair, bringing her near. Her eyes closed, but I didn't kiss her lips. Instead, I nipped the side of her neck. Her gasp of surprise quickly turned to pleasure.

As if on cue, my cock reacted, springing to life.

I kissed my way down to her collarbone, pushing aside the crisp white T, exposing a mole I didn't quite remember.

"Jake," she sighed. My name on that single breath made my pants painfully tight.

I pulled away only long enough to pull her shirt over her head and unfasten the midnight-blue bra that was keeping me from the skin I craved. I thanked the gods that it unhooked in the front. In a moment, her beautiful breasts, her nipples as hard as pebbles, spilled out. I didn't waste a single second, pulling the tip of her breast deep into my mouth, sucking one moment, licking the tip the next.

I was most grateful that she wasn't unaffected, that I wasn't alone in this storm of desire. Her hands were everywhere. First, she was pushing against the wool of my suit jacket, then her deft fingers skimmed down the front of my shirt, buttons loosening in their wake. That stiff cotton soon joined my jacket somewhere. Despite the moans she was unable to keep inside, that were like fire in my own veins, I took my mouth from her breasts, and fitted it against her mouth again.

Skin to skin was glorious. Her heavy breasts pushed against my chest. With that friction, I nearly lost any semblance of patience. I'd been waiting years, fifteen, fourteen, one, forever. And finally, finally it was right.

I could sense that we were finally in the same place at the same time. Wanting each other. Understanding each other. Intimacy and vulnerability and lust made for a heady combination.

"Bella, my God, Bella," I panted as I kissed my way between her breasts to the button of the blue cotton pants that fit like tights.

I slipped the button loose and skimmed it apart. Navy lace panties the same color as her bra greeted me. I loved her lingerie, but I liked her naked even more.

"Lift up," I whispered.

She complied. The pants were more of a challenge than I'd expected, and we both laughed as they wedged around her feet.

"Are you okay?" I asked. It was really two questions. I wanted to know if she was okay with being nearly naked. But more than that, I wanted to know if she was okay with what we were doing. If she said yes at this point, I had no plans to turn back.

Not a single one.

What I'd always wanted was too close for me to step away in three minutes or five.

"I'm more than okay, Jake. More than okay."

She'd just hooked her thumbs in the elastic of her panties when a loud crashing sound filled the room.

I jerked back and turned my head toward the door, which I could only half see from the living room area.

"Jesus fucking Christ," Liling said, standing over the remains of fish, salad, and uneaten cherry cheesecake that had toppled to the floor. "Maybe we need to rename the show Whores on Parade."

As swiftly as I could, I picked up my shirt and threw it over Bella. She clutched at it like a lifeline.

"You told her?" Bella whispered.

"What? That you fucked an old dude for money? Yeah, he told me. I'd always wondered what he saw in you. Now I know. He wanted a professional. Well, he got it."

FOR A FEW FRANTIC SECONDS, my brain ping-ponged between suitable reactions. I pushed away the Isabella I'd been at sixteen, who had skulked away when I'd realized that Jake's friends didn't think I was as good as them. I put that little girl away in the past where she firmly belonged.

Instead, I pulled out the Isabella I was now.

I had Daniel to thank for that—the woman I'd become. He'd always insisted that I be treated well. That no one treated me like the hired...companion that I was. Coupled with the lifeline he'd given me in the form of a check with eight zeroes, I didn't need to slink away ever again.

"I'm quite good at any number of things. Only one of them is sex. But I don't work in front of a crowd. If you'll excuse me."

I stood. Jake's clothes fell away on the thick carpet in a near silent tumble. Leisurely, comfortable with my near nudity, I gathered my clothes and strode through the little hall toward the bedroom. I closed the door behind me because I could only carry that façade so far.

Alone inside the huge hotel bedroom, the humiliation was almost unbearable.

With only a single cutting look, Jake's ex had reduced me to what I'd been for years.

I shoved on my clothes. Then I rinsed my face in the bathroom, careful not to look into my own eyes. I threw cold water on my skin until the heat of embarrassment receded. Then I took a deep breath.

I put my hand on the door, but hesitated. They were arguing like an old married couple. I didn't need to be in the middle of that. I waited until there was a long pause, then strode back into the main living area.

"Excuse me. I'm just going to get going." I shoved my papers and phone into my tote, pushed my toes into my sneakers and strode out the door, holding my head high.

Once outside, I debated between a cab, an Uber, the train, or melting into a puddle of goo right then and there. I picked the A train, both because of the song and because I needed the time to think. And there was nothing like a slow subway train in New York for thinking. For thirty minutes, I let the jostling of iron wheels on steel tracks and too many people on too small of a car keep me from thinking too hard about what I'd just done.

The walk to my apartment was pleasant, and I thanked God in heaven for giving me at least one July evening when Brooklyn wasn't sweltering with summer heat.

"You're not answering your phone."

Jake's voice scared the shit out of me. I looked around,

making sure I wasn't hallucinating. But I wasn't crazy. Jake was right there as if he'd sprung forth from my mind, slouching against the bricks next to my building's smoked-glass front door.

"Fuck *me*." After I said those two words, I wanted to take them back. I'd already been embarrassed today. It couldn't get any worse. I took my bag from my shoulder and rested it on my toes. "What are you doing here? Do the rich get some kind of teleportation device or something?"

"Just a regular cab, Bella. Crossed the bridge like a mere mortal." He pulled himself up to his full height. "We need to talk," he intoned.

"What do we have to talk about, Jake? I kind of want to go to bed. Forget this afternoon happened."

It wasn't yet dark, but that didn't mean I wasn't ready to put on a sleep shirt and curl up under the covers until the sting of humiliation went away.

"Jesus, Bella. Don't say that." The anguish in his voice caught me off guard. Made me lower my own—just a tiny bit.

"I'm not going to have this conversation on the street. Just come in already."

He followed me across the lobby to the glass and steel elevator. As if by mutual agreement, we were silent on the ride to the fifth floor. I dug for my keys and turned the three locks that kept my apartment secure.

I walked in and flipped on a single switch that turned on a few halogen spots, lighting the kitchen/living/dining area, but not so much as to detract from the floor-to-ceiling window view that I was paying through the nose for.

"This kind of looks like every apartment you've ever lived in," Jake said.

I didn't pretend to misunderstand him. It was generic. Nearly interchangeable with his Four Seasons suite.

"I've been living in borrowed homes since I was twelve. I'm not sure any of this makes a difference." I gestured to the muted tones of the curtains, walls, floor. I'd moved in. Bought a bunch of furniture from Pottery Barn and Crate and Barrel, and hadn't thought about it since. My last home had been in Philly. And it looked like that was about to be up for sale.

"Your mom made your house in New Jersey cozy. I always liked it a lot more than our place."

Jake walked around the room, picking up and putting down World Market knick-knacks, overpriced pillows. All the things that were supposed to make my apartment look like home. From the look on his face, I didn't think I was fooling anyone.

I shrugged off my tote. Kicked off my shoes. Dropped my keys into a ceramic bowl by the door. Then I moved toward the kitchen area. We'd gotten distracted from dinner, and I was still hungry.

"Your...mom...Mrs. Li, did not do a good job there. I could never figure it. She was always so flawlessly dressed," I said of the eye-burning décor of the original Toms River house. That had been bulldozed years ago. The new one was probably *Architectural Digest* material.

"She'd never admit it, but she was fresh off the boat." Jake shrugged out of his suit jacket for the second time. He laid it on one of the teak dining room chairs. He stood on the other side of my breakfast bar. "She was trying to combine what would have been the height of style in Shanghai and the US. It all clashed. The new house is perfect. It's been in a bunch of magazines in China. Maybe the US, too, I don't know. Liling would know."

I could tell the moment he realized he'd said her name and the moment he regretted it.

"Gave *her* a show. Did you give her soap to wash out her eyes?" I worked hard to keep my voice casual.

"I forgot she had a key." He swallowed hard.

"Don't sweat it. Consider it forgotten." I opened the fridge. Pulled out the orange-and-white-striped Junior's box. "Want a slice of chocolate swirl cheesecake? I think your ex smashed the other."

Jake didn't answer, really. He undid the top two buttons of his shirt and took one of the stools. I slid a knife through the cake once, then twice. Awkwardly, I lifted a first slice, then a second onto dessert plates.

"Is everything in this apartment gray?" he asked.

The two-bedroom accent walls were black. The kitchen cabinets were gloss white, but everything else was...gray. I hadn't thought much about it these last months. My mind had been elsewhere—Julie House, my half-brother, my not-father.

"Gray is the new beige, I think. It's like color without commitment."

Jake laughed long and hard, but it was genuine. In that second, all the tension between us dissipated. We were just us again. Two kids who'd sheltered each other through the first years in Jersey.

"You're so right, Bella. It's the same in China and London. Italy?"

"Nope, all white. They're not on board yet. Probably because it's as hot as Hades down there. No one ever mentions that. It's maybe why gelato and Prosecco are so damned popular. Speaking of. That's what this needs." I pulled a bottle of the bubbly off the lower level of the fridge and popped the top. Got flutes and poured us glasses. I wasn't drunk enough for this. For Jake and aborted sex and his ex-fiancée all in one day.

"About today, Bella..." he started.

Like discomfort was a drinking game, I downed the contents of the flute. Poured another for myself. He hadn't touched his.

"What about it, Jake? What about it? There are some people who do not need to be in each other's lives. Maybe we're those people." That's what I'd concluded after a half hour on the train. Maybe I didn't need to make this same mistake a third time. If the definition of crazy was doing the same thing twice, then us...a third time was the definition of criminally insane.

"I was thinking the exact opposite."

Of course he was. That was the problem right there in a nutshell.

"You should marry Liling or Lily or whatever her name is." If he did, we'd be over. The idea of us ever getting together would be over. That hope I secretly held out would be gone. Maybe then I'd be able to move on. Date someone else. Find another love. Lots of people had more than one. Most people, probably. I wanted to not be stuck in the same rut for the next twenty like I'd been for the last twenty. That seemed like the very definition of tragedy.

"Why didn't you marry Daniel?" he asked.

I placed my fork on my almost-empty plate, wondering if I'd told him about Daniel's proposal. But we had been anything but close by the time the two most important men in my life had met.

"What makes you think he wanted that?"

"I didn't. Not until last year, when I took a long, hard look in the mirror when I was thinking of you. That person reflected back at me wasn't hardly different from the way he looked at you."

I wanted to kick myself for the little flutter in my belly at his words. He still had an effect on me. Though the little afternoon assignation had proved that. I wanted to stamp that out. Not let the idea that this man, whom I'd loved as a boy, looked in the mirror and saw his love for me. The weakest part of me wanted to believe it. The wisest part of me knew that I shouldn't.

"Nobody marries their john. Life is not *Pretty Woman*."

I'd watched that movie a thousand times looking for clues. The only thing I'd unearthed was the fiction was fiction and my real life was nothing like the fantasy Hollywood put on display.

"That movie..." He didn't need to say any more.

"Yeah, that."

The only sound for the next few minutes was that of forks on ceramic. We finished our desserts. I took the plates. Systematically rinsed them. Stashed them in the dishwasher. Kept me from having to look at him. I don't know where his standard poker face had gone, but it was nowhere to be found. I could read him like a dictionary.

"I was serious about what I said a minute ago, you know. I haven't changed my mind about us in the last few months."

I closed the cardboard cake box. Shoved it back in the fridge. Got the kitchen towel—its teal green was the only spot of color in the room—wiped down crumbs I couldn't see. I didn't look up.

"It's not a good idea."

"You keep saying that. Why? You left brunch with a resignation letter and a plane ticket but without an explanation."

I didn't point out that he was talking about a meal from over a year ago like it was last week. I'd often thought if all the time that we'd been together had been added up. It wouldn't be more than the hours in a week, maybe a month. Any idea of us having a relationship was only an illusion.

"We were never in love at the same time." I took a deep drink of the sparkling white wine. "This is perfect though, isn't it?"

"Did you bring it from Italy?"

"I had some empty space in my luggage and too long a layover in Rome." I did a game show flourish. "From duty free to my kitchen."

"I want us to be in love at the same time, Bella. We once were. At least, I was that fall...that night of the concert."

"I was so young then. Younger than you were. I didn't know what I was feeling back then. All I remember are the nerves. That feeling in the pit of my belly whenever I thought of you, saw you, sat next to you. Love came later."

"When?" he asked.

I almost fell down because this was the Jake of my fantasies. How many times had I wanted to have this conversation? Seek out that elusive concept of closure? I knew that I should ask him to leave. Kill the stupid romantic movie ideal. Firmly eject him from my life once and for all like a DVD from the player.

But the idea that we could finally talk about all the things that we never had was more alluring than the idea of a peaceful evening. Because if he left now, I wouldn't get that elusive peace. I'd be spinning out all the ways the conversation could have gone. Better to get it over with.

I sighed loudly then dug deep for all those feelings I'd had so many years ago.

"When I got into that red SUV and drove all the way to Connecticut. I loved you so much," I whispered. "At least I think I did. I don't know now. I'd built it up so much in my mind. Our secret romance. We were practically Romeo and Juliet, or maybe a less tragic pair of star-crossed lovers, as far as I was concerned. I was defying everyone and risking everything to come see you. I'd probably shaved and tweezed to within an inch of my life because it was going to be this amazing weekend. My first time and everything. This magical mating like some...what was that director's name... like some John Hughes movie."

"I'm sorry. I didn't know..."

I waved away his apology. I'd made enough peace with the shitty way he'd treated me that weekend. Once I'd gotten beyond my hurt feelings, I was able to see what had been going on. Though Mama's words had been cruel when she'd said that he didn't love me, they had been true.

"You weren't in love with me back then. When I think about it now, the signals were clear. But I couldn't see it then. Not until I got back home." Not until after the abortion, I thought, by didn't say. "Then I went to college and life became about different things. Proving myself. Graduation. Career."

"Daniel." The way Jake said the name, it floated like a specter in the room.

"A complication I never saw coming. But you know what, Jake. Life doesn't come with any do-overs. I'm not sure if I'd really change anything anyway."

He winced at that, but I had to let him be with his feelings of regret. I'd mostly gotten past my own. That, I think, was what growing up was truly about.

"I'd change everything," he said.

I kind of wanted to shake him. I wasn't exactly one of those woo-woo California types who said "everything happens for a reason" in the kind of voice that made you want to throttle their tanned necks. But there was more than a grain of truth to that. It just wasn't the higher-power reason, but a more nuanced psychological one.

"What? If your mom wasn't your mom, you wouldn't be here. You'd be an entirely different person if Min Li was your real mom, don't you think? You'd be like those kids all over Instagram flaunting their money and their cars."

"I'd change the fact that I hurt you," he said, his voice a near whisper.

I had to turn away then. I looked out of the floor-to-ceiling windows at the Gowanus Canal. Some flyer a neighbor had slipped under the door reported that it was one of the most polluted waterways in the northeast. Supposedly life couldn't be sustained there. There'd been some cleanup, but it still smelled like death on a hot day.

"Some things can't be fixed." My mama for one. Mr. Wu for another.

"I don't believe that, Bella."

I couldn't even believe I was entertaining this—whatever *this* was. But some part of me was going soft with the presence of my first love sitting on my kitchen stool.

Who hadn't had the fantasy of their first love coming back, groveling, saying they'd been wrong? The reality, though, was so much different from the fantasy. In the fantasy, we'd kiss and...I don't know, ride off into the sunset somewhere on some horse or in the convertible I still had in storage in L.A.

The reality was that people loved, lost. Then found love again with someone different. I'd wanted that. To find real love with a person who didn't know my past and wouldn't judge me when I revealed it to them. But work and Daniel had consumed all of my twenties. When I should have been dating and just messing around exploring life, I was tied up in an unhealthy power dynamic masking as a relationship.

"Bella?"

I turned back, and Jake was no longer next to me. He was by the couch facing more of the windows that made up the apartment's walls. The lights across the canal and in all the neighboring buildings were enough to brighten the apartment.

"Where did you go?" This was the thing about Jake. The thing that got me every time. He knew me. I think most men wouldn't have known that I was in the room, but not really there in my mind. But Jake could read me in a way almost no one else could.

"To the past."

"Come here." His voice had gravel this time. This wasn't the request of a boy, but a command from a man, a very sexy one who was wreaking havoc on my emotions.

Against my better judgment, I went. I left a foot between us. Those twelve inches crackled with awareness.

In a moment, Jake pushed closer, put an arm around my shoulders, pulled me to him. He still smelled incredible. It wasn't cologne, deodorant, soap or anything artificial like that. Probably some kind of pheromone that made me crazy.

I turned to him the same time he turned to me. His hand moved from my hip, around my butt, spanned my back, then cupped my head as he pulled me toward him. He leaned in and we were kissing again.

Not the steamy kisses we'd shared earlier, but something altogether different. A third thing that was different from anything else we'd had together. A kiss that was the past and the future all wrapped up together with lips and seeking tongues. A kiss that made me want to cry.

Despite me trying to hold back, I could feel a tear course down my cheek.

"Where's your room?" he whispered into my hair.

"It's New York. Not a New Jersey mansion." I separated from him, turned, brushed away the wetness on my face, then walked down a short hall with only three doors. My office was on the right, the bathroom straight ahead. I took a left. Without words, he followed me into the room.

"Black is the new beige," I said, trying to lighten the mood. The accent wall behind my headboard had been painted black by previous tenants. I'd hung white abstract art to lighten the space.

Jake didn't laugh. Instead, he pulled me closer and kissed me again. This one wasn't an "I'm sorry" kiss. This one was real, a prelude to what he wanted. What I wanted. What had always been inevitable.

When our mouths parted this time, I was slow to release his shirt buttons one at a time, pushing the white fabric aside. I unhooked his belt, the heavy metal of the buckle clinking as it fell away. Suits weren't the mystery they had been when I'd met Daniel, so I unbuttoned the one button I could see, then felt along the waistband for the invisible one.

I gave the pants a shove and they fell. Slowly, Jake kicked off his shoes and lifted one foot then the other from the wool. The immediate need for him had abated in his hotel suite, so I took a moment to sit on the edge of my bed. To listen to my head *and* my heart. To make sure that I wanted this.

I shucked first my pants, then my shirt. Jake squatted in front of me in boxer briefs that were the brightest shade of purple I'd ever seen. Something about that color was incongruous with the image of Jake I had in my mind. I don't think I'd seen him out of black, white, or navy in twenty years.

He was unhooking my bra, when his eyes caught mine.

"What?" he asked, a half smile on his face.

"Purple is the new beige?"

He didn't say a word, but the half smile remained. He

finished with the fastener and pulled the nylon from my shoulders.

His fingers skimmed along my collarbone. A shiver of need shook me.

I scooted back on the bed, taking a moment to get my bearings, then propped myself against pillows at the headboard. Jake lay down next to me. Like a magnet, I rolled toward him. He put an arm around me, and I tucked my head against his shoulder, and just like that, two decades disappeared like smoke.

We'd lain like this watching contraband movies during those innocent days when we'd probably both yearned for more, but didn't know how to get it, or maybe hadn't even known what we'd wanted.

"I wanted to be a skater," he whispered into the dusk.

"Figure skater?" I mused, trying to imagine Jake in an ice rink.

"Skateboarding."

"The Vans." I'd forgotten about the slip-on checked shoes he'd sported that first year I'd been in Jersey. "Why didn't you?" The question was out before I thought better of it. "Sorry." I'd always thought of those six or seven acres as kind of one large playground. Now I could see that maybe it was one large, well-landscaped prison.

"I wanted to be Tony Hawk." He cleared his throat like he was giving a speech to a board of directors. "Future CEOs don't get to skateboard."

"Piano. Mandarin. English. Straight A's." I listed his parents' demands. Even when he'd done what they'd asked, they were on him if he so much as paused for a breath. I'd forgotten how relentless they were.

"It's why I didn't mind Woodward."

"Freedom from Min Li and Mr. Wu...and me." Deep shame seized me as my voice broke on that last stuttering word.

"That's not what I wanted. I think I'd have happily stayed in Toms River if it meant being with you. But they didn't give me a choice."

"It was lonely without you," I admitted. "It was hard being the only one to have to keep a huge secret. I wanted to tell so many times. To get Mama and me the hell out of that mausoleum. But we had nowhere to go. If I left, I didn't think we'd see each other again."

Jake turned his head toward mine. This time his kisses were full of apology and regret and something more I wanted to deny. They went on for a long time, those slow kisses, as the shadows deepened in the darkening room. His hands caressed my collarbone, my shoulder, my arm. I followed his lead, exploring him in a way I'd never dared to before. His body was...well...amazing. I'd never had the time to do what I was doing now.

Jake was doing a lot more than CEOing. His shoulders were broad, his abs taut. When his arm came up to brush my hair back, the muscles of his biceps bulged.

I was drawn to his lips like a moth to a flame. What had been leisurely and languorous for what felt like forever quickly became more urgent. I could feel a deep pulse starting to thrum down below. My nipples poked against his chest. When he cupped my ass and pulled it toward his own middle, I could feel his erection pressing against me.

Suddenly, I was achy and very uncomfortable, like I wanted to escape from my own skin. I could think of only one way to make that feeling go away. I shoved down my own underwear, kicking it somewhere. I did the same with his purple boxer briefs. His cock was hard. It danced with a little pulse of its own. I gave him an openmouthed kiss and wrapped my hand around his penis at the same time. He was so hard, so firm. It gave me a little thrill to think that *I* could do that for him. That I could make him that excited.

Gently, I rolled us over until he was on his back and I was straddling him.

"What do you want? What can I do to make you feel good?" I asked. For all that I knew Jake, I didn't really know this about him. What made him feel amazing in bed. What turned him on and would make him lose control.

"This. Here. Now is good," he panted.

He lifted his head and took one of my nipples deep into his mouth. The sensation was so much that I had to let go of him and brace my hands against the headboard. His other hand took the full weight of my other tit and his thumbs lazily brushed against the tip. Moisture gathered at my core. I lifted a hand and put it back on his cock. Slowly, I used his hardness to rub from my opening to my clit and back again.

Before I could think to ask about condoms or STDs, I'd taken him inside.

I lifted myself, my breast leaving his mouth, reluctant to end that contact, then sank down fully to get the other thing I wanted more—him, deep inside me. I wanted to stay absolutely still. Freeze the moment in amber so I could examine it later, relive this moment of pure connection I'd been waiting forever for, but my body wanted to move.

His strong arms banded around my back, and I pitched forward until we were face to face again. Our mouths fused. My tongue dueled with his, each of us fighting to bring the other pleasure. When he broke the kiss to slide his lips against my neck, then my ear, I was lost.

When he started moving beneath me, in and out in a steady rhythm, I sucked in a breath.

I heard an "oh God" come out of my mouth.

His hands were on the backs of my thighs, spreading me wide. His pace picked up.

"Can I come inside you?" he asked.

"Of course," I responded. "Are you!" Before I could finish my question, his pace increased as quickly as his breath. With one hard thrust, a hoarse sound left him.

After his heartbeat slowed, I disentangled our limbs and slipped from him and rolled onto my back. The room was nearly pitch black now, the only light from random windows in the building next door.

"Jesus, Bella."

We lay like that, in the silence for one minute, ten, maybe longer, the only sounds those of us breathing and whatever city noises could permeate the triple-paned windows.

Then Jake pulled me toward him again, his hands firm, brooking no argument. His kiss woke me up like a splash of cold water. This time, he rolled so that he was on top. He took my wrists in one of his hands and used the other to trace a line down my face, my neck, to the tip of one breast. I shivered even though the air conditioning wasn't on.

His head descended, his mouth taking my breast deep. His teeth grazing my nipple. Involuntarily, my hips bucked. He slid more of himself on top of me, pinning me down. His knee came between mine, opening my legs wider.

His hand let my wrists free, then his fingers entwined with my hand as his mouth licked a trail of fire from the other nipple, down my belly, until he landed at my core. His lips fastened on my clit and the pressure was almost, but not quite, too much to bear.

My insides jumbled and squirmed. He took a single finger and slipped inside, then another joined it. I couldn't have described, under pain of death, what in the hell he was doing, but it was scrambling my brain such that I was losing all rational thought. All that was left was my ability to feel.

Then he let me go, kissing his way back up as his hand replaced his mouth, flat against my clit. His hand moved slow then fast; the friction nearly killed me. I was so close, but it was so delicious that I didn't want the pleasure to stop.

One minute I was on the crest, in the next, I was riding the wave of my orgasm.

Before I could catch my breath, gain my composure, his hand was at it again. In that first moment, I was almost too sensitive for his touch, but it felt so good, I didn't pull away.

In what seemed like no time, I was winding up again like a spring. Tighter and tighter it wound, as his fingers alternated between pinching and soothing my clit. I was so close, so fucking close.

"Look at me, Bella."

I don't think I realized that my eyes were closed until then. My lids flew open, and I looked at those brown eyes I'd known for two thirds of my life, shining with lust, his full lips parted in pleasure. My own hard nipples, pointing toward the ceiling, sparked my erotic imagination in a way my own body never had before this night. The spring coiled tight and in a second, I was panting and moaning out a third orgasm.

While I was still pulsing, Jake rose over me. He fisted his cock and entered me.

Him inside me while I was coming pushed me back up the twisting spiral. It was so, so good...this...us. Better than before. Better than anything I could remember.

"I can't believe it," I whispered almost in awe, "I think I'm going to come again."

He didn't respond, just pumped in evenly timed thrusts until I was on the crest again.

"I'm so close!" I said in amazement.

"I want to keep you there," he said as his thrusts slowed. It was what I think soaring through space would have been like. I could see stars through my window. I felt like I was floating. It was almost an out-of-body experience, having Jake over me. Inside me. Around me. Everywhere. For long minutes, we kept up the rhythm, but the end was inevitable, no matter how much I wanted to fight it and embrace it at the same time.

Uncurling my toes, I stopped fighting.

Wave after wave of pleasure crashed over me. Jake held out longer than I did, but when I pulsed around his cock, his own dam broke. His thrusts went wild, and, in a few seconds, his hoarse shout filled the room. He collapsed on me for a long minute. Then he slipped to the side.

I had that urge again, to freeze time. Everything was perfect. The past wasn't our enemy anymore. The future was undecided, but still full of possibility.

"I love you, Bella. I know that I probably shouldn't say it. But I've been too quiet for way too long about too many things, especially what mattered to me. I love you, and that fact will never change."

"I...I don't know what to say," I said, because I felt like I *had* to say something, not leave his declaration of love out there hanging like a sheet in a stiff wind.

"You don't have to say anything. I'm here. I'm waiting. I'll be here now or six months from now or a year from now. I haven't wavered from how I felt last year. I think we belong together. There's nothing that could change my mind. Not Min Li. Not Father. No one."

"Does Liling know this?" I asked. I knew I'd threw in her name as a defense against my own feelings, which at the moment I'd do anything to control, cancel out, not feel. But I'd been down this road once, twice even, and I never wanted to end up as hurt as I'd been before.

"She will," he whispered.

Everyone said that pain was the other side of love, but I didn't want to believe in this, nor did I want to sign up to be hurt when his fascination faded and the woman he was *really* meant to be with came back and reclaimed her rightful place.

If Min Li was right about one thing, it was that everyone had a place. I wasn't sure I had the power to change that.

"THEY'RE COMING in to sign on the dotted line?"

I pushed my fists into my pockets, keeping my back to Liling. We were in one of CBT's Manhattan office tower conference rooms. I had to admit the views from this building were way better than those in Los Angeles. As the head of prime time, I was committed to L.A. for the foreseeable future. Committed to a future with Isabella, be it there or somewhere here on the East Coast.

I looked fifteen stories down at Central Park, full of tiny ant-sized people running and walking and probably having picnics. It was an unfulfilled fantasy to think of myself down there with Bella. Neither one of us had that kind of leisure time or that kind of relationship. The last three meals we'd had together had ended badly. Yesterday, with Liling busting in. Last year, with Isabella's resignation. In Connecticut before I took her virginity, then ignored her until she left.

If we could have a picnic, maybe I could replace all the bad memories with good ones again. It was probably going to take more than a few meals and us in bed. It was going to take a commitment on my part to be with her no matter what and where. Even I had to admit that was a lot to heap on a single night.

"Wu Jian?" Liling's high-pitched tone pierced my melancholy thoughts. "I asked you a question. If we're going to fix this...this problem your father made, we need to get this production started now or go on to the next project."

"There are a few details to be hammered out," I hedged. "Some things we can add in an addendum, probably."

"A few. Looked like the two of you had worked out *all* the details yesterday."

I thought we'd covered this last year. The "us" that couldn't be. There'd been so much pushing from our parents to get married—to each other.

Often enough to send shivers of doubt through me, I thought that maybe they were right. That maybe Liling would be the perfect wife. She could easily traverse Chinese and American culture. Her manners were impeccable in both places. She understood what it was to be *fuerdai* and knew what was expected of her. She'd been my first best friend. The first person I'd shared secrets with. The first person I'd made love with.

Unfortunately, none of that added up to romantic forever love. After thirty-plus years of watching my parents in a marriage that worked like a business deal, I'd decided that love was paramount. It was more important than money or power or status. It was everything.

I'd walked away from it once. I was never going to do that again.

"Liling, we need to talk." I really wanted to have one last discussion. One last chance to put a firm end to any romantic notions she might have.

Before I could get closure on our relationship once and for all, Alexandra burst through the doors, followed by Bella and Claire.

Isabella and her college roommate were so different. I tried to imagine them living together or even picture Claire as an escort. It's not that she wasn't pretty in a cute way, it's just that I couldn't really imagine her—or any of them really, when it came down to it—doing that job. I thought the whole point of elite schools was to save people from just those kinds of choices.

"Would you like anything to drink. Coffee? Tea? There's water on the sideboard," Alexandra was saying as she handed out thick stacks of packets.

Bella waved off the offer while Claire poured herself a Pellegrino.

I sat across from the two. Liling plopped down in the chair next to mine. She brushed imaginary lint from my shoulders in an obvious possessive move. I tried not to flinch, because I'd hurt her, too. These two women had both been there when I'd needed them, and I hadn't been able to reciprocate at the time. I had a lot to make up for.

I turned to Liling and nodded, giving her the go-ahead.

"Let's get right down to it," she said, her voice all business, belying her posture, which was still tuned to me. Despite my guilt, I realized that she was a little too close for comfort. I tried not to gauge Bella's reaction to all this. She mattered, and I'd make it my mission to get her to understand that.

Liling swiveled her chair forward and got down to business. She patted a stack of papers in the middle of the table. "These came from Legal this morning."

"Legal?" Bella asked coolly. She didn't even look at the papers Liling had pushed toward her and made no move to examine the neat stack. I tried to catch her eye. I wanted her to know that I wasn't encouraging Liling. That what had happened between Bella and I had been real. The most real thing I'd experienced in a long time. There was no way I could say any of that out loud with the others in the room. I settled for moving my chair a few more inches from Liling's.

"We'd like to start pre-production as soon as these are executed," Liling continued. "Ramp up to full production in a week. Give ourselves two to three weeks lead time before air." Meaning CBT would shoot and edit at least two but more likely three full forty-two-minute hours of television before anything aired. It would provide a buffer for unexpected circumstances. Because no matter how scripted or controlled reality television was, the unexpected still happened. Father's transgressions being a prime example.

It all sounded reasonable. Doable. Despite our complicated relationship and history, Liling was the right person for this job. I trusted fully that she could navigate CBT out of this crisis. Probably wring a bigger viewership and profitability out of the mix. If she could do it in heavily censored China, then I could only imagine what she could do with free reign in this country.

"While I appreciate you going through all this trouble,"

Isabella started, "there are still a few details to be worked out."

"We can work those out as we go along," Liling countered. "You've known Jake a long time. Surely you trust that he'll honor your wishes."

"Oral agreements are as good as the paper they're written on." Isabella was surprisingly firm. I'd never been up against her, but it seemed like she might be a formidable opponent. I was glad that we weren't on opposite sides outside of this negotiation.

"Yes, of course, but we're not strangers. I've known Jake since he was a kid. You're only a couple of years behind me. Claire is on board, and you've known her half her life. It's important that we get this on the schedule as soon as possible. Marketing a midsummer replacement is no small feat."

Bella sat back. Was quiet. I could see that it was killing Liling not to fill that silence with some kind of sales pitch. Out of sight of everyone, I put my hand on her knee to keep it from bouncing, to keep her from talking.

Isabella wasn't going to respond to bullying. She wasn't operating with the fear of missing out, either. That last worked ninety-five percent of the time in an industry where competition for airtime was fierce and cutthroat.

"Someone just said to me yesterday that there's no rush to make a decision when it's not life or death. That the person pushing us to make that snap decision is only honoring their own agenda. Is that just about right, Jake?"

Liling pinched the skin on the top of the hand I had on her knee—hard. Two could play at this game of chicken. I didn't flinch.

"It's not life or death, Isabella. What it is, is important to CBT," I said, trying to play to her sympathy. Whatever feelings she had for me, I had to assume that even if she wasn't cheering for my success, at least she didn't want me to fail. "It's important...to...*me*."

I picked up the pitch where Liling had left off. We were a team—at CBT, at least. "We need to replace *Screenplayed*. This seems like it would be an excellent opportunity for both of us. Sex sells. I'm not going to lie about that. I think this would be a ratings booster for us. Maybe even better ratings than *Screenplayed*. That's *our* agenda, of course.

"What we think, though, is that this could be a show that helps your goals as well, which is to transition these women from one line of work to another, less...personally exploitive job. What you're doing is working, but slowly. We think bringing in more top-of-their-field experts and even some outside pressure could jumpstart that process," I explained.

Liling's sigh was a little dramatic, but that was Liling. "What *are* your concerns, Isabella?"

"I was at CBT for five years, so I'm not unaware of the kind of 'pressure' these kinds of shows can bring on the participants." Bella leaned down and pulled a portfolio from her tote. Nearly as dramatically as Liling had pushed the papers across the table, Isabella opened it and took out a pad that had a neat list of bullet points.

"First, no writers. I do not want lines fed to our girls. You're going to have to work with the footage you get. No booths where they read scripted responses to producer prompts."

"No writers," Liling conceded. "But we will have

producers working to make sure there's a narrative thread. People are tuning in for stories. It's not a documentary."

Bella's nod was brisk. "Who?"

Liling gave a couple of names, and I took Bella's stiff bob of her head as an agreement. It went on like that for the next forty-five minutes.

Bella's demands weren't outrageous. Most were actually thoughtful and protective. I'm not exactly sure how she'd been promoted early and often over others like Connor, but she'd obviously been good at what she'd done nevertheless.

"We will get these over to Legal and have documents for you to sign in the morning," Liling said, passing her own notes over to Alexandra. "We'll need the names, addresses, and all other pertinent information on your clients for those releases. If we could have them signed this week as well, that would be helpful."

Bella took an embossed card from the leather card case in front of her and slipped it to Alexandra. "That's our attorney. Please have your legal department interface with him before they go through all that drafting work. She's assured us that she can keep this week clear to expedite this. We good?"

It was Liling's turn to nod stiffly. Then she was up and out of the room in a shot, presumably to start "interfacing" with Legal Affairs. Alexandra followed her.

"I need to get back to Julie House and think about what we'll need to say to the girls. I'll meet you back there. Okay? We'll talk to them after the two o'clock group session." Claire excused herself.

"Sure," Bella said to Claire's back. Then the two of us were alone again, sitting on opposite sides of a table that was suddenly too wide. I needed to touch Bella, make sure the woman across from me was real.

In a few steps, I crossed the room and closed the conference room door. I twisted the lock for good measure. The last thing I needed was to be disturbed while I talked to her, maybe even pleaded for her to give us another chance.

I went back to the window and stood for a long time alone, watching so many New Yorkers enjoying themselves in the park. She joined me this time with a different set of floor-to-ceiling windows and a different view in front of us. I'd grown up with cityscapes in Shanghai. All the buildings and people and controlled chaos was oddly soothing.

This was an altogether different game of chicken, and she wasn't budging. Finally, I broke the silence.

"Well played." I had to admire her cool, both in dealing with Liling and admittedly with me, too. There wasn't going to be any swooning or falling into my arms. That would be too easy. Nothing with us had ever been easy.

"I wasn't playing, Jake. This isn't a game. These are women who need help, and Claire and I took on the task of doing that. Please tell me that I'm not going to regret this."

Liling hadn't been wrong. Bella was placing her trust in my hands, probably because of our past. If she didn't know me from Adam, this would probably have been a complete no-go. I didn't want that trust to go misplaced.

"Obviously I'm not going to be involved day to day, but you let me know if anything doesn't seem right and I'll do my best to fix it." I held out my hand. "Deal?"

"Deal." She shook. Her fingers were smooth, cool,

perfect. It didn't take much to remember what they'd felt like all over my body.

"What happened to *Screenplayed*?" Bella was asking when I steered my thoughts back to what she was saying now and not the moans she'd uttered just yesterday. "I loved that show. It was one of the good ones. About creativity and making the best product—kind of like a cooking show. Not twenty girls chasing some mediocre guy or even a bunch of comedians in a house playing a game of who can gross out the audience faster."

I ignored that sleight to *Heir to the Throne*. That one had been someone else's ugly baby. *They* could defend it.

"It'll be back. Just a glitch with this season."

"Glitch? That was one tightly run show. Two of the producers from that are going to be working on this. I think I have a right to know if something hinky is going on."

"What does that even mean? Hinky?" I asked, stalling for time. I'd often used the fact that English was my second language to stall a conversation when I didn't know what to say.

"Suspicious—like you right now." Knowing Bella half my life was an asset in one sense. But a complete liability in this dodge and feint.

"Nothing hinky."

"Why won't you look me in the eye?" She put a hand on my shoulder, concentrating my attention on her. "I love Central Park as much as the next person, but a bunch of trees in the middle of Manhattan aren't that fascinating. You want me to turn the lives of these girls upside down. I will not put them in the path of any proverbial oncoming train. I just won't do it. Nothing is worth that to me."

I wanted to pull her into my arms. Kiss away the frown between her eyebrows. That would have been unwelcome, at least now at CBT. Maybe later. I held that vision close to me, then spoke. Bella wasn't going to like what I had to say. Anything but the truth wouldn't be right, either, though. There was no way to get around this one thing I didn't want to talk about.

"What I'm about to tell you is confidential. Only a few at the network know."

"That says sex scandal or drugs. Those are the biggest liabilities. Unless someone brought a real gun on set. Please tell me there were no guns. I was so focused on the psychological implications, I didn't think of the physical. Goddammit. Tell me Jake."

I rubbed at the space between my own brows. I was trying to ease the ache I always got when it was time to face up to my father. He wasn't even in the state, much less this room, yet I was still stuck answering for his misdeeds.

"There were allegations of sexual harassment from one of the contestants on the show. She got a pay-to-play message. Obviously if she won *or* lost, there'd be some kind of violation of game show rules, so we shut it down. I'm not going to lie. The Me Too movement prompted us to take quick action. I didn't want that to be the start of Dyno's media legacy. Us on the front page of *New Yorker* magazine with Ronan Farrow's byline underneath."

"You say legacy like it's a dynasty. It's just television."

"Reputation is important. These scandals have been

pretty brutal. I want CBT to be a place where professionals of all genders and races thrive."

Bella nodded neither in agreement nor disagreement.

I watched what looked like tiny sailboats on a fake lake. Kind of like the ones in Luxembourg Gardens in Paris. I wondered if you could rent them or did you have to bring your own. Where would you buy a miniature sailboat anyway.

"Who's the culprit? CBT is like every other company, you know. There's a whisper network. Men who should be avoided."

I made a mental note to task Alexandra with getting a list of those names. I didn't want to be blindsided a second time.

"It's no one you've worked with," I grudgingly admitted. There was probably no way to avoid this particular revelation.

"Geez, one of the guys you brought with you? I wondered how that would go, these guys who were star-fuckers having too much influence. It takes cool to work in Hollywood."

"Bella?" I tore my gaze away from the park. Looked her directly in the eye. There was going to be no good way to do this, so it was best to get it out of the way.

"What?"

"It was Father."

Her eyes went wide with shock, then outrage. Probably for her mother. I was so busy being angry with Father and trying to keep his damned secrets that I'd forgotten all about her mother, and my stepmother, for that matter. The enduring victims of Father's feckless actions.

"Wait? What? Mister fucking Wu. Jesus Christ. Jesus

fucking Christ! So your father fucks up, and I'm the first person you call. To fix your fucking family problems? I've taken the hit one too many times already for something that wasn't my doing."

"Bella—"

"Maybe you should have called Maria Sofia Aconi, she's a much better Mr. Wu problem solver than I am."

She turned away. Not being able to read her expression was hellish. If I could just figure out how she felt, maybe... I don't know how or what I thought could be better.

"I can't believe this. You did a total bait and switch on me. Was all that seduction part of it? Isabella Aconi must be lonely. She can't find a normal guy, given her messed-up background. I'll fuck her, then fuck over the women who mean the most to her right now."

She paced the room angrily, leaving heel marks in the carefully vacuumed maroon carpet.

"Isabella..." I reached out for her. To stop her. To soothe her. But she eluded my grasp.

"Jesus fucking Christ." She banged her fist against the window for good measure.

"You already said that." I felt useless. There seemed to be no limit to the damage my family could do to hers.

"Because you're making your father's problems *my* problems. Every time *he* messes up, *I* lose something important.

"You.

"My mother.

"My college tuition.

"And now the one thing I care about, this organization I've co-founded with Claire, put up on the altar of sacrifice for Mister fucking Wu. Do you even care about me or the mission of Julie House?"

"No one is sacrificing anything. You negotiated pretty hard there with Liling. I think your girls are protected."

Bella lifted her right hand and covered her entire face with it. She bent her head. Her shoulders shook.

Damn, she was crying.

I went to her.

The urge to comfort her was too strong to resist even though I was also the source of her pain. I smoothed a hand against her hair. Put my thumb under her chin to lift her head. She wasn't crying.

She was laughing. But there were tears.

Which was it? Sadness? Mirth? Exhaustion?

"I'm so confused. Are you okay?"

"I'll never be okay, Jake. The Wu family is like a curse. Or maybe a really bad gift that keeps on giving."

"Father agreed to leave CBT," I offered, like it was a gift. It was a shitty gift, but it was all I had to give. My word that he wouldn't be around to wreak more havoc.

"And go where? New Jersey? I wonder what disease he'll pass on to my mom this week."

I didn't want to know, but my mouth spoke first. "Disease?"

"Did I tell you about the time Mama almost died of gonorrhea?"

"Your mom was sick?" It didn't compute. When Min Li was done arranging my life and studies, she was full of gossip about everyone in her orbit.

But who would tell me about her mother? Father only

referred to Maria Aconi as a very loyal employee. We never again spoke of the scene Bella and I witnessed. And of course, Min Li didn't even mention her by name.

"As a dog, Jake. Sick as a dog. But did she go to the doctor? No, because Mr. Wu needed this or Mr. Wu needed that. My SATs weren't great the first time I took the test," she started.

I wanted to ask what in the hell a college admission test had to do with anything, but I held my tongue and just listened.

"I got Mr. Wu to pay for one of those expensive prep classes. My practice test scores were way up after that.

"I figured I'd definitely get into Owen regular decision. But I missed the final SAT exam. Instead of sitting for a test, I was at the emergency room, watching Mama get an infusion of IV antibiotics. She was a middle-aged woman being treated for an STD. And when the county worker asked how she'd gotten sick, she didn't say a word. Kept Mr. Wu's dirty little secret."

"I had no idea." The moment the words were out of my mouth, I realized how inadequate they were.

"Of course not. You were probably in Cambridge by then, doing whatever rich kids do. Planning winter break trips to Aspen or spring break trips to the Caribbean or whatever. For keeping that secret, I got a guarantee of admission to Owen. For keeping another, I got tuition. You got to run a network. Like I said, Mr. Wu...the gift that keeps on giving. I'm done Jake."

"You're not going to do the show?"

"I'll do the show. Unlike Mr. Wu, I honor my promises.

But after this, we're done. After this ten weeks is over, I never want to talk to anyone with the last name Wu again. That means your father. That means you."

"How can you say that after yesterday, after last night?" I wanted to reach out to New Jersey and do bodily harm to my father. There's no way I was going to let him mess up the best thing that had happened to me.

"Jake, I can't change the past. I can't change twenty years ago, or ten, or twenty-four hours. But I can change my future. And it could only be better without you in it. The Wu family runs on lies, secrets, and half-truths. I'm not perfect. Far from it. But if I want a better future for myself then I can't make the same mistakes. I can't try to relive the past or fix the past. I need to make some entirely different choices."

"What about love?"

"What about it, Jake? Love from Mama got me kicked out. My father's love dried up over DNA." She paused a long time. Ran her fingers through her hair. "Love...Jake? Love is fickle."

"I love you, Bella."

"I love *you*, Jake. I have probably since the first day I met you, when you gave me dumplings and taught me how to use chopsticks. I think I'll always love you. No, I know that I'll always love you. But what you love isn't always what's healthy for you."

"What are you saying?"

"That last year I said goodbye to Daniel. This year, I'm saying goodbye to you. It's time to build my future."

"Are you just leaving?" I looked around the conference room. I could not think of a single reason for her to stay. I couldn't think what I had to offer. If I'd had more time, more notice, I would have worked hard to figure out something. Anything to keep her from walking out the door.

"I think I am," she answered before I had time to hatch some sort of plan.

Her kiss was unexpected.

I wrapped my arms around her and pulled her close, kissed her back. Without words, she needed to know how important she was to me.

With her this close, I went from cold to hot in under a minute. I pushed up her white and red striped shirt. It was up and over her head in a minute.

Her fingers were at my pants. They fell to the floor in another moment. I pushed up her bra. She pushed down my briefs and had her hand fisted around my cock. I took a nipple in my mouth while I pulled at her white pants. I felt them give way, then I pushed my hands down her panties. She was as wet for me as I was hot for her.

I took my own cock in my hand and fitted it to her opening. She moaned when I thrust into her.

"This is us," I grunted as I set up a fast and furious rhythm.

"Yes."

"You'll *always* be mine," I said as my pace continued without interruption.

"This has to be the last time."

"Chemistry like this...fire like this is rare."

"Shh. Just fuck me, Jake. I want to remember this part."

"You don't need to remember. I'm not going to let you forget."

I lifted her higher, onto the table.

"Oh God..."

"Everything about you is beautiful. Everything. I want to see you come. I want to see you get as much pleasure as you deserve."

"Oh God!"

"Open your eyes. Look at me. I love you, Bella."

"I love you, too, Jake. I love you, too."

"Then this can't be the end. This has to be the beginning."

"Stop talking! Just fuck me."

And so I did. I bent over so that my mouth fused with hers. I kept a hand in the silk of her hair, making sure she wasn't able to wriggle away. I bent so that I took her nipple in my mouth again. I used my other hand to spread her moisture against her clit and rub until the nub swelled under my fingers.

I wanted to leave my mark on her. It was stupid, but when she was close, so close I could feel her walls starting to pulse around my clock, I sucked a cord hard in her neck.

My rational mind knew that giving her a hickey like we were teenagers was stupid. But my caveman mind, the one that was fucking her, the one that wanted her to be mine forever, wanted to put an indelible mark on her, and this was the only way I could think of in this moment when thinking was nearly impossible.

Wherever she was later today or tomorrow or for however long this physical connection between us lasted, I didn't want her to forget. I wanted her to remember. I wanted her to come back.

"SO I KNOW this is unconventional, but we want to do it."
That was Claire speaking to the group after the two o'clock
therapy session.

We'd asked Dr. Banks to stay. Both to assure her that we
weren't here to interfere with her therapeutic objectives, but
also to help us manage the clients. Figure out a strategy for
those who didn't want to participate. "Let's open it up to
questions. Isabella and I will try to answer everything that we
can."

"How long?" one client was asking.

I'd let Claire take the lead in laying out the vision for the
TV show, but I answered this one. "Eight weeks initially. To
be completely honest, it's filling in a schedule hole at CBT."

"You worked there, right?" a client asked. I think her
name was Kristina, with a Russian last name I couldn't
pronounce without practicing it first. She was tall, blonde,
cool.

I nodded. I'd been completely honest and upfront about

my past. To show them two things. First, that we could be out in the working world without our pasts clouding things. But also to own up to the fact that Daniel had placed me in those jobs at CBT. I needed them to know that continued contact only led to our sugar daddies continuing to control us like we were marionettes and they were master puppeteers.

"I was with CBT for a lot of years. First in New York, then Philly, then Los Angeles."

"Are you getting something out of this? Money or something?" Kristina's eyes were coolly assessing. I thought it was a shame that she still lived in the head space that everything was a commodity.

"CBT will be making a one-time payment that we will use for our operating budget, pending board approval. Neither one of us will be getting any money, if that's what you mean."

Lola raised her hand. I pointed to her, encouraging her to speak.

"All the stuff you're saying sounds good. More counseling, better access to career services. The shame factor propelling them to cut contact once and for all. But what about the other way around? Who will hire us if they know we were escorts? It's not as if we live in a society that doesn't crucify us for our pasts."

"Bill Clinton did fine," Claire said.

"Monica Lewinsky didn't," Lola shot back.

Arguing the relative treatment of an impeached sitting president and one of his interns would derail the argument. Our clients were smart, so there was no snowing them.

"What Lola brings up is a legitimate concern. I don't

know the answer to that. Monica Lewinsky *was* skewered. We hope that the opportunities opened up outweigh the close-minded bosses and businesses that wouldn't hire you. That said, you may be better off pursuing opportunities on the coasts than you might be if you want to go back to a small town. At least initially. Memories do fade, though."

I wondered at the truth of the platitude the moment it left my lips. My memory of Jake would never fade. Nor would the betrayal of Mr. Wu. These women were facing different memories. For their sakes, I hoped theirs faded faster.

"But the internet doesn't. Clips of us on YouTube or Facebook or whatever may be forever," another woman piped in.

I was quiet and shared a look with Claire. Honestly, I hadn't thought about that. What I'd had with Daniel and what she'd had with her sugar daddy had been the kind of thing that had stayed out of the papers. The compensated dating relationship was the kind that both parties wanted to keep to themselves to avoid the stigma. Where privacy bene-fitted both parties.

The men desperately wanted everyone to believe that young, smart women wanted to be on their arms for who they were, not what they could provide. The women learned quickly in today's Instagram age to keep it low key. In a click-bait news environment, there would be no such reticence.

I felt stupid now, for being so gung-ho about the idea after my initial hesitation. Fucking Jake had blurred my vision of what we wanted to achieve here, and the shame that I'd lost sight of the mission that quickly was almost too much.

"What about prosecution?" another woman was asking. "How do we know there won't be some big operation set up to try to take down our non-profit or something. Somehow criminalize what we've done and we end up as felons instead of independent? What if you're setting us up to trade one kind of prison for another, well, more literal prison?"

"The crimes—if you want to call it that—are receding into the past. That's one of the reasons we wanted all of you to cut off contact. Every day you're closer to clearing the statute of limitations."

Two of the women looked at another in the back. A phone slipped from her hand to the floor.

It was a Samsung. We'd given them all iPhones.

"Pass it up to Claire," Dr. Banks said.

"Barney," Sarah Roy said. "I keep it in case Barney calls! He says he wants to marry me."

"When?" Claire challenged, as she smoothed her fingers on the glass of the contraband device. I leaned against a wall. I knew where this was going. We *all* knew where this was going, but Claire was willing to play along, probably as an abject lesson for the others.

"Well. It has to be after his daughter's wedding. He doesn't want to upstage her."

"When is his daughter getting married?" Dr. Banks asked.

If I were a betting woman, I'd have placed a bet that the daughter wasn't even engaged, maybe didn't even have a boyfriend. Could have been twelve.

"They haven't set a date. She's trying to get on the cancellation list at the Plaza or New York Public Library."

"What happens in that year or so while you're cooling your heels?" Claire asked.

She shrugged. "Things would stay the same. I'd stay in the loft. He hasn't rented it or anything since I moved out. But I'm thinking maybe graduate school during that year. Most Master's programs are only a year. Then after we're married, I can start my career."

"How often does Barney travel? Or rather, how often do you travel with him?" I asked.

"Once or twice a month. But if we're living together, then maybe I could stay in the city?"

"Why not get married at city hall?" Claire asked. It was a question Dr. Banks wouldn't have asked. She was all about letting the women come to their own solutions. I was thinking with that prohibited phone in her hand, Claire was all out of therapeutic patience.

"What?" This girl, who'd graduated magna cum laude from the most competitive liberal arts college in the country, looked dumbstruck.

"If he wants to marry you. Why not have a civil ceremony downtown? You get to be man and wife. No one gets upstaged."

"He says nothing but the best would work for me. So he wants Gotham Hall or even the Museum of Natural History. Isn't that sweet? But he wants to give his daughter time. To find her own venue first. Get married. Have a honeymoon. Settle in wherever her and her fiancé land. So after that?"

"That sounds like four or five years. Why do you have to put your life on hold for the second half of your twenties?

What sacrifice does Barney make? He'll still...what? Put you up at that loft in Soho?"

"It's the Meatpacking District."

"Sorry. The Meatpacking District then. You'll spend your days at the gym, or getting manicures, pedicures, waxed. Be at his beck and call while he is still CEOing. His daughter is planning and executing her future. When do you start to live *your* life?"

"I said I was thinking about graduate school. Maybe psychology or social work or something like that."

"You took the GMATs, right?" I asked.

"I aced the GMATs," Sarah said with pride in her voice. My memory was that she'd gotten a perfect score.

"You were admitted to that Owen program."

"Hanover Scholars," Sarah answered. It was the US equivalent of the Rhodes Scholarship. "I would have to be in residence in Connecticut, though, so I turned them down. Barney didn't think it was the right fit for me."

"It wasn't the right fit for *him*," Claire said. I was thinking that her experience with Leland the third, Finn or whatever, had given her a front row seat to watching a woman's ambitions be sidelined. She'd wanted to study in England, travel the world looking at ancient religious texts. Sounded as dry as dust to me, but talk of the future used to light up Claire's eyes. "Would you have to sign a prenup?" she asked.

"If...when...if we got married." Sarah nodded. Not one of us commented on the shift from certainty to uncertainty in just the time Claire had been interrogating her. "It's for both our protection," she rushed out. I could tell that was the line he'd fed her. Felt rehearsed. "That way, if he dies or divorces me, I get a preset amount of money. Inheritance is too compli-cated because of all the family trusts and whatnot, so he thinks it would be a good idea. Otherwise it could turn into one of those Anna Nicole Smith cases or something."

"We're getting distracted from the topic at hand," I said. This girl was the reason I'd agreed to do the show. I was sure that if she spent twenty minutes watching herself tie herself up in a pretzel to meet Barney's needs, she'd wise up. Or any of her friends from college might call her on her bullshit.

Sarah Roy was too damned smart to be spouting the crap that was coming from her mouth. But this wasn't another group therapy session. We needed to be ironing out the issues related to the show. "Anyone else have questions about doing the show?"

"What would it be called?" someone asked.

"To be honest, we hadn't gotten that far, ladies. We wanted to talk to all of you first. You're the ones who would be affected. It might turn your lives upside down more than they've already been flipped about by the kind of work you've been doing.

"Look I don't want to exert any peer pressure, but can we get a show of hands from anyone who strongly objects?"

The only hand raised was from Sarah Roy, of course, our weakest client. The one we knew was a long shot. And with that secret phone she'd somehow stashed, it was looking like a longer and longer shot every day.

"If anyone else has an objection that they want to talk to me about in private, my door is always open," Claire said.

"Why doesn't everyone take a breather before dinner," I said. "Let's tentatively say that it's a go. We do take your concerns seriously, though, and I think in addition to our contracts attorney, we're going to get some guidance from a criminal attorney as well. The last thing we'd want to do is expose you guys to any more harm than necessary."

Our little meeting broke up. I followed Claire to her office, shutting the door behind me.

"What do you think?" Claire asked. She looked a lot less sure than she had this morning, or even earlier this week, when the rosy picture that Liling painted had been fresh in her head. Now with our clients' faces fresh in her mind, the glamour of television was fading fast. I'd tried to tell her that TV lost all its luster once you'd been behind the scenes. But I think it was a thing every soon-to-be disillusioned person had to experience for themselves.

"Maybe we shouldn't do this," I said. "We haven't signed on the dotted line. How much would it cost to hire a career counselor and coach?"

"For someone who's not at the tippy-top in terms of cost, but hopefully effective? Maybe a hundred and fifty, salaries combined. With taxes, unemployment, yada, yada. Maybe two hundred thousand. We don't have the budget for it right now."

But I did have access to a couple hundred thousand dollars. If I sold my interest in the house and after capital gains taxes. Wisely, I'd already used the Daniel money to buy a fifty-year annuity. It provided me with an income for the next fifty years and eliminated any possibility of a crazy splurge spend. I'd learned a valuable lesson at Daniel's knee. Keep your net worth to yourself. That didn't mean I couldn't make investments, though.

"What if I put up the money? Committed to two years. By then we'll have figured out if the idea works and if we could raise the funds to continue."

"Where are you going to get money like that?"

"I may be entitled to a little inheritance," I said truthfully.

"I couldn't let you do that. If this doesn't work out for any number of other reasons, I don't want you to be vulnerable."

"I would not go back to Daniel." I was vehement in my objection to that scenario. I couldn't believe she would think I was *that* vulnerable. Of all of us in the building, I thought myself the most impervious to returning. I'd still lay odds on Claire going back to Rolland, even though she'd been out of contact for over six months.

"He's not the only one," Claire said, unable to look me in the eye.

"What do you mean?" I asked. There had only been Daniel. I'd been lucky in that way, that I'd only had one sugar daddy. I think some of the women who'd had several had really taken a blow to their self-esteem. They very much saw the commodification of sex. They couldn't—like Sarah Roy, or even me, for that matter—indulge in the *Pretty Woman* fantasy.

"Jake Wu."

I tried not to start at his name. From the look under Claire's lashes, I wasn't successful.

"Even a blind woman could see that man wants you. That he would do anything to get you back."

"Back. We were middle-school sweethearts for a minute. There is no going back."

"Honey, I lived with you for four years. Do you remember your little drinking-and-hookup phase?"

I felt my forehead and cheeks, happy to find them cool and not warm with the heat of mortification. Acting out had not been my look.

"What about it?"

"After you came home, drunk off your ass, and already regretting whatever guy you'd just done, you'd go all wistful about Jake. Most times. Once in a while, you were all full of anger at him blowing you off in high school. Either way, that —excuse me—shit with him was very unresolved."

"There's no future there. It's all resolved now."

"Have you told *him* that?"

"He knows. We talked about it today."

"From the way you looked when you came in here, I'm not thinking you did much talking at all."

I'd tried to rush by when I'd finally made it to Julie House. To get into the bathroom to straighten out anything that might have gone crooked. I guess I hadn't been as stealthy as I'd thought.

"It was just a last fuck." My language was intentionally crude. I wanted to throw Claire off the scent. Get her to not think about Jake and me. So that maybe *I* could stop thinking about Jake and me.

"So it didn't mean anything?"

"Does sex have to...mean anything?" I gestured around the room, meaning to encompass all of Julie House. "Henri's lesson on that was valuable, I think. She preached that just because we were naked and vulnerable, it didn't have to mess with our brains. That sex was something to enjoy, to make sure our partner enjoyed, and that was it. Kind of like making him a good meal, or making sure the conversation flowed smoothly."

I thought I'd done an excellent job of compartmentalization. I could kiss someone. Even give and take oral sex without attaching a whole lot of meaning to it. I got off. The guy got off. Then I went on with my day, doing the next thing that needed to be done. Whether it had been making sure Daniel's desire for Dutch gin was satisfied or picking up my dry cleaning. Once you treated it as part of everyday life, it took all the power away.

"Did you ever have a boyfriend?" Claire asked. Her eyes had gone soft. I hated that look of pity, like I was broken.

"Not really. Why?"

"Can I be frank?" Her voice had gone whisper-soft.

"As long as I can still call you Claire," I quipped.

"I'm serious."

"Please go ahead," I offered, throwing my arms wide. "Tell me what's wrong with me."

"I wasn't exactly going to put it that way."

"What way were you going to put it?"

"As long as I've known you, you've been avoiding intimacy."

"Jeez. Did you just jump into the DSM there? Dr. Banks is rubbing off on you." I kept my voice light to make sure she couldn't see how close she'd come with her aim. In the middle of the night, when I couldn't sleep, and my mind spun out all my life regrets, there was a little niggling of that bit of truth. I usually jammed ear buds in, turned on music that would drown out all thoughts and lull me back to sleep.

"I'm not a therapist," Claire said. "I'm not trying to psychoanalyze you. It just sounds like Jake wants to have a relationship with you and you're using sex to push him away. Because you think sex means less to you than it does to most people."

"I had sex with Jake, because sex is fun. I'm pushing Jake out of my life because he's not the right man for me." I was proud of myself for that analysis.

"Why?"

"Why what?" I tried not to let the frustration fill my voice.

"Isn't he the right man for you?"

"Are you kidding?" I tried for a big laugh, but Claire didn't join me. Not even a smile. "No? No, you're serious." I stood and double checked that her office door was not only closed but bolted. We'd added locks so that the clients would feel safe knowing no one could barge in on them spilling their guts. Now I was the one using the lock. No one else needed to hear my dirty laundry.

"You grew up together. He's the boy next door. It's an adorable story."

That was the story I'd told. When I was new to Owen and saw how casual kids were about their wealth, what I'd shared about growing up in Toms River had been kept to a bare minimum. The car and the clothes and the fact that I didn't have to do work study had help prop up the façade.

"My mother is his dad's housekeeper, Claire." My voice was matter-of-fact. "That's how we know each other. Please eject any sepia-toned images you have from your mind."

"Does that matter? Does class matter now that you're

both older and on more equal footing?" She was dismissing what I'd said like I was Sarah Roy.

My bark of laughter sounded harsh in the office with all of its soft furnishings and seal-gray tones "Equal footing? He went to Harvard and Wharton. He's the president of a national television network. His father's a freaking billionaire, for fuck's sake."

"You went to Owen," Claire said. I wanted to laugh in her face. There had been a time when I'd thought that getting into Owen would put me on equal footing with Jake and his Woodward Tillman friends. About two months into college, I'd been disabused of that notion by Claire herself, when she'd come back from her work-study job in student dining smelling like a bad combination of French fry grease and harsh detergent.

"It's way more complicated than that, Claire. It's not just a class issue." I closed my eyes. I wonder who'd said we were only as sick as our secrets. I was tired of keeping quiet. I wasn't even sure who I was trying to protect anymore. I'd already suffered all the consequences.

"What's the complication?"

"About my mom..."

"What about your mom? Lots of people come from humble beginnings."

I wanted to laugh or cry, I wasn't sure which. That had been coming up a lot lately, those dual feelings.

"My mother has been having an affair with Jake's father for at least twenty years, Claire. That's just one of the issues between me and Jake. Just one. Liling is another. Their families practically have them married off. They should probably be married so they can combine their billions and…run the world or something."

"Your mom…" Her innocent, fresh-from-Maryland's-shore face was back. It was like we were freshman again. I could tell from the features she couldn't keep straight that she had no good way to process what I'd just shared.

"On our first date, Jake and I walked in on them in bed. It's a secret the two of us have kept from various people for years. That's trauma bonding or some shit, not a boy-next-door, rom-com relationship," I said disabusing her of that notion once and for all.

"I had no idea." Her voice was a whisper again. "You never said."

"Because I can keep a damned secret. I remember getting your wedding non-invite and wondering why I couldn't just be at your wedding playing the role of your college room-mate. It was like you thought I'd blurt out that we'd been escorts between hors d'oeuvres and speeches. *I* wasn't the one who'd pulled the rug from under you."

"I'm still really sorry about that."

"It hurt." So much had hurt that day. I couldn't say if it was her more than Daniel or Cole and Jake. It was wrapped up in one big Philly-cheesesteak-sized shit sandwich. I looked pointedly at Claire. "It really did hurt. It was like I didn't belong anywhere in polite society if Daniel wasn't paying or paving the way. In his world, he paid everyone enough money that no one said what they thought of me, though I could see it in their eyes. But you and Jake, two people I'd loved so much, told me in a million subtle ways what you really thought of my worth."

"I don't know what I can say to make this any better. I'll never forgive myself for how I treated you. I can only hope that one day you can forgive my shortsighted behavior."

"I think I've already forgiven you, Claire." I think I had. I'd been the victim of some fucked-up thinking like Lola and Sarah here. I didn't want to let that control me any longer.

"Then what about Jake?"

"That does not follow."

"Forgiving him."

"Maybe I will one day. Maybe in my mind, I already have. I can't say. Forgiving doesn't change the past."

"So are you going to give him a chance?"

"That ship sailed. Got boarded by pirates. Then sank."

"Do you want love? To get married? Have kids?"

"I have no idea. Maybe? Maybe not? Doesn't matter. I have a lot of time to think about all that. What we really need to figure out is if we're going to do this show, the best way to maximize the benefit for the girls and minimize the downsides."

I wasn't subtle about my change of subject. Fortunately, she didn't push the issue. Instead, she followed me back to the real reason we'd started this conversation. To make a final decision about CBT.

"Does that mean you're on board?"

"Yes." I nodded emphatically. "Yes. Television will always have its own agenda. But Oprah really turned the tide about fifteen years ago, and more and more producers want to do uplifting shows. I mean, Brené Brown got a Netflix special. That's huge. Let's put our heads together and make sure our clients are safe. We can't deny them the huge potential upside. It's not fair. I'll leave my baggage out of this one. Let's go for the greater good."

"Okay. Okay. I'm excited for them. Maybe you're right. Maybe it's too late for us. We're too broken. Too jaded. Too something. But our clients are on the other end, where the possibilities are endless."

"YOU'RE STILL IN TOWN?" Isabella took a seat in the screening room. She'd left an empty one between us.

"It's a new show. A lot is riding on it. The rest of L.A. is on hiatus, so there aren't any fires to put out there."

"Ready?"

That was the engineer. He probably wanted to hit play and get the hell out of there. But union rules required that he be the one to hit that button.

"Claire coming?" I asked.

"Can't. She's got Henry tonight. Her nanny does get vacation, apparently. So Claire's a full-time mom the next week or so."

"Sweet." I pointed to the tech. "Let's do it."

The opening was a gritty black and white. It was all smash cuts of streets. Of the lobbies of high-end hotels. Of Ibiza or maybe Antibes, it went by too quickly to tell.

"It's like *Law and Order* meets *Lifestyles of the Rich and Famous*," Bella whispered.

I'd been thinking exactly the same thing.

"There are approximately one million sex workers in the United States. Of those, very few reach the upper echelons. Those who work for one man only. Welcome to *The Girl-friend Experience*."

Isabella didn't turn my way, but I did see her wrinkle her nose. That had been the least salacious name that Claire, the producers, and marketing could agree on. The format of the show was going to focus on a single girl per episode, with some input, reactions, interactions from the others.

Given that Claire and Isabella thought Sarah Roy was most vulnerable, her episode was first.

The scene opened like a documentary.

"Hi, I'm Sarah. I'm twenty-three years old. I'm from Rocky Shores, New York. That's on Long Island."

Smash cut to some pictures of her growing up, full Technicolor filters in effect. Some teen prom photos with the guy blurred out. A couple of college shots.

"How did you start dating?" The host asked, the back of her carefully coiffed head visible on camera.

"My dad used to have the snow plow contract for our town. It had been like that growing up. Each town hired a different local guy to do the plows in the winter. do the landscaping in the summer. While I was in high school, a few towns got together and decided it would be cheaper to consolidate. My dad didn't have the equipment or manpower, so he was beat out. We were doing okay, I thought. But when I got my financial aid package, it was half grants and half loans. Dad had used my credit to float us through my last year of high school. That first year of college, I only qualified for variable-rate high-interest loans. My grades were impeccable, but there weren't enough scholarships to make up for the forty-thousand-per-year tuition. An older girl took me aside at a party when I was discussing my money issues, and she proposed a solution."

"And that's how you met your sugar daddy—we're calling him Bob."

"I didn't think I could do it at first. I threw up three different times on the night I was supposed to meet him. Finally, I pulled it together and took the train from school uptown down to the restaurant where I was supposed to meet him. The thing that was most surprising was that he was nice. I think I was expecting him to be some lech or creep who'd want to tie me up in a dungeon for the rest of my life. But it was kind of the opposite. He was interested in what I had to say. He wined and dined me. He didn't even want to sleep with me that first night.

"My next week was spring break, and he took me to the Cayman Islands for a week."

"Did you sleep with him then?"

Sarah nodded, a slight blush on her cheeks. "It wasn't like you're thinking. He was a perfect gentleman the whole time. We had separate hotel rooms. He asked me to breakfast or dinner. I had time to myself to study or just lay on the beach.

"It was a lot more than most boys at college did for you. They bought you a slice of pizza and expected you to go to bed with them. Then they wouldn't even call you the next day. Just move on to the next girl at the next party on the next weekend.

"Bob remembered my name. What I liked. What I

disliked. My opinions on local politics, social media, global warming. He didn't always agree. But he treated me like I had a brain, at least. So I was happy to sleep with him. His interest in me and desire to make me happy made him extremely attractive. At least I learned *that* in this job. That the outside package isn't as important as how he treats you."

"Why are you at Julie House?"

"Because..." Her voice dropped to a whisper. The camera zoomed in for an extreme close-up for emphasis. The music became a crescendo. "I think I'm ready to live a different life. I want to get married. Have kids. Pursue a career as a psychologist maybe, and I'm not doing that now."

"You said that your sugar daddy wants to marry you. Why haven't you taken him up on his offer?"

Sarah looked down. Played with her necklace, her rings, her bracelets. I thought the producers were pretty brave to have allowed such a long moment of television silence.

"I think I want to do things differently. I think I want to fall in love the regular way."

"Don't you love your sugar daddy?"

"I do. Of course I do. He's been amazing. But maybe I love him in the way you love your high school sweetheart. It's amazing and precious while it lasts, but it's not forever."

"So why not just lose his number?"

"I'd have to find a place to live. A job. While my class-mates were doing that kind of thing. I was traveling the world with Bob. It was amazing. I've been to all seven continents. I wouldn't trade that for anything in the world. But..."

"But..."

"Rent is expensive. I don't think I want to move back

home. There aren't a lot of opportunities out there. And traveling back and forth to the city every day isn't realistic. I haven't worked since high school graduation. I didn't have summer jobs or internships. I've never had an entry-level job. I don't even know if I have any skills."

"You were awarded the prestigious Hanover Scholarship. Wouldn't that provide a year of housing, and an all-expenses-paid education while you complete graduate studies?"

Sarah turned away from the camera. "Bob traveled a lot. I couldn't be in residence and continue my relationship."

The screen went dark. Then it opened with the psychologist CBT had hired.

"Sarah appears to have the perfect out. She has an all-expenses-paid opportunity to go to graduate school. So her excuses don't make sense. Why is it that she can't leave her sugar daddy?"

"How many people have we met in our lives who claim to have problems? And you can see the solution. It's clear and straight forward, but it's like they're walking through life with blinders on?"

They both smiled knowingly.

"The dependence isn't monetary. I mean, that's part of it. But in Sarah's case, the dependence is completely psychological. Essentially, Sarah's life is entwined with Bob's. She's never lived life as an adult without him. It's not much different than if she'd been in a sheltered religious community. The outside world that most of us were exposed to one bit at a time is big and overwhelming to her. That's a big leap for anyone to take. The human brain is wired to avoid adversity. Probably stems from a time when we had to avoid death on a regular basis. Even though this is one of the most peaceful periods in human evolution, our brains haven't evolved as quickly. So we resist change and what isn't easy. What's uncomfortable. What's potentially painful.

"We're asking Sarah to give up someone who's been her companion for five years. Her apartment. Almost every possession she's used to, and take a freefall without any real friends or support system.

"This lifestyle is essentially isolationist. The fact that they're doing it is a secret. Whether it's because it's a crime or because it's a social faux pas, doesn't really matter. What's happened to these women is that most of them don't have the usual safety net that others share. She was never able to come home and complain about her job. And even if she did, you can imagine that most wouldn't be sympathetic to what they considered to be her moral failings or specious complaints.

"No one wants to hear about your horrible private jet ride, or the time you were sabotaged by the help because they didn't like prostitutes in their establishment. Or the fact that you met your sugar daddy's family and they pulled their father aside and pushed him to seek out psychological evaluation because he thought your paid relationship was real.

"These are two people in a relationship that's very present and very real, but isn't acknowledged in any way by the outside world except to be made fun of or censured."

The rest of the episode was a blur. A kind of montage of Sarah being glamorous and Sarah crying with Dr. Banks, the career counselor and the life coach.

Twenty minutes later, though, Sarah was getting in a car, her next stop Thimble Islands, Connecticut. The producers had worked with the scholarship committee and wrangled back her scholarship offer. She was going to move in to the free housing the scholarship program provided and brave life in a completely different way.

"Do you think she'll make it?"

"We're not TV producers, Jake. This isn't the end of the story. What we'll do is provide her with continuing support. Most importantly, we've found a therapist who she can see there. She needs someone who can help her continue to choose the future instead of the past."

"How was it?" I asked. I didn't want to need her approval, but I did.

"Better than I thought. Or almost as good as I thought it could be."

"I'm glad."

"Thank you."

"For what?"

"For this. I had almost forgotten the power of television. A call from CBT and people are ready to bend over backwards. You got her the scholarship back," Bella said with genuine appreciation.

"Her perfect grades and GMAT got her that scholarship to begin with. We just helped her to not squander the hell out of that opportunity." I looked her directly in the eye. "Is that what it was like for you?"

"Sorry?"

"You and Daniel."

Like Sarah, she turned away from me. Fiddled with the bangles and cords at her wrist.

"Girls with good families and strong support systems are

not poised to give the girlfriend experience. Lots of people in elite schools are in difficult financial straits. These schools are ridiculously expensive and financial aid relies far too heavily on loans. Yet most women aren't dancing around a pole or dating old rich dudes."

"You didn't answer the question," I probed.

"What question?"

"Was it like that for you? Is that the reason you stayed with Daniel for so long?"

"Maybe, Jake. Maybe a little bit."

"EVERYTHING'S FINE at Julie House, right?" I asked. Concern lined Claire's face when she came through my front door. I think this was the first time she'd come to my apartment. Her presence only reinforced how odd my life was.

Most people probably would have had a housewarming party or some other kind of thing at their new place. Other than Jake, furniture delivery men, and the building super, no one had been in here besides me in a year. I felt like a dog who holed up in a den at the end of the night. Maybe that comparison didn't work because dogs were more social than I'd ever been.

"Your place is nice," she said. Politely, she stood by the door, shifting her purse from one hand to the other. It was a long, awkward moment before I realized that I hadn't invited her in.

"My manners. Sorry. Come in. Do you want water or something?"

I didn't wait for an answer, but padded to the kitchen in

my cotton ankle socks. I pulled two tall glasses from the cabinet and filled each with water from the sink filter. I drank mine down completely, trying to soothe the unexpected lump in my throat, then filled it again. This time I put it on the counter, rather than chugging impolitely.

"Are you okay?" Claire asked. She extended a hand and laid it on my forearm. I didn't want to but flinched at her unexpected touch.

Most of the times I'd been touched in my life, the person reaching out had wanted something from me. My time. My body. It was ironic then that her friendly touch made me the most uncomfortable. I backed away the few inches it took for her arm to fall away. I sipped at my water again, wondering at the source of my nerves. I didn't need to wonder long. I was desperately afraid that she'd ask me to appear on screen, admit in public that I'd been no different from the Julie clients.

"Other than a bit of thirst, I'm fine," I lied. "It's kind of hot. August in the city isn't the best." I picked up a restaurant menu and fanned myself in the air-conditioned apartment. Suddenly seventy-two degrees wasn't cool enough.

"Where did you spend August when you were with Daniel? I was in Maine a lot. Rolland liked New England.

"You guys went to watch the leaves change the first time I learned you were a Julie." I don't know which had been more startling, Claire's sudden upgrade in luggage and wardrobe or the fact that she was a high-end escort.

Claire's voice cut short my walk down memory lane. "Kennebunkport was warm during the day, but cool at night. I liked the Atlantic Ocean there. Always made me think of the Gothic novels my mom had on a shelf in her bedroom. Women in long dresses who always looked like they were at risk of falling in love or falling to their death on the rocky shore.

"Love or death. That's a hell of a choice," I said. Though at this point in my life, only death was certain. Love was more elusive than ever.

"Lola's been asking about you."

The break from working on site at Julie House had been for my mental health. I'd developed a bit of a rapport with the girls there, but was surprised that someone had asked for me by name.

"I'll give her a call tonight," I offered. Lola did seem vulnerable. To tell the truth, they all seemed endlessly vulnerable. From a distance, it was easy to see how they'd let life jostle them about like a dinghy in an ocean storm. I wanted them to be fierce captains of their own ships.

"You're avoiding Julie House, aren't you?"

Even though it was true, my insides squirmed. I wanted to be tougher than this. I didn't want to be someone who was unable to handle the least bit of stress.

"I don't want to get in the way of filming," I said. "Nothing's out of whack? You've seen the next two episodes?"

After Claire's nanny was back, I'd e-mailed her and bowed out of discussions about the show. When Claire had first called me in Italy, I'd somehow imagined that being involve with Julie House would cleanse me of the feeling that I'd done something wrong, been wrong all of these years I was tethered to Daniel, but on too many days, I was feeling worse, not better.

"We're good. It's better than I thought. I'm so glad you were there during negotiations. You kept it from being a tabloid show. I totally chalk that up to your expertise."

"Expertise. I was just a network censor. Keeping the airwaves penis-free since twenty-fifteen. Wait. I failed at that too. I was barely in entertainment. More like a government job, for sure."

Watching Claire's face made me shift on my feet. I'd had so many disguises over the years. Mafia princess, rich dilettante, impressive TV executive. All of them had been a front for a poor girl in a rich town, an escort, and lastly, a woman who had a job at CBT only because the FCC was breathing down every network's back.

I hadn't been trusted with anything as important as deal making or storytelling. Just limiting the number of swear words and mentions of genitals on the air. Once I had to prompt animators to add seat belts to a kids' cartoon show. Another time I had to ask a producer to put a character on a smoking-cessation program. High glamour, that. I didn't give Claire chapter and verse. But I was out of the business of pretending to be something I wasn't as well.

"But you've been on set and seen how people are really treated. Don't downplay how much you've helped make *The Girlfriend Experience* a pretty good experience." Claire took a seat at the counter. Took another sip of her own water. "Looks like we've got a placement for Kristina."

"You said something in your e-mail?" It was another thing I'd left dangling. My emotions had been wildly out of whack these past couple of weeks. I alternated between wanting to light a fire under our clients and feeling envious of their ability to start a new life in their twenties. That envy I kept tucked far away from public view. I had ten million reasons not to envy them, yet I did for all the years I'd lost, not getting to be who I wanted to be. I was staring down the barrel of my mid-thirties and I didn't even know what I wanted for my future anymore. At least it was happening for our clients.

"It's for an editorial assistant at a publishing house. She developed a passion for reading when she was filling all those hours of traveling and sitting and waiting."

"Yes, the hurry up and wait. I would never put on a gown until five minutes before we actually left. The first time Daniel and I went to some fundraiser in New York, he had a call with Amsterdam and I nearly suffocated in a dress that was, let's just say, form-fitting...not too much for taking a full breath."

"Maybe I lucked out because Rolland was more outdoorsy. Maybe a dress for dinner or something, but never a formal."

"Probably because he took his wife."

"Or that." Claire sighed, looking almost as tired of revisiting the past as I was. "I just came by to see if you were coming tonight."

"Tonight?" I played dumb, hoping to avoid having to say no again without giving a reason.

"We were all going to watch the premiere."

"I'll pass."

The buzzer sounded. *Saved by the bell,* I thought. It was buzzing for the second time in less than an hour. The only time that had happened is when the food delivery guy had gotten locked in the vestibule and I'd had to come down and let him out.

"Hello," I said into the intercom phone, expecting to deliver the news that they had the wrong apartment.

"It's Jake," the disembodied voice returned.

I debated a long minute before pressing the blue button that unlocked the downstairs doors.

"I'm sorry, are you expecting someone?" Claire called from the kitchen.

I gestured toward my sky blue and purple yoga leggings and lavender lotus tank with the word "Namaste" across my breasts. "Nothing says guests like Lululemon. It's only Jake."

"He was asking about you today."

I rolled out my ready litany of excuses. "My God, I was only out of the building for a couple of weeks. I submitted three grant proposals and went through the entire backlog of applications. I wanted to be caught up because I thought there may be an influx with the show. Even though we're not named specifically, some girls are going to figure it out."

"I get it." When a knock sounded at the door, Claire rose, hefting her purse onto her shoulder. "Let me answer that for you. This is my cue anyway."

"Didn't expect to see you so soon," Jake said, bussing Claire on the cheek and pulling her into a half hug L.A. style. "You don't have to leave on account of me," he said to my friend's back retreating through the front door.

"Nope, not because of you. I have to get back home and get Henry to bed before the show."

I was disgusted with myself because I even envied Claire her maternal responsibilities. She had a small person to whom she could give her undivided attention, get out of the loop of thoughts in her head.

"Let me know what you think," Jake said to Claire. "If there's anything that doesn't come across, let me know so we can fix it before number two airs."

Jake didn't wait for an invitation. He strode past me, dropping his bag by the door, and took a seat at the kitchen counter. I took Claire's glass from the counter, extracted another and poured water for Jake. He took it without comment and swallowed deeply. I glanced outside, only to see that the few people walking by looked like wilted flowers. It was no wonder people with money escaped the city in the sweltering summer.

"Who are you and what have you done with Jian Wu?" Even though my voice was bordering on the sarcastic, there was some truth to my question. Nice and accommodating weren't among the first thirty adjectives I'd have used for Jake. I turned away and opened the fridge. The only things in there were green tea and wine. One would wind me up too much. The second would make me too vulnerable. I pushed the door closed and rested my back against the sink. Looked Jake in the eye.

"Do you really think I'm wishing for bad luck for you?" He looked genuinely aggrieved.

"Jake." I sighed. Rolled the tension kinks out of my neck and tried not to wish like hell that I'd ignored the buzzer today. "It's television. The goal of television is to get high ratings to sell ad space at a higher rate. That's it. There's really no more to it. There are only so many hours of ad space you can sell in a day, so the only way to increase profits is to raise the price. I didn't need to major in economics to do the math on this one."

"What was your major?" he asked. The question completely caught me by surprise because I'd expected the usual lecture on how television was the new hotbed of Hollywood creative energy. A lot of producers, mostly to their detriment, plugged their eyes and ears when it came time to face the bottom line of the almighty dollar.

"Are you serious?"

"I have no idea what you majored in at Owen."

"Humanities." I'd never gone back and changed my concentration to something more challenging, like I'd promised myself during those early days at Owen. Keeping up my relationship with Daniel had been all the challenge I could muster.

"What does that mean?"

My mother, Mr. Wu, and countless employers had asked that one. It's probably why I'd taken Daniel up on his offer of assistance for that first job. I'd wanted to show what I could do, not spend an entire year trying to convince someone I could do the work.

"That I designed my own major. Took the classes that interested me. Graduated with decent grades."

"I majored in economics," he offered. Of all the things I knew about Jake, I hadn't known this. The last time we'd had a "getting to know you" conversation, I'd been twelve. Getting to know me then had consisted of telling him about my parents' divorce, my favorite movies and video games.

"Not marketing or business?" I probed. Those laser-focused majors had seemed like the kind of thing Mrs. Li would have insisted upon.

"Fortunately for all of us, we didn't have that in Cambridge. Having worked with people who majored in such narrow subjects, I think the liberal arts approach is better."

"What did Mr. Wu think?" I couldn't resist the question. What Mr. Wu thought had dominated so much of my life, of Jake's life, that I couldn't have imagined him making something as big a decision about a major without having to run it past the man who paid everyone's bills. I certainly hadn't felt much autonomy when Mr. Wu supported me under the guise of bribery.

"Mr. Wu thought his son was in the most prestigious university in the country and it was not best to second-guess the American way."

"Another shield?" I pointed out. Jake had been a master at doing what he wanted while practicing obedience. My own failure at the same had cost me the promised tuition.

"Come again?"

"Like Woodward Tillman. A way to do more of what you wanted in an approved way."

"Why aren't you at Julie House tonight? Or why weren't you there the last couple weeks?" He deftly changed the subject from Mr. Wu. It was probably for the best. That way would eventually lead to some kind of argument we didn't need to have—again.

"Grant proposals. Applications. Lots of paperwork to get through." I peppered him with my well thought out excuses. "I can work here uninterrupted. Between the clients and

Claire and all the cameras, I needed a place I could put my head down."

Tucked somewhere in his pants, Jake's phone beeped.

"If that's work, you should answer."

The sooner he left, the sooner I could push away the discomfort.

He lifted the phone from his pocket. Swiped. Put it back.

"Not work. Alarm. The show starts in five minutes."

That damned show. It was too late to go back, but sometimes I wish I'd never said yes to *The Girlfriend Experience*.

"I have a ton more stuff to plow through," I demurred.

"You'd better get to the network. Maybe you can be there in time to catch the Midwest feed." Most shows were broadcast three times a night, for eastern, central and mountain, and the western time zones. It was that space between broadcasts that had allowed us to fix mistakes like Blue's penis, and limit the havoc live shows could wreak on the air.

My words didn't prompt Jake to lift his butt from my kitchen stool.

"I'm here because I wanted to watch it with you. You didn't respond to any of my e-mails."

I'd ignored the five e-mails from Claire, the three from Jake, and the single one from Liling, all asking about where I wanted to watch the broadcast premiere.

"I didn't? Oversight." I shook my head. My ponytail swept against my neck. I left the kitchen and took up a perch at a living room window. I could hear the creak of the seat, the footsteps across the wood floor. Feel the presence of Jake next to me. Even if he never made another sound, I was convinced that something about Jake changed the very air around me

"Stop." He laid a hand on my shoulder, half turning me toward him. "What's going on?"

"I already saw it."

"Just the rough cut."

"I don't need to see the final." I did not want to tell him how much I could barely stand the idea of looking at that show again or going to Julie House while the taping was ongoing.

"Bella. The producers reordered—"

"I don't want to watch it." My voice was louder than I intended. I couldn't help the surge of feelings rushing through me, pushing to get out. "That's final. It reminds me too much of Daniel. Brings up a lot of issues that I'd rather not think about." I was surprised at my own honesty. I guess that little self-directive to stop playing games was overriding my usual censure.

"Oh...oh." Jake's face displayed something I'd never seen before. Embarrassment. Maybe I wasn't the only one who'd gotten tired of wearing masks. "I didn't think—"

"Now there's the Jake Wu I know. Profits over people."

"That's not fair. At all. Talk to me."

"What is there to say? I hate the word triggered. But maybe in this case it's true. Watching the Sarah Roy episode fucked me up. Okay? That was evidence front and center that I'll never be normal. Can't hope to ever live any kind of regular life. That's what I've been holed up here thinking about the last couple of weeks. The grant proposals and applications were real. But I needed that as a distraction from having to face a past I'm not proud of and a completely uncertain future."

"What do you want?" Jake's voice was unbelievably soft.

The way he asked the question made me feel like he would, if he could, give me whatever was necessary to make me happy. Daniel had assumed, on more than one occasion, that money was the key to happiness. After all these years of having a front row seat to the lifestyles of the rich and famous, I wasn't so sure.

When I allowed myself just this tiniest of space to think about my wants, my mind flashed back more than a dozen years.

"During my junior year abroad, this guy Mathijs, he asked me out on a date."

"A date?" Jake's face screwed up, though I couldn't quite read his expression.

"We went to have coffee...no, beer. It was later in the day and I think I remember him ordering me a Belgian beer. We flirted. Talked about Dutch culture and made a second date. Like a go-out-with-each-other-and-hang-out date."

"Did you guys get together?"

"No, because Daniel nipped that in the bud. I'm not sure if it was an unspoken agreement or something I should have figured out, but he required exclusivity." Which had been okay ninety percent of the time. The other girls at Owen who had boyfriends had time. I couldn't quite put together how it would be possible to finish school, date *and* have Daniel. How would I explain my unavailability? My need to travel at a moment's notice or be ready to have a formal dinner at the drop of a hat?

How would that conversation go?

Him: You want to catch a movie marathon at the Temple Street theater, maybe get some pizza after?

Me: I'd love to but I have to meet the limo at 5, which is going to take me down to the Sound for a dinner party on a friend of a friend's yacht. How about a rain check?

"But I've always wanted that. A real relationship. A guy I can call my boyfriend. Maybe something more in time. I just want to do life normal."

Do life normal. Sounded like something I should get printed on a t-shirt or maybe even mantra jewelry. Maybe then I'd be sure not to relapse.

Jake looked around my apartment. "This looks normal."

"But it's not. Something about my time with Daniel changed me in ways that I don't ever think will change back. I lived in a big, larger-than-life kind of world for years. I've lived with rats in the walls and stayed in the most expensive suites on earth. What am I supposed to do with that? Get up tomorrow morning and swipe right on Tinder?"

"You've heard of Tinder?"

"I don't live under a rock. This is Brooklyn, where every other billboard is an ad for online dating." The rest were for iPhones. The latter seemed unnecessary, since everyone under forty seemed to have one permanently attached to their hand.

"I was kind of hoping you'd swipe right on *me*." His earnest face nearly broke my heart.

"Oh Jake. How could we do that?" I abandoned the window and sank into an armchair that wasn't as comfortable as it was aesthetically pleasing. My heart was pulling for Jake and second and third chances. My head couldn't wrap itself around how that could possibly work. If some people had baggage, we had steamer trunks.

"The same way other people do it. The way people on Tinder probably do it. Get to know each other—again."

Jake took a seat on the couch across from me. His hands dangled between his legs, spread wide, in that way that said a guy was comfortable enough to talk. For once, my heart wasn't in overdrive nor was my belly twisting. It was the first time in a long time I was sitting near Jake and he was just a person. He may have been the most attractive man in the world—to me, at least. But he was just a person. Not perfect by any means. But neither was I.

"What's your favorite movie?" he asked, his voice loud in the long moment of silence that had stretched between us.

"*Pretty Woman.*"

It took him a long minute filled with only the sounds of the air-conditioning unit cycling on and off before he realized I was kidding.

"Oh God, that's a joke." His voice was tinged with relief.

"I used to be funny sometimes. In all seriousness? Maybe *Donnie Darko* or *Lost in Translation.* How about you?" I asked, playing along with the getting-to-know-you game.

This conversation was the oddest I'd had in a long time. I could describe the contours of Jake's childhood bedroom, the way his father cleared his throat after eating Mama's pasta, Min Li's perfume, but I didn't know any of the innocuous things about him.

"*Napoleon Dynamite,*" he answered.

Was I supposed to make something of that choice? Or

was it just a fact that I was to tuck away for later? With Daniel, I'd filed away every little fact for later use. His favorite pastry would be a surprise one morning. His favorite gin had always been in my freezer so he could have a nightcap without having to try something new and unfamiliar or too American. He'd nearly spit out the Bourbon I'd once offered him.

"What's your favorite food?"

Dutch wasn't the answer. I'd never wrapped my head around that, with its hearty soups, heartier beers, and all the cheese you could eat. It was like they'd never seen a tomato.

"Italian? *Pitta rustica.*" Mama only made it once or twice because Mr. Wu didn't much like potatoes. But I'd probably gone overboard last year. It had become a comfort food when the family I'd gone to see had run cold. "American? I still think the burger is a pretty great invention. Chinese. *Xiao-longbao.*"

"They were in the steamer that time your mom came for the job interview."

"I was so hungry the first time I tasted them," I admitted. "I probably hadn't eaten a proper meal in a couple of days."

"I'd always wondered about that. Did you guys not have enough food?"

I scanned Jake's face, but didn't see an ounce of pity, just empathy. Relieved, I answered.

"Nope. I think the electricity had been turned off and Mama couldn't really store anything in the summer heat, so it was peanut butter sandwiches. The sugary peanut butter, not the Whole Foods kind that really tastes like peanuts. I forgot how hungry those could make you after your body had worked through all the carbs."

Jake's jeans rustled against the couch cushions as he leaned forward, his elbows landing on his thighs. "Did you ever have a boyfriend?"

"That lasted longer than a night? Nope. There was you. There was hooking up. There was Daniel. Maybe that Dartmouth guy would have dated me if you hadn't come into the room."

"He wasn't known for his 'dating' techniques at the club."

"Every guy has a reputation. They probably cultivated it. I'm not sure half of them are real."

"What's your favorite color?"

"Midnight blue."

"It's a good color on you."

"Thank you, I think." I tried to remember what he'd seen of me in midnight blue, then remembered it had been my lacy underwear. I wasn't touching that one with a ten-foot pole.

"Dogs or cats?"

"I don't know. Cats, maybe? We had one when I lived in Philly."

"What happened to him? You guys didn't bring a cat with you."

"Her," I corrected. "Her name was Mittens. I think she went to live with my aunt and uncle when we moved. I'm not sure. I kind of blocked a lot of that out. It was a super confusing time. No one ever explained to me what in the heck was going on. It wasn't some Disney Channel movie where the parents sit the kids down and tell them they love them, but not each other anymore."

"What happened?"

"My grandma came from Italy."

"The one your brother wants you to give the house over to?"

"That one. She yelled at my mom. Later, my dad and mom fought. Then they stopped speaking...and a couple of days later, Mama said we had to leave. I stopped asking her questions because she always refused to answer."

"Where do you want to live?"

"When?"

"Now? Later? Do you want to stay in New York? Move back to Los Angeles? Live somewhere else in the world?"

"For now, New York is fine, I guess. I don't have long-term plans or long-term answers. Do most people? Or do they live day by day?"

"Probably about half-half. I don't know. There are a lot of people who say, 'I've always wanted to live in San Francisco, or London, or Paris.' Then there are people who probably have never thought about it. They stay where they were born or go where the next job is. I'm just wondering in a perfect world, what would you like?"

"You go first."

Jake was quiet. He sat back. Crossed one leg over the other. Closed his eyes. Opened them.

"I'm going to lay my cards on the table here. There's no reason to play games."

"I didn't know we were in a game."

"We've always been in a game, Bella. Whether we were

on the same team playing against our parents or whether we were on opposite teams keeping our cards close to the vest. We were in a game."

"I guess I see what you're saying. So?"

"So. I bought CBT because I wanted to be near you. I moved to Los Angeles because once and for all, I wanted to be with you. But the adjoining penthouses? That was a coincidence, I swear."

"Wait. Did I hear you right? You bought an American television network because you wanted to renew our acquaintance?"

"When you say it like that, I sounds kind of crazy."

"Sounds kind of crazy. Kind of. Crazy." My brain got hung up on the math of that like a computer hangs when I've tried to ask it to make too many calculations. "The CBT deal was valued at something like ten billion dollars. Billion with a 'b.'"

"A combination of cash and stock transfer."

"How did you convince Mr. Wu to join your little scheme?"

"Liling's father owns a network. He's competitive. Owning a network in America was more prestigious."

Ten billion made Daniel's ten million seem like a drop in the bucket. Either way, I'd been commodified. If one of them wasn't trying to buy me, then it wasn't Wednesday.

"I'm not for sale."

"That's not the spirit of the deal."

"With all this talk of my favorite foods and movies, I thought something was different. But at the end of the day, we're back to money. Always money. If you spend enough.

If anyone spends enough, they can have me. That ship sailed."

"I realize it may have been a mistake."

"Maybe? You think? You could have just...I don't know... called me on the phone or something. Or e-mailed me."

"But you wouldn't have responded. You shut me out until I pushed my way in."

"At least the other would have been honest."

"I'm being honest now, Bella. I love you. I always have."

"Always?"

"Since I was thirteen and you were like this whirlwind of smart-mouthed Philly girl who came into my life. You were like love and light and fun. You were willing to try anything. To do anything.

"You even made middle school fun. That whole Shorty Aconi thing? It was freaking brilliant. No one dared mess with me or you after that. My first year in Toms River was shit. After you got there, nothing could bother me. Not Father. Not Min Li. Not the stupid boys who tried to bully me. *Nothing*. I just had to look out of my window toward yours and I knew my other half was there.

"The network thing was heavy-handed. But it's not a bad investment. My father and his friends wouldn't have put up money if it was just a vanity project."

"Do you know how I got the job at CBT?"

Jake shook his head. I'm not sure if the change of subject was going to give him whiplash. I didn't really care.

"When I graduated from Owen, I had no job. No money. Nowhere to go. Every summer, while people were doing internships or whatever, I'd been in Antibes or in the Alps—

Swiss and Bavarian—or once Australia, where it was winter. When it came time to send out resumes and look for work, mine was thin.

"Daniel is the CEO of—"

"The largest staffing company in the world," I finished. "He asked me what I wanted to do. My goals were modest. I just wanted to try the Page Program at CBT. The day after I mentioned it, I got a call from the program head offering me a job. The pay? Ten dollars an hour."

"I had two choices. Take that job, which felt like a dream job...and the strings that came with it...and stay in Daniel's New York apartment. Or try to figure it out on my own. Taking my humanities degree and finding a job in a smaller city where I could afford to live on an entry-level salary."

"You chose CBT."

"After the program, I was offered a job in the one of CBT's stations in Philadelphia. Again, Daniel offered an apartment. All I had to do was see him from time to time. Maybe once every other month. That seemed a small price to pay for a career. Then I took that show on the road to Los Angeles, where he got me a different job and a different apartment. When I gave up CBT, I gave up Daniel. When I gave up CBT, I also gave up you. I want a relationship, Jake, where there's no exchange of money. Ours is already corrupted. I'm not sure if there's any way to go back. Any way to begin again. To start over."

"What could I say to convince you?" Jake's question was a plea.

"I don't know if I want to be convinced." It was an unconvincing lie.

"Let me try."

"What would that mean? The past is our problem. If we met now, maybe things would be different. Or maybe not. Maybe we're fooling ourselves. Maybe the past is all we have."

"Come sit next to me."

"We're not having sex, Jake. That is not going to help."

"Oh, it could help a lot of things." He barely hid a small half smile. "It feels great. Helps me feel closer to you. Helps me get to know you better."

"Helps distract us from the hard conversations."

"That's true," he admitted.

"If we're going to try this...what would the plan be?" I asked, making the most sudden and rash decision of the day.

"Serious?"

"Jake, I've always loved you. If we didn't try, I'd probably regret it for the rest of my life."

"Then let's neither of us have regrets."

"A SURPRISE? Do I seem like a surprise kind of person?"

"Honestly? No. You are the exact opposite of a surprise kind of person. But I don't think what I'm about to do would have the same impact if you knew about it in advance. So I'm taking the risk."

"Am I dressed fine?"

"You look absolutely perfect."

"That's a come-on, not actionable information."

"As long as you're comfortable."

"Let's go then, so we can get on with the surprise."

"Is it always going to be this hard to do nice things for you?"

"Nice things have always had a price tag attached, Jake. Give me a minute to adjust."

"Point taken."

Turns out CBT had as many cars, if not more, in New York than they had in Los Angeles. The black car I'd ridden over the bridge to Bella's Brooklyn apartment was idling outside her front door. Before I could lift my hand, the driver opened the rear passenger door with a flourish. Isabella slipped in like a natural, even in her casual clothes.

She had been right about those with money, versus those without. There was a certain comfort those with money had with being served. The women at Julie House were the same in that way. They did not step up to open their own doors or lift heavy bags. I could see how their dependency would seem more feminine to men used to taking care of everything.

It was hard sometimes to reconcile the pre-teen girl I met with this woman who'd become worldly in this way when I wasn't looking.

On the ride back across the bridge, we talked a bit about how much New York had changed in the last couple of decades.

"We were so bridge and tunnel," Isabella said. "At least I was. Maybe you never were."

"New York overwhelmed me back then."

"But you seemed so sure."

"I think it was because Father gave me a few hundred dollars to keep in my wallet. It was the security of knowing that no matter what happened, I'd have a way to get back home."

"No situation you couldn't pay your way out of. That's a completely different perspective on life."

"We're here," I announced. I wasn't ready to reply to her comment.

"It's a movie theater."

Isabella waited until the driver parked, opened the door, helped her out. She looked around, uncertain.

I texted the number I'd been given and a man appeared behind the diamond-paned metal gate covering the door opening.

"Jake Wu? We're all set for you. Follow me to theater two."

Without second-guessing, I grabbed Isabella's hand and we followed the man to the theater. The lights were dim, but not yet dark.

"You want anything? Popcorn? Candy? Wine?"

"Maybe popcorn," she answered. In a few minutes, the man was back with two bags of popcorn and a couple of green bottles of sparkling water. He disappeared behind us, then a curtain parted, the lights dimmed further, and a single picture of Led Zeppelin appeared on the screen.

"My God. Is this what I think it is?"

"What do you think it is?"

"The Led Zeppelin documentary that's in post-production while looking for a distributor. It may be on the festival circuit soon. That documentary."

"You still reading the trades?"

"Habit. Somehow the *Hollywood Reporter* and *Variety* found my new address and are in the mail every time I look up."

The credits were over and there was a cut to footage from years past. Eventually, Isabella shifted her popcorn to the seat next to her. I slipped an arm around her and pulled her closer for the two-hour show.

"That was incredible," she said while the end credits rolled. "My dad... Well, he probably would have loved it. What's it called?"

"Still doesn't have a title. There's somewhere else I want to take you."

Twenty minutes later, we were just off Herald Square at the same place we'd had pie after that concert.

"It's still here. I can't believe it. An article in the *Times* said that diners were going the way of the dodo."

"Fortunately not this one, then." I opened the door. We took seats at the same booth we'd sat at years earlier. A waitress was quick to come to the table, pad in hand.

"If you want pie, we've got lemon meringue, key lime, cherry, Boston crème. What are you guys in the mood for?"

"Cherry," I ordered.

"Boston crème," Isabella ordered for herself. "Not the season for pumpkin. Not everything needs to be the same. Actually, maybe it's best it isn't."

"I'm glad you liked the documentary. They haven't played a concert in probably a dozen years."

Please tell me you didn't think of booking a private concert?"

"The thought crossed my mind, but it would have been too much, right?"

"Yeah." Bella eased her fork into the cake and custard combination. "Do you think they've ever changed the recipe?"

"Probably not. Why?"

"This is like taking a bite of childhood. No offense to Magnolia and Sprinkles and all the so-called *elevated* cupcakes, but this is divine. Too sweet. Cold. Perfect."

Following her lead, I took a bite of the pie. She was right.

This probably had every forbidden ingredient on Earth, but it was sinfully nostalgic.

"Money is a huge cushion. Or maybe it's like the safety net you can barely see at Cirque du Soleil. It's nearly opaque, but it's there."

"Before Mr. Wu gave me the credit card, I didn't really know what it was like. To go out and not worry that you'd get stuck with some guy with no way home. Or stuck somewhere without enough gas. Or stuck in the city with no ride back to Jersey. Then he gave me the card and that phone. I sort of realized then what it was a little bit like to be you."

"Consequences became a little less consequential. I did like it. That freedom. To the girls in town, I appeared to be one thing. But in my heart, I knew it was another thing entirely. It was a bribe. It was a payoff."

"Do you want me to apologize again?"

"Not about that. None of that was your fault. That was two adults who wanted to continue to do whatever they wanted and had zero compunction putting the burden on me. The really sad part is that I thought I had gotten the better of them. Driving around in a brand-new cherry-red SUV. Wearing the latest in Jersey mall chic. Being only the second girl at school to have a cell."

"Let me guess, the first was Johnna Rossman."

Her laugh was big, beautiful, hearty. Real.

"Oh my God, you're one hundred percent right."

"I can't believe I dredged that out of my memory. I remember you being jealous of her because she got to wear makeup, short skirts. Had a piercing."

"Did I tell you all that?"

"Not in so many words on any given day. But yeah, you told me more or less when you used to complain about your mom."

"After the concert, she wasn't so strict, but I never did work up the nerve to get the piercing. Then later, I was glad I didn't."

"Do you remember what happened after we left?"

"It was our first kiss, Jake. Before the whole night went sideways, it was one of the best nights of my life."

"Me too. Can a guy still say that?"

"No hashtag and you're good."

"I'd been fantasizing about kissing you for weeks, maybe months, I don't know," I said. "I'd spent days working out that shed idea before Min Li came in and ruined it."

"It's like she had a sixth sense."

"We were probably more obvious than we think."

"Oh God!" Bella dropped her fork and covered her face with both hands. "You're probably right! We were probably mooning about looking like teenagers in heat."

"I slipped out for a few days looking for a place that we could be alone without the possibility of someone walking in on us, which left out your house and mine. I'd planned to take you to the shed and then kiss you after showing you the rats."

"Only a boy would think rats a good prelude to a first kiss."

"It was my best move."

"I hope your moves have gotten better."

"I still think you're the most beautiful girl...woman, I've ever known."

I watched a blush, as rare as seeing a snow leopard in the

wild, creep up her cheeks. She dipped her head. Took another bite of pie.

"Thank you."

"Do you have a house that you dream about?"

"A house?"

"I've heard that many people have a house that recurs in their dreams. In most dreams, it's not a real place. But at night, during REM sleep, it becomes this place that you can revisit. Some professor once said that this house represents the self.

That was a little too hocus pocus for me. But in my dreams, you were always there. You at the age you really are. But you were always outside, walking by, running away. Laughing. Crying. No matter how hard I tried... Opening doors. Opening windows. What have you. I could never reach you."

"That's how I felt when I was awake."

I took her hands in mine. Rested our hands on the Formica-topped table. Held them.

"I don't want to ever have that feeling again. I want to be able to go to sleep and wake up knowing that you're near me."

"I think I want the same thing."

"But?"

"But I worry we'll destroy each other. We've come shockingly close before."

"DO YOU WANT HIM? Or do you just want to relive your past? Work out your frustration? Then leave him high and dry?"

I knew Liling was going to get to me one day. I hadn't banked on it being today. Especially when I wasn't in the mood to explain myself to anyone, much less Jake's ex.

"There were about a thousand assumptions in that question," I demurred. If she were half as polite as she always pretended to be, she'd act like she hadn't just asked the world's most inappropriate question and instead would get back to doing whatever the Wu family had hired her to do at CBT.

I hadn't regretted coming to Julie House until just this moment. I probably could have worked at home forever, but I didn't want Lola or any of the other girls to think I was abandoning them. I also wanted to meet two of the new girls who were moving in. Let them know that someone who'd walked in their shoes had their backs. But

Liling had ambushed me before I could do what I'd come here to do.

I figured I could pop into the little office space Clair set aside for me. Look through the accumulated stack of mail. Talk to the girls. Then head out. The daily e-mailed call sheet had indicated that there was no filming today. A concession made so we could move in the two new women.

No filming had minimized the chance of contact, had given me a false sense of security.

I wondered how long Liling had been waiting for me to show my face. I was one hundred percent sure that her wandering in to "touch base" was not a coincidence.

"Have a seat," I said. I pointed to the other small white plastic chair in my office. Usually I used it for files, but my productivity of the last two weeks had made hash of my backlog. "What is or isn't going on between me and Jake isn't really any of your business," I laid out as plainly as I could, hoping she'd take the hint and find someone else to bother.

"I'm his friend." She set her work papers on the floor next to her chair, abandoning any pretense of this being a work meeting. "How his other so-called friends treat him is totally my business."

"Jake Wu. Wu Jian, is an adult capable of making his own decisions and living with the consequences." I wasn't proud of my use of his full Chinese name and the excellent Mandarin pronunciation, but I couldn't help a little bit of one-upmanship.

"I'm not so sure about that. He has a particularly large blind spot when it comes to you."

Jake and I had done a lot of talking over the past few

weeks. It had been good. Great, really. We'd made space for each other to say many of the things we'd resisted, hid, lied about, and stuffed down for years.

Despite all of this openness and honesty, there were still a few things that we hadn't touched with a ten-foot pole. One was my abortion. I pushed away that last thought and the dread that came with it. That was a grave worthy secret.

The other was Liling.

I wasn't jealous of her exactly. All my love, anger, sadness had been directed toward Jake, who I still think was the most appropriate target of those feelings. The fact that she'd been among Jake's lovers made me crazy with envy at the oddest moments. Most of the time I understood why he'd sought out a relationship with her. Other times, it ate at me that he hadn't waited for me to find a way to come to him, to be ready for us.

I stuffed all that other stuff down and pointed a clear-eyed look at the other woman who'd been in and out Jake's life almost as much as me.

It was now or never.

"I am a grown woman who makes all my own choices. You have something to get off your chest. This is the one and only time we're ever going to have this kind of conversation. So say your piece."

"I think you should stop seeing Jake."

I'd like for that to have been unexpected, but it wasn't. She'd probably been trying to excise me from Jake's life for years, like Jake's mother and father. None had been successful.

"Why?" I leaned forward in my chair to get closer to her.

To hear all reasons loud and clear. Liling leaned back in hers like I was going to smack here. For a fleeting moment, I wondered if I was wearing my Mafia princess face.

"Because you don't belong together. I know he's stuck... no, fixated...on you because he didn't get to kiss you or date you or whatever in nineteen-ninety-something. But that's silly. He has a big and complicated life and you're not the right person to help him live it."

I wanted to tell her she didn't know from big, complicated lives. I'd watched Daniel live one for years. I could manage a working billionaire's life with one hand tied behind my back. My mother had done it *on* her back.

I pushed away thoughts of Daniel and Mr. Wu and concentrated on Liling.

"Let me guess. You are."

"We have the same background. Early years in Shanghai, high school and university in America. Our families have been friends forever. And no offense..." She glanced down at my clothes, simple ones from the Gap. I still hadn't gone back to the designer suit and pencil skirt days of the recent past. I glanced toward her ensemble then back at her face. One glance and I knew that she found me wanting.

Before Liling spoke again, she pushed up the sleeves of her shirt. I knew that move. She wanted me to see the diamond Rolex that dangled casually from her left wrist and the Hermes bangle that hung from her right.

I scrutinized her in the same way she'd done to me.

My quick assessment? She probably had ten or fifteen thousand dollars' worth of clothes and jewelry on her rail-thin body. Except for my own understated Tissot sport watch, my outfit probably didn't top two hundred. With the watch, I didn't break five.

For once, I was glad not to be blinged out. If Liling... Lily...whatever, was any reflection of what I used to look like, then I was kind of embarrassed for my former self. As if more money on the outside made a person more worthy on the inside.

"Whether Jian stays with CBT or ends up being the head of one of the Woo concerns," she continued, "he's going to need someone in his life who can help him with that. Who speaks Mandarin, English, and French? Not to mention a little Cantonese."

I sat back, letting her feel like she'd won the argument. I took a long breath. Extended my legs. Crossed my feet at the ankles.

"If love were a job, then you'd win."

I let that sit there for a moment while she tried to figure out if she'd convinced me or had just been insulted.

"Marriage *is* a job. A full-time one, which I'm qualified for." It was a closing line for a job interview. Too bad there wasn't a job opening.

"Then maybe you should get married. I know firsthand that there are a ton of rich CEO types who would be happy to hire you." I mimed as if I were going for my office phone. "Want me to put in a call?"

Liling huffed. She puffed. Too bad it wasn't enough to blow my house down.

"I can't believe that you'd compare me to..." Her arm shot out, Hermes bangle spinning as she gestured toward what I could only assume were the Julie House inhabitants.

"I'd be careful if I were you. Compare you to what? Because what I'm hearing is that you're perfect for the job of wife to a rich CEO, but are about to shit on others who play girlfriends to rich CEOs. Certainly that wasn't what was going to come out."

More huffing from Liling. I don't imagine this was how the conversation was going to go in her mind when she'd waylaid me in my office.

"You're very clever with your English," she admitted.

"That's what an Ivy League education gets you." This. *This* was the reason I'd needed to go to Owen. Not because the Ivy League was inherently better than other schools.

It was because people believed *I* was better for having gone. If I hadn't, I have no idea how I would have deflected these kinds of barbs. This wasn't the first. Probably wouldn't be the last.

"I...I went to graduate school at Owen."

"Now that you've listed your qualifications and resume, is this conversation done?" I scooted my feet back and half lifted my ass from the chair like I was on my way out the door.

"You don't belong with Jake."

"And you do?"

"Of course! That's what I've been saying. Maybe your English *isn't* that good. I just want you to agree that when this show is over, you'll not see Jake. That would be the best, wouldn't you agree?"

This girl was like a dog with a bone. I was going to have to yank it from her mouth.

"Liling."

"Call me Lily."

"Lily, then. Let me say this. I've had some time to think. Two weeks. A year. Twenty years. In all that time, I've tried to forget Jake. I've been sad, angry, happy. All of the emotions. You want to know what I am now?"

"What?" Liling asked. I could tell she was finally starting to rethink her ambush. Not because she'd rethought her position, but because she couldn't put a finger on the thing that would control me.

"Resigned."

"Resigned? What does that mean?"

"It means," I started, patting myself on the back for not inserting a bad-at-English comment directed at her. "It means that whatever Jake and I have is not going away. No amount of trying to forget, pushing it away, running away, or being prohibited from seeing each other has made a difference. Not in the last year. Not in the last twenty. I'm tired of fighting what we have. So you know what?" My shrug was intentionally dramatic. "I'm not going to anymore. I'm going to do everything in my power to continue loving Jake and figuring out if we really are destined to be together. To find out if we have a future."

"Uh..." I could see in her eyes that this was one hundred eighty degrees from her expectations. That her brain was prompting her to bail, but that her heart wanted to stay to hear what was coming next because she couldn't leave without some kind of finality. Some kind of closure.

"I know, Lily. I get it. I know what it is to have loved Jake for most of my life. To have idolized him as a kid, have him be my first love. To want this man in my life as an adult. This is something that we have in common. We're the only two people in this world who've had this big, great, nearly lifelong love for Jake."

"But—"

I cut her off before she pointed out the obvious—that we couldn't both be with him.

"There have been buts for years. There aren't any more. I'm all done making excuses. I don't have too many regrets in life. I can tell from your face that you're surprised to hear that. But it's true. For the most part, I've done what I think is right. Last year, for the first time, I went against my heart. I followed my brain and it wasn't the right thing. But Jake has given me a second chance, or maybe it's a fifth chance. Either way, it's probably a *last* chance, and I'm going to reach out and grab it with both arms."

"Are you serious?"

Lily and I both turned swiftly toward the door. We rarely closed them here, and Lily hadn't pushed it shut behind herself before she'd confronted me.

"How much of that did you hear?" I asked Jake. I didn't know what else to say. My little confessional had gone much further than I'd anticipated. Once I'd opened my mouth, I hadn't really been able to stop. All of the emotions I'd bottled up over time had spilled out like Henry's juice had on too many mornings when he tried to pour it himself.

"Enough." His voice was rough with emotion.

I wanted to stand up. Walk over and take him into my arms. A sense of workplace decorum and Lily's dagger stare kept me in my place.

The person who stood up and closed the distance between her and Jake wasn't me, but Liling.

"Wu Jian." She grabbed his lapels. Shook him the tiniest bit. "You can't be serious! You and Isabella? There isn't any way to make that work. You *know* that. Mrs. Li...Mr. Wu. They could disown you! Then how would you live?"

Gently, he removed her hands from his suit collar. He strode in and retrieved her papers and bag from my office floor. Joined her again near my door.

"Liling?"

"Yes?" She looked up at him then. Tears were shining in her eyes. I had to blink and look away because it was all so familiar. Like some kind of weird mirrored déjà vu where she was living my experience, only in another time and location.

"We need to talk. And not here in Bella's office. Let's take a walk."

"It's hot outside," she protested. Stood stock still. As if not moving could somehow stave off the inevitable.

"Then we'll take the network car."

Some quality in his voice broke her. Made her move again. She snatched her bag from him, threw open the flap, grabbed the papers and jammed them in without a care as to their condition.

"Fine, Wu Jian. Fine!" she snapped. "You can explain to me what's going on in your mind. Because nothing I'm hearing makes any sense. None at all. Not one English word."

"DID you really hear everything she said back there? That girl? That *Isabella*. Your housekeeper's daughter?"

Liling and I were in the car. I'd asked the driver to take us on a very scenic route—like hour-long scenic—back to CBT. We needed to talk, and neither Julie House nor CBT were appropriate venues for the kind of conversation I thought we were about to have. The Four Seasons hotel room was the last place I wanted to have a talk as well. Mixed messages could come from that place.

As we rounded the Brooklyn Botanic Garden, which had to be in the opposite direction of the city, I made a mental note to give this driver a large cash tip to help him remember that the most important part of his job was discretion.

"I heard enough," I answered.

I swallowed. Tried to school my expression so that it was only shades of neutral. I had heard enough from Bella to make me feel like I was floating.

For the first time in years, the stirrings of hope filled my chest. Made my heart speed up with anticipation for a future that seemed infinitely brighter than it had only hours earlier. I wanted nothing more than to be running around New York city like some Asian romcom hero buying flowers and spinning around light poles.

But before I could get to the good part—the hands-on figuring out how we could really be together—I had to get through the hard part. The hands-on crushing of Liling's dreams.

There'd been so many hard parts, but as a person who was working to be compassionate, who was trying to be considerate, I couldn't skip this conversation, no matter how much I'd have liked to avoid it. My father would have walked out on Liling without so much as a backward glance, leaving her to pick up the pieces of her heart. I'd seen that firsthand and knew I needed to develop my own way of handling things, starting with this very hard conversation.

"So is what she said true?" Liling asked. She turned away from the garden, bursting with bright and cheery summer colors, and looked at me full on, her own face devoid of it. I tried not to shrink from her stare of condemnation. I hadn't done anything wrong.

Loving Isabella would *never* be wrong.

"Which part?" That was a delay on my part. But I needed a moment to get my bearings, figure out the best way to put the truth to her.

"That you and she have talked and have somehow decided that the two of you are going to...what? Go steady? Be boyfriend and girlfriend? God forbid, get married?"

Usually when someone said those combination of words,

their voice was filled with love, with hope, with wonder at a future where two people who'd been apart their whole lives, would now face a future together. Liling's voice held none of those. Probably bitterness more than anything else. Envy or jealousy—I could never figure out the difference—made Liling unattractive.

The truth was that I *wanted* to marry Bella, though I wasn't entirely sure it was for the right reasons. I wanted her to be legally bound to me. For us to be so tied together that we couldn't run away when we got to the hard parts. Because for all the hard parts we'd already had, I knew that the future held more. Nobody rode off into the sunset and lived happily ever after outside of Grisham novels and Hollywood movies. I looked at her, spoke in Mandarin so my meaning was crystal clear.

"That is for me and Bella to discuss." There was no way I was going to talk about my plans, hopes or dreams with Liling. For one, it would be cruel. Also, I was learning my own lessons on discretion. I wanted to keep what was growing between Bella and me just between us until it was strong enough to withstand daylight and the scrutiny of others.

"So that's it," Liling huffed in English. There was a stutter in her sigh, as if she were forcing tears back down her throat. "After thirty years. That's it. You made a choice. It's not me."

Liling's lip was trembling just enough for me to know that she was truly devastated, that she couldn't keep all of her emotions in check. All the breaking up and the official end of our engagement hadn't been the end in her mind. I could see that now as clearly as one could see a school of fish while snorkeling off the coast of the Caribbean.

"Lily. We officially broke off the engagement four years ago," I said, stacking my evidence like a lawyer ready to mount a case. "You didn't speak to me for a solid eighteen months. Then you turn up in Los Angeles, acting like all is forgiven."

"Why did you *think* I was here?" She asked the one question I'd been avoiding for months.

"The truth is, I didn't have the guts to ask. I half thought that Min Li had asked you to come here and check up on me. But I didn't want to encourage that." Min Li and I had reached a kind of truce. We smiled when we were together, but stayed well out of each other's lives. I could count on one hand the number of times I'd seen her in the last decade. After a couple of false starts, Father had well and truly left our relationship alone.

"That is partially true. I'm not going to lie." Liling opened her hands in a pleading motion. "She's worried about you, Jake. On the one hand, she's happy that you aren't running around drinking champagne out of models' navels. On the other, she worries because you've been so fixated on work that you haven't really looked for a wife."

Min Li and I would probably have agreed that doing shots off women wasn't going to lead to any kind of successful marriage. But neither was spending more time with Liling.

"Hadn't you and she tried to do that for me? Find me a wife?"

"I...uh..." Liling looked away. Commenting on her and Min Li's scheming was bordering on rude, but I was done coddling them. Trying to consider their feelings had practically led me down the aisle. "She didn't want you to keep moping after Isabel."

"She knew?" After I said it, I realized how stupid I sounded. My teenage self thought I was keeping secrets. My adult self quickly realized that my hormones had fogged my brain from seeing the reality that any adult out of adolescence could have seen. "Anyway, it's Isabella," I said, then felt stupid for feeling the need to correct her.

"Everyone within a three-square-kilometer radius of you knows, Jake. She's...*Isabella*...is like...what's that American phrase...a bad penny that keeps turning up. Your mother blames herself, you know. She regrets letting your father isolate you out there in the middle of New Jersey. If you'd been in New York or even Shanghai, you'd have had the proper exposure to all the people in our social circle. I wouldn't have been the only appropriate woman you would have dated."

That last had me reeling. I sat back hard against the leather of the limo's seats.

"*That's* what she thinks the biggest mistake of my childhood was? Not being in the right club or escorting the right girls to the right debutante balls or whatever? That's rich."

"What are you talking about?" Liling's face was innocently unaware.

My parents had snowed her.

Money did that even with others who had it. People wanted to believe that money made you good or righteous, when all it did was make you rich, and probably unaccountable, too.

"The reason I never wanted to date or get married was because of them," I explained out loud for the first time. I paused, waiting for God to strike me down with lightning, but outside, there was nothing but blue skies. "They had...*have* one hell of an unhappy marriage."

"I don't think that's right," Liling said. She looked up, and I could tell she was shuffling through the Rolodex of memories of times she'd spent with my parents. She shook her head because her own experiences were not matching up with what I was saying. It was incongruent in her mind and therefore easily discarded. "They look great together at fundraisers. Her hand on his arm. His hand on the small of her back. They smile at each other." I could see her reaching further into the recesses of her brain for evidence confirming what she believed to be true. "They redid that house together. Did you see the picture of them in *Architectural Digest?*"

I'd seen that picture. No less than ten friends had sent it my way via e-mail because they were as impressed as Min Li had wanted them to be. Father is leaning against the kitchen counter. Min Li is leaning against him from a snow-white upholstered stool impractical in any universe where people actually eat.

"Really? You think those things make a marriage happy?" I asked, wondering for the first time if the depth I'd ascribed to Liling was all in my head. "Galas and magazine-worthy interior design?"

"It's not what anyone imagines comes after the end of some fairytale princess movie, probably, but it works." Now Liling was laying out her own evidence. I had to wonder who she was trying to convince, me or herself. "She provided the capital and he multiplied that times a thousand," she continued. "Mrs. Li gets to travel the world and spend time with her friends. He gets to do the work he loves. Together, though, they've built this amazing empire. Their only son has double Ivy League degrees and has even expanded the business some more. But Mr. Wu can't work forever. What, maybe ten more years? Then they're going to want to enjoy grandchildren. Maybe move back to China permanently. Who knows? But you need to be thinking about a succession plan."

She made it sound like a dynasty and not just a group of publicly held companies that anyone could run.

"Your succession plan—for me—is to do exactly what they did." I didn't want to step into those same ill-fitting shoes, and even if I did, I didn't want to drag her along with me. That would be bad for us both. Another generation tolerating each other, living vicariously through their children, shopping or having inappropriate sexual relationships to bury discontented feelings. It sounded downright awful. "Don't you want to be better, or at least be different?"

"The difference is that we love each other." My carefully neutral mask must have slipped because Liling course corrected in a single sentence. "That we could love each other differently than they have. It wouldn't have to be so cold and clinical. Maybe we wouldn't have to work so hard. We could probably enjoy the whole thing more. It's a lot of work, but we could have fun, too."

I hadn't ever thought she'd spun out this level of fantasy in her head. I mean, I knew she'd probably imagined our wedding. Some of it she'd talked about—the two wedding dresses, one red silk, the other white. Chinese and American traditions coming together in harmony, is how I think she'd put it. But what came after had been as dense as fog for me. I hadn't asked her about her vision of the future. Probably because I knew, even back then, even in my subconscious, that there wasn't going to be one.

I leaned forward a little, feeling the need to disabuse her of the notion that everything was perfect in Toms River.

"Did you ever ask Min Li why she and my father aren't close?"

"You know I could never ask that. Your mom and I are close, but we don't talk about those kinds of things."

The way she was examining her nails, I knew Min Li had snowed her ten ways to Sunday. She thought what she was seeing was the same as her parents. Love that had matured, didn't need to display itself every moment of every day. I'd seen her parents when no one was looking, though. They were affectionate with each other in the same way that her dad had been with Liling when we were kids. Lots of hugs and kisses. Nothing like the stoicism he displayed in the boardroom or C-suite.

I was done keeping my father's secrets. He could take over that job for himself. He'd been handling much of it for years. He was the expert. I needed to leave Father to his field of expertise.

"What happened at CBT. Those weren't isolated incidents. I'm not sure Father has been faithful even a single year during his marriage."

"But you're nothing like Mr. Wu." Liling acted as if Father and I weren't two sides of the same person. I lowered my own head, looking at my onyx cufflinks. Maybe in many ways we were. I tried not to take on that feeling of shame that shimmied through me as I considered our collective behavior toward women through a clear-eyed lens.

"Aren't I? The way I've treated you. The way I've treated Isabella. The moves are exactly from my father's playbook. He's always done what he wants. What makes him feel good. What serves his purposes. And when people get hurt, he doesn't apologize. He doesn't have remorse. He just plows on as if we should all be grateful for his largesse."

"He's a different generation, Jake."

I wanted to be a fairy, wave a wand and give Liling a backbone. I hope whomever her parents married her off to was nice, even if he was rich.

"That may be true. But there's no reason I need to move ahead and repeat the mistakes of the past. I want to break the mold. Create a different future."

"What if he disowns you?" she asked, as if I was only a single step from pitching a tent on Skid Row.

"Which is it? He needs me to carry on his legacy or he's going to toss me to the curb? I'm not sixteen anymore. He can't banish me to Shanghai or Woodward Tillman. I can do what I want."

"Damn the consequences?"

"The consequences will effect no one but me and Bella."

"And me, Jake. And me..."

I looked down at the bag at her feet. The CBT-logo-headed papers were spilling out. Then I took a look out the window. I don't know what part of the city or even which borough we were in now, but there was what looked like swampland out the window.

"I'm sorry. You're right. Kind of." I had no idea what my father would do to me or Liling when he found out about me and Bella. If I had anything to do with it, my father would be the recipient of that knowledge sooner rather than later. I was done hiding. But I didn't want to plow through Liling's life like my father did everyone else's, indifferent to the collateral damage.

"Do you want to quit now? Do you want to go back to Red Dragon before the shit hits the fan? Before my father figures out a way to have you fired from CBT?" I asked, considering her alternatives if she wanted to continue working in entertainment in the States. I didn't know about any other business, but I was a thousand percent sure her father would take her back, make sure she had a soft place to land.

"So that's it? We're just driving around endlessly so you can do career counseling? I can stay on as head of scheduling or I can go back to Red Dragon. Or take some unknown third choice while I watch you commit career and social suicide."

"Those aren't the only choices, Liling. Your options are probably infinite. I was just trying to solve a potential problem and save face at the same time."

"I don't want you to fucking solve my problems, Wu Jian!" she yelled. The driver hit the brakes unexpectedly, jolting us. Then he lay on the gas, no doubt sensing that we needed to be at our destination sooner rather than later. "I want you to love me!" she wailed. "Is that too much to ask?"

"Yes."

A single sob filled the car's cabin. This was the very hard part, but I continued on anyway.

"I'm very sorry, but the answer to that question is yes."

When the crying started in earnest, the driver went even heavier on the gas. I wanted to kiss him as the Battery Tunnel came into view.

"So that's it, then? After all these years. This is it." The way she asked, I knew it would be my last chance. It was one I was willing to forgo.

"Liling. There's nothing I can say that's going to make this better. I wish only the best for you. I want you to tell the stories that you want, make the art that's inside you. Find the love that you deserve." I reached across the narrow strip of leather separating us and laid my hand over hers, which was damp with the tears she'd swiped away as we'd zoomed up the West Side Highway.

"Please. Please don't touch me. I don't think I can be around you right now. I don't think we can be friends anymore. Maybe later. Maybe another time. Just not now, okay? I'm going to fly back to Los Angeles tomorrow. I'm sure the producers can handle this...this show. Or you can keep an eye on it, since you're staying put. I wanted to get my hands dirty in marketing anyway. Oh, look. We're here."

Her hand was on the door handle even though the car was still moving. Even though the driver hadn't come around and opened it for her. I couldn't remember a single time I'd seen her open her own door.

"Let me run upstairs. Gotta get some paperwork done before it's too late on the West Coast. Alrighty then. Thanks for the ride." She pushed open the door the minute the car stopped. "Good luck to you."

With barely a wave, she disappeared through the smoked glass revolving door.

I'd done the hard thing. I hoped that would be enough to break my father's mold, or at least put a crack in it. I directed the perplexed driver to make a U-turn back to Brooklyn. It was time to do the easier thing—pursue Bella.

I STOOD ON THE TARMAC, my hands shading my eyes over my dark polarized sunglasses. I couldn't see the water from here, but I could feel that late-August breeze coming off the ocean. It was anything but warm.

"You've never been to Nantucket?" Jake asked after he was done talking to the charter jet pilot. For some reason it had seemed important to him that we take our first weekend away to someplace neither of us had been. It was probably part of what I was coming to think of as his "fresh start" policy.

He was insistent that things be different this time. That we deliberately make thoughtful choices about us and our future. Those last two words made me shiver where the breeze had not. I poked my hand into my huge plaid tote and pulled a similarly plaid scarf from its depths and arranged it around my neck and shoulders. I peered at Jake through my lenses.

"Martha's Vineyard a few times. Here, never." I didn't

mention that only one of those time I'd been on the Cape, I hadn't been with Daniel. I'd been with Claire. One of us, I can't remember which, had been scouting for a future trip with our sugar daddy. Henri often cited the Boy Scout motto when coaching us.

My relationship with Daniel was an awkward topic that we kept off limits by silent agreement. Even when *The Girlfriend Experience* brought back all sorts of memories I'd tried to forget. If Jake's eyes squinted or forehead lifted in a way that made me think he was going to ask something, I quickly deflected. Changed the subject or brought up a new one. This time, I'd put on the scarf and refused to elaborate.

Like every previous time, he took the hint. He pulled his own sunglasses from his head and fitted them against his nose.

"Here's our car now," Jake pointed toward the large blue-gray SUV headed our way. The driver stopped by the belly of the plane, hefted our luggage from the padded cart into the back of the car. With the liftgate secured, the driver then drove the few feet toward us. I let myself be helped into the backseat captain's chair. Jake took himself around to the other.

Once belted in and the nearly silent engine started, the driver turned to look at us. "Siasconset is only fifteen minutes. I'll have you folks there in a jiffy."

"Thanks," I said offhandedly. I was usually more friendly with hired help because I knew what it was like to *be* the hired help and to be ignored, but I didn't have it in me today. The idea of a weekend with Jake without the distractions of work or the city scared me.

Instead of looking at Jake or the driver, I craned my neck toward the tinted windows. I don't know if it was the tint or if every house was covered in faded gray wood siding. One after another, gray siding, white shutters, gravel walkways, and American flags passed us by. Maybe it was some kind of preservation scheme.

Make New England gray again.

"How long have you folks been together?" the driver asked, his Massachusetts accent seeping into his words. His brown eyes connected with mine in the rearview mirror. I wondered if he could see right through me. Knew that I was more like him than like Jake. Knew that I really didn't belong in the backseat, but should be up front with him.

His eyes and that simple question paralyzed me. Our story was so muddled it didn't even have a proper beginning.

"T-two-two months," I stuttered, out at the exact same time "coming up on twenty years" came from Jake.

"I'll let you guys work on getting your story straight," the driver said on a hearty laugh.

My eyes ping-ponged from the driver's—now a squint—to Jake. His smile was rueful. He slipped his hand across the empty space between us and grabbed mine. After a shock of awareness ran up my arm, my heart calmed and my anxiety went back to zero from where it had been hovering by one hundred for the last few hours. His touch could thrill or calm me in equal measure.

The drive was as short as promised, and in a moment, we were at our own gray-shingled house with its steeply pitched roof sections joined at odd angles and bank of white-paned windows. The driver scurried to get our few bags into the house, then with a jaunty wave, he drove off and we were, for the first time in weeks, alone.

When he pushed the front door closed, Jake glanced at his watch.

"I hope you're hungry," he said.

Even though the big flutter of nerves had abated, my stomach was still a bit tied up in knots. I had zero idea if I'd be able to put any food down there. But the idea of being in this big house with its bigger beds and just Jake and I was more nerve-wracking than trying to stuff down some kind of seafood or boiled potatoes.

"You have a reservation?" I asked. When Jake had suggested a weekend on the Cape, I'd said yes, and left the planning to him. I wasn't his employee, and I appreciated not having to make sure everything was perfect. Daniel would never have admitted it, pretending to be a devil-may-care European, but his needs and demands were exacting. I, along with his other staff, made sure they were all met and there were no mistakes. I couldn't think of a time that I'd ever been pampered. If pampered meant someone else making accommodations and restaurant reservations.

"At the Summer House in an hour and fifteen," Jake answered.

"Then I should probably change out of jeans," I said after looking down at myself. The casual me was more comfortable. But I wanted to dress up for Jake. Make an effort. Be the beautiful woman that he saw in me.

"The driver will be back in an hour."

Relieved that there would be no time for sex, I let out a

breath I hadn't been aware I'd been holding. "Let's see the upstairs, then."

Jake lifted my bags and I followed him to what was clearly the master bedroom. A huge king-size four-poster dominated the room. Its rich, dark mahogany stood in deep contrast to the cloud of luxurious white bedding and light gray walls.

"It's lovely," I said, more for something to say than any thoughts about the house itself. In July, I'd had no problems having sex with Jake. Last year had been even easier. But now that my feelings and hopes and dreams about the future were getting all twisted up with desire, I was so nervous I could barely swallow.

I'd done sex without love.

I'd *mastered* sex without love.

I was co-running a nonprofit full of women who had that particular skill. I had no idea how people were vulnerable enough to mix sex and love. I didn't know anyone who'd done it. Which was half the problem right there. And in these weeks since Jake and I had started down a more serious road, I hadn't found a Google search result that had given me the answer.

Jake's voice interrupted my thoughts. I had no idea how long I'd been silent.

"Why don't you get changed in here? I'll use one of the other bathrooms so we're not stepping all over each other."

Grateful for the momentary reprieve, I closed the door behind him, then launched myself onto the bed, shoes and all.

What had I been thinking? Jake and I couldn't do this.

How did we go from best friends, to awkward near-strangers? How did we now transition into something normal?

Something real?

Something true?

I lay in the pristine all-white bed that I'd be sharing with Jake later and tried to think of a single healthy, happy relationship that I'd ever witnessed. My mother and father came to mind first. I'd *thought* that was happy, but obviously I'd been very wrong, as we'd all learned when that broke up in spectacular fashion.

Mama and Mr. Wu obviously weren't that. Neither were Jake's parents—though whether that was Mama's fault or Mr. Wu's fault was a bit hazy. Claire hadn't had it. Jake hadn't had it. Daniel and I hadn't had it.

I wanted something different...deeper and more meaningful somehow, but had zero idea how to go about getting it. Or even how to figure out if I had it once I got there.

Instead of spending time journaling, meditating, or kneeling in gratitude, or whatever it was that touchy-feely California people did to get in touch with their feelings, I jumped into a stinging-hot shower, getting all the travel grime off.

Then I did what any self-respecting Jersey girl did —armored up.

I slipped on an Alice + Olivia sheer silk dress. It's creamy white background stood in full contrast to the midnight blue and burnt sienna velvet flowers woven into the fabric. The tie at the front, which I looped casually around my neck, and long bell sleeves kept the dress modest. Though the mid-thigh hem hinted at sexy. The contrast was deliberate. I knew from experience, wearing this kind of dress for Daniel, it pulled a man right in.

I smoothed my hair back into a bun. My makeup was a sheer matte except for a slash of dark red lipstick. I knew it was cool, unapproachable Isabella on display, but I didn't know how to be anyone else right now. I was afraid to show the vulnerable girl who worked with former escorts. It had been hard being myself and vulnerable for the last year, and I needed a break from being her.

When I came down fifty-five minutes later, I could see the Escalade idling outside. Without any fanfare, Jake and I got back into the SUV.

"You'll like Summer House," our driver, Cliff, said on the way over. Fully suited up, this time I'd introduced myself, gotten his name, and made nice when he'd opened the back passenger door for me at the house. "It's got some great traditional seafood, which is fine, hearty, but it's the view that's the real reason for eating there. It's amazing."

Cliff was right about the view. He dropped us off and I let Jake's hand rest on my back as he guided me up to the restaurant's door. We were quickly seated outside on a porch, our table and chairs facing ocean.

Thousands of generations of humans have flocked to the water and up until now, that basic human desire had been a mystery. I've been on so many crowded beaches in my lifetime, seeking that communion with water. This by far, though, was the most soothing. It was nearly empty. The waves made for a quiet cacophony of sound as the sun set behind us. This was better than the Jersey Shore or Ibiza any day. I wish my insides felt like the outside looked.

Small talk was the best I could do while we made our way through a shared appetizer of raw oysters. When my sword fish and Jake's halibut came, he took a single bite before lowering his fork.

"I wanted to come here this weekend so we could talk about the future. What that looks like."

I cocked my head to one side. "The future?"

"There's no reason for me to be in New York any longer. I've pushed that as far as I could. Now, I need to get back to Los Angeles and really dig deep at this job if I want to succeed."

A little bubble of panic welled up inside, piling on top of the discomfort I already felt. He had to leave. He was telling me that he wasn't going to be in New York or on the coast much longer. Not only did we have a fractured past and uncertain future between us, now Jake was saying he was going to add distance.

I knew enough about relationships to know that I had to ask for what I needed. No one had told me what to do if I didn't know what that was. So I did what I *did* know how to do—deflect.

"Do you like television?" I asked, as if it were the most interesting fact I wanted to know about him.

He didn't address my avoidance in any way other than a slight nod that let me know that we were going to get back to the "us" part of the conversation, but he'd humor me for now.

"If you'd asked me ten years ago, it's not what I'd have predicted for my future. It's more satisfying than appliances or cars, though. What made you stay with it after the Page Program?"

I was plumbing my brain for the truth when I was inter-rupted, but not by Jake.

"Now there's a question I could answer," a deeply accented voice said from behind me.

I closed my eyes like a kid did after having a bad dream, as if not seeing would make the scariness go away. It didn't work. Of all the people in the world, *his* voice was the last I'd expected to hear.

I laid my own fork down. On automatic pilot, I did what I always did when I heard that voice, stood and turned, tugging my hem and straightening my posture.

It was no surprise to see that Daniel was behind me. He'd been following the hostess, but had stopped at our table. The woman with him could have passed for my sister, if that sibling were a decade and a half younger.

"Daniel, it's so nice to see you." Standing on my tip toes and kissing him on both cheeks was so automatic, I didn't think of the propriety until I landed on the stacked heels of my sandals. I didn't dare glance in Jake's direction.

"It's been too long, Bella." He'd grabbed my upper left arm with his right hand when we'd kissed. He hadn't let go.

I pivoted the best I could in his grip and used my free right hand to gesture toward my actual date for the night.

"You remember Jake Wu? We grew up together in New Jersey?" I silently cursed myself for my tone, but I couldn't help the obsequious uptalking voice that had come out of my mouth.

"Yes, of course. I hear that your family is in television now. Quite the diversification you've got going on there." Daniel finally released his grip on me, only to extend his hand toward Jake, who had to stand to complete the polite exchange. Now all four of us were standing on the porch while the hostess shifted uncomfortably on her patent-leather Mary Janes. Eventually, Daniel's date signaled and she and the hostess disappeared around the corner.

"I seconded at Red Dragon in China and fell in love with the medium," Jake said.

I wondered if I'd known that about him, that he'd worked at a Chinese network? I'd self-centeredly assumed his investment in CBT had been all about me.

"That's one reason," Daniel responded cryptically. His voice grew light as he dropped another kiss on my cheek. "Well, Bella, it was lovely seeing you tonight. I always did love that dress. The contrast of velvet and silk is lovely under the hands." Daniel let that sit there for one beat, two, before continuing, "I shouldn't leave Giulia alone for too long. Pretty Italian girls have a way of drawing other men's attention. Have a wonderful evening."

To Jake, he said. "I do hope you're finally worthy of her."

Then he was gone. He hadn't changed in the year and a half, except to get a tiny bit older. He was still dapper, his clothes still impeccable without looking too formal. For one piercing second, I missed him down to the bottom of my heart. Our relationship hadn't exactly been fulfilling. But it was a lot of other things. Loving. Predictable. Uncomplicated.

"Of all the islands..." My voice trailed off as I sat back in my seat, placing the linen napkin carefully on my lap. What little appetite I'd had was long gone. I took a bite, but the fish had gone cold.

"Is it okay if we go?" Jake asked. "I don't seem to have much appetite."

When I nodded, he flagged down our waitress.

"We'll take this to go."

"Are you leaving so soon?" she asked. I could see her calculating the tips that wouldn't materialize if we didn't drink more and linger over dessert. "The pianist is about to get started. She plays from dusk on. Most of our guests love to have port or sherry or one of our unique liqueurs while she plays."

I wanted to tell her that it all sounded divine for any couple other than us, the broken one, the one that "normal" dating might not fix. I hoped that Daniel and Giulia were one of the server's other tables. Daniel had always been a generous tipper.

"Thanks. Maybe another evening," Jake said briskly.

Taking the hint, the waitress whisked the plates from the tables.

I nodded and stood, my usually steady legs a bit wobbly.

"I'll meet you outside," I said, and placed my napkin on the table. I detoured to the ladies' room and took a seat on one of the couches in the lounge outside the bathroom. I looked at the straps crisscrossing my instep and tried to work out the chances of running into Daniel.

Purportedly the world had seven and a half billion people. Daniel was European. He lived on an entirely different continent—most of the time. Nantucket was a smallish island off the coast of Massachusetts. The population during the summer maxed out at fifty thousand. How in the world could the two of us end up in the same place?

For something to do more than need, I got up, used the bathroom, then washed my hands. I fished in my tiny purse and reapplied my lipstick.

I met Jake, paper shopping bag in his hand, in the forecourt.

"Is he stalking you?" was his first question the moment my feet crunched the gravel at the bottom of the short staircase.

"No, Jake. No. I'm sure it's really an unfortunate coincidence." I wasn't one hundred percent convinced of my own answer, but there was no reason to speculate further. The damage to the evening was already done.

"My father says there are no coincidences."

"That's maybe because he hires his lovers to work for him." I could hear the bitterness in my own voice, but I couldn't help myself. "I'm sure Mr. Wu's world is carefully controlled and curated."

Cliff turned up at that moment, his raised eyebrows the only acknowledgement that he was surprised to see us so soon. The SUV was as silent as a tomb all the way back to the gray-shingled house. I took the food and set it on one corner of the vast black granite kitchen counter, while Jake took care of things with Cliff. He found me sitting on one of the counter stools, looking through the kitchen window toward the large and unruly garden. He took a seat next to me, but facing toward me instead of outside.

"Did you ever love Daniel?"

His question forced me to turn, look into his searching brown eyes to try and figure out what my answer should be. I wanted to run away to the beach or anywhere I could go where I wouldn't have to answer the hard questions. But we'd promised not to do that anymore.

Run away.

Avoid what was difficult.

So I told the truth.

"Yes," I exhaled on a deep sigh.

"Wow. I didn't expect that."

I could see I'd missed the cue. He'd wanted reassurance, not facts. He probably should have asked a different question. Or I should have said something about loving him first. I laid my elbows on the cool counter, giving some thought as to how I could best explain Daniel.

"He was in my life for more than a decade. I'm not sure our relationship was ever one of equals, or ever could have been. But I'll always be grateful for what he taught me. The lessons were invaluable."

"Taught you?"

"So much about navigating life as an adult. He was sometimes more of a father figure, though that sounds a bit creepy now that I say it. Look...Mama didn't help me much past high school. Nor did Mr. Wu, though he did teach me to drive. But there was no one who helped me figure out how to find a place to live, balance a checkbook, make a budget, or even get a job. Owen's college counseling only went so far, and I needed to know so much more to be an adult. Daniel was patient with me. Taught me so much of what made me successful."

"It's not like he didn't have an agenda."

"Of course he had an agenda. Fortunately, it was clear

and up front. I think of it as kind of a paid internship in some ways."

Jake snorted his disbelief.

I laid one hand on Jake's knee. "Look, Jake, he's not a threat to you and me. What we're trying to do here. But I can't just erase him from my past."

"Does he still call?"

"No." I stood and got my purse from the edge of the counter. I took out the only phone I had in there. I held it up. "No Blackberry. He only used those because of their security. I broke it off from him once and for all...before that time we were together in Los Angeles. Other than a couple of holiday cards, and birthday cards, it's been radio silence."

Then *we* were silent.

"Why are you so far away?" Jake asked.

I hadn't moved from the end of the counter, a good five or six feet from where he was. His question caused a fine wave of tremors to shoot through me. I did a tiny one-foot pace that ended in a nonsensical spin. I forced myself to stop moving.

"Because I don't know how to be around you. I don't know how we do this thing."

"What thing, Bella? Us? You don't know how to do us?"

It was so very weird. But I didn't want to say that. Here I was, standing a few feet from a man I'd loved for what felt like nearly my entire life.

I'd wanted him more times than I could count.

I'd craved him on so many lonely nights.

I'd ached for him when he'd rejected me.

"To be honest? Not really. I can't decide who I need to be around you. The glamorous woman I was with Daniel? The pencil-skirted executive I was at CBT? The casual-dressing woman I am now at Julie House?"

"I want all of those or none of those. Above all, I want you to be yourself. You can be anything or nothing with me. I just want to be with you."

"How do you know who 'me' is, Jake, well enough to love me? If I don't know who that is?"

He came over to me. For every step he took to close the gap, I took a step back. The awkward dance stopped when my back hit the white wood panel covering the fridge door.

Jake's hand fitted against my jaw. My stomach roiled and I was transported back to being that girl on the New Jersey Transit bus, hoping against hope that Jake would kiss me.

His eyes fluttered closed, and his mouth descended toward mine.

That first touch of his lips was so electric that I gasped and tried to jump back, but was stopped dead cold by the appliance.

"You're as jumpy as a cat." He took my hand and tugged me toward a living room or family room. He gently pushed me down on the blue and brown jewel-toned cushions. He shed his blazer on the arm, took a seat next to me, and undid another button of his crisp shirt, revealing the tan skin of his throat and the top of his chest.

"I don't know if I want to have sex with you tonight," I blurted out.

Jake's blink was slow. "Okay."

"It's not that I don't want to. I just—"

"Shh. I didn't come here with a list of expectations. I wanted to spend time with you out of New York, out of L.A.

Okay, I lied. I did have a single expectation. Like I was going to say before dinner went sideways, I think we need to talk about how we're going to tackle the future. Not too sexy, but practical."

"Like how to handle distance?"

"Like whether or not we *want* distance. Whether one of us relocates."

"I've only been at Julie House for a year. I'm not sure—"

"This is just talk. I'm not dictating what happens next."

Jake leaned forward, kissed me again.

This time, I didn't pull away. I leaned into the pleasure of it. His lips against mine. His tongue exploring mine. His hand sliding down the silk and resting against my breast. This time, my gasp was one of pleasure and not fear. Then he sat back. His eyes were a little fogged, as I imagine mine were.

"I love you, Isabella. I've loved you as long as I can remember knowing what love is. I can't imagine my life without you in it. Geography is just a small problem to solve."

I couldn't say those words back. Not in the romantic, forever way. I wasn't ready to make the commitment. Once I said it this time, there would be no going back.

I was still on the "one day at a time" diet. So I deflected, again. I hoped that one day I'd have more tools in my personal arsenal. Until then, I would do what I could. He'd have to love me enough for the both of us right now.

"Geography?"

"Would you be willing to come back to Los Angeles? Not today. Maybe not for months, but is it in the cards at all?"

I tried to think. I took Jake's hand in mine and held it

against my thigh. I wasn't ready for the big words like he'd just done. But suddenly I didn't want to be without his touch.

"I don't know much about life in Los Angeles," I admitted.

His brows knit together in disbelief.

"I lived there for five and a half years. But I lived to work. I walked to work and back. Drove from one studio to another, to hair and nail appointments. Drove to go shopping. Maybe went to a few parties with college friends or work friends, but that was it. I never went to the beach in the afternoon to watch the sunset or the mountains in the morning to catch the sunrise. I've never driven up the coast. I'm not sure what it means to really inhabit that city. New York is the same, I guess. I've been to all the popular shows. All the hip restaurants. This time around, I mostly stayed in my apartment and worked or was at Julie House."

"It sounds like you never worked to live."

He was right about that. Sounded like something the well-off could do...or Europeans. Put in some hours at work, then get off and live their real lives.

"Have you?" I realized then that I had zero idea what he'd done in all the years we'd been apart. I'd always imagined he was a workaholic like his father.

"Not exactly," he hedged, not answering the question. I wasn't the only one who could deflect. "You know what? I'm not sure we're coming at this problem the right way. Let's sleep on it."

"Together?" My belly was doing flip-flops again.

Jake nodded. "I want to sleep with you. Wake up with you. The rest, we have the rest of our lives for."

I'd probably had more sex than most people on earth. I never thought I'd be here, now, as nervous as a virginal bride before her wedding. I was suddenly glad it was Jake, because I don't think I'd be anything less than mortified to share my fears with anyone else on Earth.

CHAPTER EIGHTEEN

JAKE

NOW

"BELLA, HONEY. WAKE UP."

Her face was scrubbed clean of makeup. Her hair was in some kind of messy ponytail. I wanted nothing more than to lie next to her for an entire morning. Kiss her awake. Maybe kiss her some more. Breakfast in bed, maybe. But none of that was going to happen. At least not today. Probably not tomorrow, either.

I rolled my neck. I needed to get on the road. I wondered if I'd be on the road alone, once she found out why I was waking her.

"Bella."

She blinked awake, her eyes clearing slowly. "What time is it?" she croaked out.

"I have to go to Toms River," I said without preamble. It was best to get out ahead of the bad news.

"What? Now? It's Saturday, right? I thought we were staying here for the weekend." She blinked again, trying to work out the confusion I'd introduced.

I sighed. "It's my father." Of course it was my father. It was always about my father.

"Mr. Wu?"

"Your mother called me," I said. I was still holding my cell in my hand in case it rang again with more bad news, or worse news. "My father is in the hospital."

"Is it an emergency? What's going on."

"The doctors think he's had a heart attack."

"Think?"

"I'm not sure if your mother's minimizing, or if there's testing to answer that question, or what's going on, to be honest."

For every question I'd put to Maria Aconi, the answers had gotten fuzzier. I could tell they didn't want me to come, but from what I could piece together, Min Li wasn't there. Someone needed to make the hard decisions, and I was the only next of kin in the tri-state area.

Bella sat up, drawing the covers up to her neck in the cool room. "Are you going?"

I didn't want to say it directly, but I didn't want to face New Jersey alone. Not anymore. "If we take the seven-forty ferry to Hyannis, we'll be at the hospital before visiting hours end."

"We?" she asked. She had not missed my deliberately chosen pronouns.

"I'd like it if you came with me. If we're together now, I want us to face these kinds of things together." These kinds of things being our parents' unconventional relationship. It had kept us apart for too long. It was time to face the issue head on.

"It's six?" Bella turned her head toward the giant bedside clock numbers. "Seven-forty?"

"We can make it if we pack now. It's only a few minutes to the ferry."

Decision made, she ducked her head. "Give me thirty minutes. Forty-five at the most."

At seven, Cliff was waiting at the door. He hoisted our bags in and we were back in the car for the fourth time in less than twenty-four hours.

"Leaving early?"

"Family emergency," I supplied.

Between Cliff picking us up and the ferry dropping us off in Hyannis port, there wasn't much talking. Isabella had stood quietly and watched the waters of the Sound during the whole ferry ride and while I'd completed paperwork at the rental car office.

We'd been on the road for half an hour before Bella spoke.

"Thanks for the double cappuccino." She'd been sipping quietly since we'd picked up coffee and doughnuts in Hyannis, once we'd gotten into the car.

"Might be a long day." I pinched the bridge of my nose, trying to relieve some of the stress.

"Do you think this is a good idea?"

"Taking the Bourne Bridge?"

"No, New Jersey. Us going there. Together."

"It was going to have to happen sometime."

"Was it?" I'd thought of one hundred ways we could skirt a New Jersey visit. Near death hadn't been among my scenarios.

I took my eyes off the road while we waited in bridge traffic. "I'm too old for secrets, Isabella."

I had no idea how our parents would react. I found that I no longer cared. What they'd been doing for years was wrong for many reasons, but they were adults. So were we. There was nothing wrong with what we were doing, and I didn't want or need their approval, but I wasn't interested in hiding, either.

Neither Bella nor I talked much during the drive along the interstate until we approached Olde Haven. Bella sat up in her seat suddenly.

"Thought you were asleep."

"Just thinking." Her eyes were fixed on the gritty industrial downtown, then the tree-lined highway that followed. "Wow. I haven't been this way in years."

"Did you like Owen?" I'd always thought it was curious that she'd chosen a top Ivy League school. I never remembered her being that interested in her studies when we'd lived together. There was so much I wanted to know about her. So much that I'd missed out on. I wanted nothing more than time to fill in the gaps.

"No one's ever asked me that."

"Well, did you?"

"There were some really good classes. The Science of Well-Being was the best one."

"The happiness class?" It was the major difference between my college and hers. Owen may have been one of the oldest schools in the country, graduating a few presidents. But it was the first Ivy League to have gotten rid of formal grades as well as introduce a bunch of interdisciplinary majors and touchy-feely classes.

"You heard about it?"

"Not from anyone who ever took it. What was it about?"

"Bottom line? Money doesn't make you happy, but can make you secure. Happiness is about savoring and joy and gratitude."

Of course, I knew that money didn't make anyone happy. Despite that people played the lottery and worked more hours and did almost anything they could to get more because it always *seemed* like more could make you happy. I'd been guilty of it myself. Maybe having more of my own hadn't made me happy, but it had helped me gain independence from my father. My father, though, was still playing the lottery of life.

"Money doesn't make you happy? Huh? Someone should tell my father." The acquisition of millions of dollars and billions of yuan is what drove him every day. He was at his most jovial when he was talking about mergers or acquisitions or container ships.

"I'm pretty sure Mr. Wu is wedded to his life philosophy."

"Do you think your mother makes him happy?"

"Seeing them is one thing. Not hiding our relationship is another. I think we need to stay away from the third rail of conversation."

"What's that?"

"Talking about *their* relationship. It's probably best to leave that to the three consenting adults who are most affected by it."

I had about a million questions about her mother and my father, but she was right. She wasn't the one I needed to process that with. My father was the one who needed to answer for his behavior, make amends or whatever. Not me. Not Bella.

Taking my right hand off the wheel, I grabbed her left in mine. Shook it.

"Deal. We're us. They're them. Let's not bring the past into the future."

Her grip was as firm as mine. "Deal."

CHAPTER NINETEEN
ISABELLA

NOW

DRIVING up to the hospital gave me a shiver of recognition. I thought I'd put all that stuff from Mama and Mr. Wu and their complicated past behind me. But maybe I hadn't. Or maybe it was just that very real fear I'd had of losing my mother that put me off hospitals, and this one in particular.

"We'll get out of here soon. No valet." Jake leaned through the driver's window, pulling a ticket from the machine. "You should have told me to turn off the air if you were cold." We wound through the nearly full lot while Jake scouted for an empty space.

"It's not the A/C. It's déjà vu," I admitted. I covered his hand with mine, stopping him from turning off the climate control.

Jake maneuvered toward a free parking space. Once we were out of the car, he didn't hesitate a moment before grabbing my hand, spinning me toward him so that we were practically nose to nose. His other hand pushed a hank of loose hair behind my ear.

"Sorry. I didn't put two and two together right away. It was that day you were supposed to take the SATs." Jake glanced at his watch. He did nothing to hide his frustration. "I shouldn't have dragged you here. There's no time to find a hotel or drop you at home right now."

I jiggled his hand with mine. "It was just...the last time I was here, I thought my mother was dying. The last time I was here, my future felt like it was way outside my control. Although now, the hospital seems about three times bigger. I thought things were always smaller than you remembered?"

The way the building had appeared to triple in size was the stuff of horror movies.

A smile snuck past Jake's knitted brow. "It *is* bigger, actually. There were two new wings added after that book about the cancer cluster won the Pulitzer. Father made a big donation to the building fund. I'm sure there's a brick or ten around here with his name etched."

For a second, I was pulled out of my own self-centeredness. My concerns felt petty in light of the cancer surge that had killed children right and left in this little corner of New Jersey.

"Gosh. Geez. I guess we're lucky, huh?" I said. Compared to rare cancers, our parents' betrayal felt minor in comparison.

"I don't think either of us was here long enough."

"Being banished wasn't the worst thing that could happen."

"Guess not." He shook my hand and arm, focusing my attention once again. "You ready?"

"Or not. Here we come."

After getting directions from a receptionist, we walked a long corridor. Then Jake and I rode an elevator to the cardiac care unit. A duty nurse informed us that Mr. Wu was in room 1672. Any bravado I'd worked up left me in an instant when we got close to the wide wooden door.

I shook off Jake's hand and turned my back. I looked up at Jake, silently pleading with my eyes. We'd talked about this in the car. About how there was no going backward now, only forward. How we were a united front from now on.

"We're not moving back in, Bella. It'll be fine." Jake's voice was far calmer than I felt inside.

What I didn't say was that I had zero idea who'd be there in the room by Mr. Wu's side. I hadn't had the guts to ask. Either it would be Min Li, who'd look down on me like I was one of those rats that had infested her barn way back when. Or it would be my mother, clinging to a man who wasn't hers. Who would never be hers. I'd waffled for six hours and still hadn't decided which was worse.

What I did know is that it didn't matter. Neither woman could determine my self-worth, not anymore.

I caught Jake's eye. Nodded. He took my hand again. This time, I didn't let go. He pushed the extra-wide door and we stepped in.

Mr. Wu was...alone. That was a third option I hadn't considered. He looked somehow diminished without his trademark suit and slippers. Without his ornately carved wooden desk before him, its gold fittings gleaming in the lights around his study, he was just an ordinary man. An ordinary man in a too-thin hospital gown, tubes coming from his arms to bags of mysterious liquid. Wires connected his heart to a pulsing monitor.

"Is he sleeping?" I whispered to Jake, who looked between us and shrugged.

"No, Isabella Aconi, I am anything but sleeping." Despite lying down, and being much grayer than I remembered, his heavily accented authoritative tone was the same as it had always been. "What are you doing here?"

"Dad," Jake answered for the both of us, though he didn't take any steps to close the distance between himself and his father. "Maria called to say that you'd had a heart attack. How are you? Who are your attending physicians? Where's...Mother?"

"It wasn't a heart attack. It was just a little chest pain. I'll be out of here tomorrow." Mr. Wu pushed a button and the head of the bed rose about a foot. "Since you're here, you can call my assistant. I don't have my phone, and without it, no numbers. I need to talk to her about some problems at the plant here. There have been all these protests from people talking about pollution and the environment. No such problems in China. Also, you'll need to call there to handle the issues with a delayed shipping container, and—"

Jake held up a hand, putting a halt to Mr. Wu's lecture.

"Father, there's probably a reason they won't give you a phone."

The air from the hastily opened door lifted the hairs at the nape of my neck. Before I could turn to see who it was, my mother strode in like a woman on a mission.

"Darned right, there's a reason. He needs rest. I took that damned thing. Cemeteries are full of men who thought the world couldn't live without them. But look at us, living, and them...dead."

I couldn't remember the last time I'd heard my mother's voice. It had to be at least a year. When Francis Aconi had died, I'd sent her an e-mail. She hadn't replied.

"Isabella Maria Aconi, what in the hell are you doing here in Mr. Wu's room? You're not allowed—"

"Or what, Mama, he's going to disown me? Leave me stranded? Already did that. I'm not here to see either of you. No offense. I'm here to make sure that Jake was okay."

"Oh God, are you trying to be with him again?" She asked the question like I was the most pathetic girl on Earth, desperate for a boy who wouldn't have me.

I'd thought it was that for so long. But it wasn't that at all. If anything, *she* was that desperate woman, not me.

For the first time ever, I was sure of Jake's love. His devotion. Sure that no matter what life threw at us, he'd be by my side.

"We're already together, Mama." This time my voice was strong and clear—unwavering.

"Did you know this?" Mama asked Mr. Wu, like he was the omniscient leader of the free world.

"I am as surprised as you." His assessment of me was cool and appraising this time around.

"Do you think this is a good idea? He'll hurt her again," Mama said to Mr. Wu.

"*He* will hurt *her*? How is she a good match for him?" Mr. Wu shot back.

The two of them glared at each other, not even acknowledging that the people they were talking about were in the room with them.

Jake stepped forward, slicing his hand in a motion that halted their speech.

"Father. Stop it. Isabella *is* a good match for me. She's been the *only* good match for me. This isn't why we're here. This isn't how we'd planned to talk to you about this. But you're sick. Maria, what did the doctors say?"

"They're saying something about bypass surgery. Maybe triple or quadruple. I'm not sure I understood everything, but there's seventy percent blockage. He will be in the hospital for one week, if all goes okay. Then he'll be off work for six weeks at least. They'll do a check here. If all is well, he can be back to work in three months. That's why I called you."

"*That's* why?" Jake's voice was incredulous.

"You'll need to take over. Mainly the New Jersey stuff. You can stay in the house, of course. I'll get your room ready."

"Father, are you going to be okay? What's the prognosis?" I knew Jake and his father had their issues over the years, but I could hear the love and concern in his voice nonetheless.

"They say it's one of the safest surgeries. They do half a million a year in this country."

"Have you considered going to China? Are the outcomes better there?"

"He can't go to China. There's no one to take care of him there. He can get the best that money can buy in the US. They say the best options are New York Presbyterian or that school where you went in Philadelphia. What do you think? You'll have to help with that decision as well."

"Where is Min...where is my mother?" That honorific was Jake's attempt at equanimity.

"She's in Nanjing," Mr. Wu said.

"Did you call her?" Jake pressed.

"Not yet." Mr. Wu waved his hands dismissively, like Jake was asking about the Jell-O selection. "I didn't want to worry her. Her friends are visiting Mount Huangshan."

"They have phone service there."

"Later. Later. Can you go into the office?" Mr. Wu's voice dropped an octave, like he was going to dictate.

"It's Saturday."

"Monday, then."

"I'm going to find your cardiologist. Bella?"

"I'll help." Heeding his signal, I followed him to the hall. "What in the hell is that? Are they done pretending? Have they just cut your mother out altogether?" I'd always hated their hypocrisy, but for today, I wished they would have gone on pretending like they'd used to.

"I have zero idea. I haven't been home for more than a couple of days in years. And Min Li was always at the house when I visited. I'm going to have to call her."

"Do you think you should? It doesn't look like she's missed."

Jake winced at my characterization. "Her husband is slated to get a quadruple bypass."

I pulled Jake farther into a corner so that some doctors or nurses or whomever in the white coat entourage could pass.

"One thing I learned is that other people's marriages are just that—other people's. Maybe they've come to some kind of agreement."

"They didn't tell me."

"It's not appropriate to share with you. Plus, they're not the kind of people to share anything personal. You know that better than I do."

"So you're saying I shouldn't call her."

"If you think she needs to know, and really doesn't know. You could e-mail Liling and tell her that you'll be away a few days because of your father's procedure. Then you can be sure your mother will know, and she can make whatever decision she wants without feeling pressure."

"You think she'd feel pressure?"

"Do you think of all the people on Earth, somehow *she* doesn't know about my mother and your father? I mean, we've all pretended we didn't know what was going on. But we all knew. I'm guessing they made some kind of deal where they're socially monogamous. He gets to have his...I don't know...life here, and she gets to have her life there. Maybe she has a great guy who loves all her quirks and that's who she's seeing the mountain with."

"She...I've just always assumed Min Li was in the dark. Oh my God. I don't know anything about their lives, do I?"

"Do you want to? Keeping secrets was the worst part about living here during high school. Taking the gifts. Knowing they were bribes. You being sent away. Maybe they learned that keeping other people out of it is for the best. Or your stepmother has no clue he's been fucking another woman under his roof for twenty years. Take your pick."

From Jake's nod, I assumed he took in what I said and would consider it.

"I'm really going to find the doctor now. You'll be okay waiting here?"

"It's fine."

After he stalked off, I fell in one of the beige upholstered wood chairs, put my feet up on another and closed my eyes for a minute. Not because I was tired, but mostly to pull myself together. I was in the last place I'd wanted to end up. Yet I was here, and so far, the sky hadn't come crashing down around me.

Then I heard my mother's footsteps and reconsidered my good fortune.

"Where are you staying tonight?" was her second question after years of not seeing me. Was she missing the gene that fostered connection? Had she passed that defect down to me?

"Mama, I hadn't thought that far ahead. Jake was in such a rush to get here before visiting hours ended. To talk to the doctors and get information on Mr. Wu's condition. He's saying he's fine, and you're talking about quadruple bypass."

"You know Mr. Wu, honey. His manhood is all tied up in running those companies. He'll get the surgery. He'll be better, and his companies will be fine. He's a very smart and successful man. That won't go away in two or three months."

"I should go find Jake." I didn't want to have to get on the Mr. Wu cheer squad. I was happy to leave my mother alone with her pompoms.

"That boy is going to be busy a while. I'm really beat, though. Why don't you drive me home? I really would like to get a chance to talk to you. I've really missed you."

Curiosity won over my better judgment, and next thing I

knew, I was texting Jake and getting in my mother's car—a new or nearly new Woo DynoAutomotive luxury sedan. This one was a dark seal-gray color on the outside and full of smooth-as-butter leather and burled mahogany on the inside. I wanted to enjoy the smooth ride and nice appointments, but it felt like I was riding in a padded jail cell. I pushed down hard on the gas to cut this part of the trip short.

I didn't need any directions to make the drive, but when I turned onto Old Freehold Road, everything was different. As if my childhood had been bulldozed in one fell swoop.

Where there'd been an open gravel drive lined with trees, now stood eight-foot iron gates, in front of even taller hedges. This rich man's barrier now signaled the entrance.

Mama handed me a slim white card. "Swipe it over that black knob."

I did, and the gates swung open like a cool embrace. When space allowed, I pushed the gas just a bit and the car crawled up multicolored pavers. In the place where the red-sided structures had stood, was now one large house. Probably fifteen to twenty thousand square feet, was my guess.

Once I pulled up to the top of the circular drive, I cast a critical eye about. I knew they'd bulldozed what had been there, but if there was only one house, where was my mother sleeping? At least when Min Li was there?

"Where do you live?" I asked.

"We can leave the car here. I'll have Albert put it away. I'm in my own apartment over Mr. Wu's office in the east wing. It has a guest room."

I followed her along an outside path, trying not to dwell on the convenience of them being less than a few feet apart for these last few years. Practically, it probably wasn't any different from him being in the main house and her in the guesthouse. Exterior walls hadn't been any sort of barrier.

Mama put a key in the lock of a side door. I followed her up a long staircase to another door. Inside was filled with Pottery Barn and Crate and Barrel kind of furniture—warm-toned, but not immediately inviting. The kitchen was the same. It was tastefully decorated. It also looked like no one really lived there, kind of like a luxury hotel room. Our guesthouse had had a comfortably worn-in sofa, and all sorts of Italian bottles of oils, vinegars, wines and liquors had lined the counter.

Maybe she'd put everything away, but I suspected that the kitchen of the main house reflected Mama a whole lot better.

"I have some iced tea." Mama bustled about, opening and closing drawers. "Let me make you a plate. You're very thin."

I sat silently at her kitchen table, next to plantation shutters as she put together a platter. In a few minutes, she had *panino con porchetta*, some cheese and some olives, along with the previously offered tea. Hunger tore through me at the familiar food, and before I knew it, I was halfway through the pork-filled sandwich.

"This is good. Thanks," I said around my last mouthful before I set the food down to wipe my mouth and take a breath.

"So, you and Jake." Mama's sigh was dramatic and drawn out.

I braced myself. Jake's instinct to get out in front of this with our parents had probably been right. But if I could have avoided this conversation with my mother forever, I would have.

"Don't beat around the bush." I took a last sip of tea, wiped my hand with a napkin, then beckoned toward Mama. "Out with it."

"I'm happy for you. You guys have always belonged together."

I was glad that I'd put my drinking glass down, because I'd have dropped it otherwise. I nearly fell off my chair in disbelief.

"Seriously? Mama! You said that he was just playing with me or using me or something like that." Those words had hit very hard when we'd been on the way to the clinic.

"Was I supposed to be happy taking my Catholic daughter to get an abortion?"

"You have a point. I made a mistake back then." I was no longer filled with regret, but there was still a bit of shame I couldn't shake.

"You were sixteen. I'll assume now that you have your wits about you."

"I won't have an unplanned pregnancy." If there was one thing I'd mastered completely, it was birth control. Well, that and pencil skirts, which were probably their own form of birth control.

Mama's face softened. "Now, Isabella, that wouldn't be such a bad thing."

"I'm not sure I'm ready—"

"No woman's ever sure." Mama took my hands in hers. Squeezed hard for emphasis. "It would certainly tie you two together. You wouldn't have to work again. Especially if you get married."

"I don't mind working."

"Owen was a fancy school, I'll give you that. But it didn't give you any particularly useful skills. Managing the Wu house is honest work, but I don't have the kind of security you could. If you married Jake, Mr. Wu couldn't really fire me, could he?" Her voice got whisper-conspiratorial quiet. "We'd both be set for life."

"Mr. Wu does pay you, right, Mama? Haven't you saved all of that money over the years? You're probably pretty well off in your own right."

Fortified with the strong iced tea's caffeine, I was doing some rough and dirty calculations in my head, and she had to have at least half a million stashed away somewhere.

"I have a little bit of savings put away. Most of the cash I've put into Dyno. Bought shares. He said those would be worth more than any interest I could earn from the bank."

Is that how he got women to stick with him, I wondered? Took their money. Invested it in his business. That way their fates were tied to him forever. I'd thought he stayed married because Min Li was the rich one. Maybe it was just about keeping all these women tethered to him.

"I don't want money from Jake, Mama. It was never about the money."

"You love him. It's fate, kismet, soul mates or whatever. I get it. But don't overlook the obvious benefits. They say it's as easy to fall in love with a poor man as a rich one. You fell for a rich one. You've hit the lottery. If he comes in and takes over the business, we'll probably all be better off. Mr. Wu can retire, and you two can live here while Jake takes home a CEO salary. I've seen Mr. Wu's taxes, and his salary is nothing to sneeze at."

I didn't want to talk about Mr. Wu. It was like being back at Julie House. I wanted to talk to Mama about her own autonomy. She probably needed to break the bond as much as any of the Julie House clients did.

"Have you ever thought of moving back to Philadelphia?"

"What? Philly? I couldn't afford to live there now. It's gone and gotten all gentrified, hasn't it? Like all the other big cities. Young hipsters like you paying high rents. I couldn't even afford it when Francis Aconi threw me out of my very own house."

I let go of the young hipster comment and soldiered on with the idea I'd been working through the last couple of months.

"I inherited the house, Mama."

"*What?*"

"The house on Pemberton Street. In the eyes of the law, I'm still Francis Aconi's daughter, and I've inherited the house. He never sold it. It's been a rental all these years. Between that and odd jobs, that's how he supported himself in Italy."

"I can't believe it!"

"I know, Mama. I get half of his estate. I've put aside a little bit of money, enough that I could buy Arturo out. Buy the other half, and you could live there free and clear. Just taxes and utilities. You could make a fresh start."

"What would Mr. Wu do without me?"

"Hire another housekeeper, Mama. You say that you

think I should marry Jake, so I'll be set. How about I give you this house, and you'll be set without needing a man." I shouldn't have said the last, but I couldn't help myself.

"I don't know anyone in Philly." Her face looked panicked. "I don't have any friends there."

"Maybe you could pick up with some old friends. Everybody's kids would be grown up. Probably a lot of old friends from high school who have empty nests and time on their hands. Even if you don't hook back up with them, you could make new friends. It would be a fresh start."

"I don't know..."

"What if Mr. Wu goes back to China, Mama? Then what?"

"He wouldn't leave me," she whispered. "We're almost as good as married."

"Oh, Mama." All of my fears for her were bound up in those last words of hers. In my heart, I knew she couldn't pack a few boxes, move to Philly, turn her back. But I'd hoped the idea would sit with her. Give her that security she so sorely craved. Move her to make a different choice. "Good as married" scared the crap out of me.

"Don't 'Oh, Mama' me. I know it's unconventional, but it's what I have. Feng Wu has loved me and taken care of me for almost twenty years. That's longer than a lot—a LOT—of marriages.

"Thank you for the offer of the house in Philly. I haven't always been there for you, but it means a lot that you'd think of me. You don't need to worry. Mr. Wu has promised that he will always make sure I'm taken care of. Right now, my place is here, helping him recover."

"I think I need to go," I said. I didn't have anywhere *to* go, but I needed to not be here where my mom was stuck like a fly in amber.

My brain scrambled for purchase. Maybe I'd get an Uber or a cab to the hospital and figure it out from there. But staying here was a no-go. My mother and common sense had long parted ways. There was no way for me to bring the two back together. It wasn't my responsibility. I'd tried.

"Where? The guest room bed is already made up. I keep it neat in there."

The knock at the door couldn't have come at a better time.

I rose and strode to the front entrance. Jake stood there. A bit disheveled. A lot sad.

But he was there.

For me.

"I'M sorry that you're sick." I kicked myself for sounding so stiff and formal, but what did a son say to his father after a heart attack that was going to disable him for months?

"I'm not sick. It was only an episode. The doctors will do a procedure and I'll be back at work in a few weeks."

Sounded to me like he was minimizing his pain. But I didn't have time to deal with his denial. I had to work with the facts before me. That fact was that he hadn't involved his legal wife of thirty-plus years in life and death decisions.

I didn't beat around the bush. "Have you called Min Li?"

"I didn't want to bother her with this." He waved his hands in a way that said he was firmly into minimizing his health rather than owning up to what it really was—a serious, life-threatening heart attack.

"Father, she's your next of kin. She needs to be here...to make decisions...in case."

"In case of what? Got me dead and buried already? Going to take over my job?"

I wanted to both laugh and cry at Father. The thing about life is that we all know that no one gets out alive, yet death is always a surprise. Even though I had a lot of ambivalent feelings about Father and how he'd moved us all around like pawns in his game of relationship chess, I wasn't ready for him to die just yet. Not the least of which was because I wasn't interested in becoming the head of Woo's various enterprises. I'd gone along as the expected heir apparent for years. It wasn't until I'd become serious about Bella that I realized I wasn't interested in following in my father's footsteps. He'd never believe it, but I wanted a different kind of life.

"I'm not interested in taking over your job."

Father's look, even partially obscured by a handful of tubes, was cutting. "Still playing at entertainment executive?"

"I have enjoyed my work there," I admitted cautiously. "But I'm ready to roll up my sleeves and do what needs to be done here," I said. I was unwilling to leave him high and dry, but that didn't mean giving up the rest of my life, either.

He nodded, satisfied that I'd fallen in line.

"Four weeks. Six tops. You'll have to be here, though. Someone else is going to have to take care of things in L.A. So you won't be able to see Isabella during that time."

Of course he hadn't been privy to Bella's change of career or any of that. Wasn't the kind of thing he'd have bothered himself with finding out. I could see that he was trying to control us the same way he'd had for all those years when I'd let him.

"My relationship with Bella isn't up for discussion."

"Why are you still chasing that girl? I can't see how she's any good for you. Why don't you just fuck her already and get her out of your system? You're getting up there in age and need to settle down. Start having children."

If sleeping with her had been the antidote for my feelings, I'd have been cured a long time ago. Being with her had only made me crave more.

"Father, Bella is going to be that person."

"Good God, are you serious?" Father's face was a mirror of what I imagined Min Li's would be when she found out.

"As a heart attack."

"That's not funny. You wouldn't be so insolent if I weren't tied to this bed with these tubes and wires."

His threat was hollow. Physical intimidation had never been his thing. Emotional manipulation had been his specialty. I had thrown off those shackles, though. For the first time, I was thinking freely, doing what I wanted without regard for Father's irrational feelings.

"I love her, Father. All that you've done to keep us apart hasn't worked. So we're going to give it a try...being together."

"She...she's..."

"Careful, Father. Were you going to say she's only the housekeeper's daughter? Because the housekeeper seems to be good enough for you."

"I'm not sure what you're talking about. We have a strictly professional relationship, Maria and I."

"Do you think I'm blind, deaf, as well as dumb? We walked in on you, Bella and I. It's not the kind of thing we were likely to forget. Maria Aconi is still employed even though you have a new housekeeper from Nanjing who handles the heavy work and most of the Chinese cooking. Am I supposed to believe the 'house manager' bullshit?"

"Language! You were not raised in this way. To talk back. To use bad language."

"My language isn't the problem here. Your infidelity is. There's no amount of money or stuff you can buy to keep us quiet anymore."

Father wilted back onto the raised mattress. I wondered if he were truly tired or if it were an act. I hated myself for doubting his sincerity, but in many ways, he was the man who cried wolf. I didn't know when to believe him or when to disregard his self-serving lies.

His sigh was long, edging on pitiful.

"I have a weakness, okay. Maybe it's excessive hormones. Maybe I'll talk to the doctors here about it. Maybe they can give me a pill that will set it all straight."

"You needed that pill thirty-six years ago."

"This again. You're full of yourself today."

"Maybe what I'm full of today is the truth. I'm tired of brushing everything under the rug, hiding from reality."

I was happy when the door opened and a woman in purple scrubs bustled in.

"How are you feeling, Mr. Wu?" the nurse whisper shouted like he was hard of hearing.

"A bit tired."

"Are you in any pain?"

"Only a little."

The nurse turned a tiny plastic knob on a clear plastic

tube connected to an IV drip. In moments, Father was visibly relaxed. The pinch in his face from his earlier agitation gone.

"Visiting hours are over in forty minutes," the nurse said to me, her urging that I leave not subtle. "He'll need his rest, to get his strength up for the upcoming bypass."

"I won't stay long. I'm going to be handling his affairs during his hospital stay and recovery, and just need to get a bit of information."

"No business is worth jeopardizing his health, okay?"

"Got it," I said. She took the hint, wrote a couple of things in his chart, clicked it back into the holder by the door, and exited.

"Baba." I'd barely uttered that word in years. "Tell me about my real mother."

Father's sigh was long and deep. For at least a minute, his lids came down over his eyes, remained closed. I took a seat at the bedside, wondering if he'd fallen asleep and I'd missed my opportunity. He wasn't asleep though. I could tell when I touched his shoulder and he flinched slightly.

Resigned, he opened his eyes and looked straight at me.

I braced myself.

"My father used to sell fish to lots of nightclubs and other similar types of establishments in Shanghai. For years, when I wasn't in school, he'd take me along. It was important to him that I knew how business was done. How to make sure you could deliver to your customers on time. Also to make sure that we weren't cheated. It took me a long time to realize that while some of the clubs were legitimate, many weren't. It's how he made money. In exchange for his discretion in their business, he would charge them a higher price, but also keep his mouth shut when the authorities came sniffing around.

"There was a girl who was at one of the clubs. I met her when I was young, before I met your...before I met Min Li. I loved her, or at least wanted to spend more time with her than the few minutes we shared during deliveries. So I would sneak out to see her.

"In the meantime, though, I met Min Li in college, and Father insisted that she would be a good match. I met Min Li's father, and he admired my business acumen, and gave me a job after graduation. Min Li and I got married even though I was from a poorer family. Her father allowed it because he could see that I had enough ambition and drive to make sure Min Li never lived any lower than he could provide for her.

"But I still visited this girl and, as American's say, one thing led to another. She became pregnant. I was distraught, frantic, because I didn't want to have to tell Min Li's father that I needed money to pay this woman. At the same time, though, he was paying for doctors from all over the province to find out why Min Li wasn't becoming pregnant. She has some problem that's left her barren. Her father wanted male heirs. I brought him to Jian Mei Zhen's establishment and made a deal."

"Her surname was Jian?" I was stunned. The clue to my origins had always been right there in front of me. In what I'd been called every day that I could remember.

"I gave you her name to honor what she'd given to us."

If my father and Min Li's father were involved, the word "give" wasn't. They were businessmen, not philanthropists.

"How much?"

"What?"

"How much did you pay her to have her give me to you?"

"Two hundred thousand yuan."

I nearly fell back from my perch on the thin hospital blanket. That would have been a small fortune thirty-five years ago. The equivalent of thirty thousand dollar would probably be a small fortune for many families in China now.

"I thought Chinese babies were cheaper." I couldn't help my sarcastic rejoinder.

"You were not sold. We were solving two problems. Min Li and her father wanted a child and heir. Jian Mei Zhen couldn't continue with her job and have a baby. She was able to leave the profession and not have the stigma of having a baby with no father."

"All tied up in a neat little bow." I didn't need to try too hard to imagine the looks of smug self-satisfaction the men had probably shared.

"It was the best for everyone. You were born and raised with all your needs fulfilled. You'll inherit a fortune and a legacy you can pass on to your own children one day."

I'd been bought and sold like a new Mercedes and Father didn't see a single thing wrong with it.

I needed some space.

"I'm going to call...Min Li." I rose. Pulled my phone from my pocket. Began backing out of the room.

"I hate it when you call her that. She's always been and will always be your mother, Wu Jian. I really don't think you should disturb her vacation."

"She needs to be here. Maria Aconi is not in a...position

to make decisions for you, if you can't make them for yourself. I'm not either. In America, next of kin is the wife, not a first son." This was a lie. I knew that the doctors would be happy to make me the on-hand decision maker. I didn't want that burden on my shoulders, not when his wife was far more capable of doing so.

"Fine."

"Where does Maria stay?"

"She has an apartment in the house. Min Li stays in a guest room next door to my own bedroom."

I didn't know why he'd provided that last bit of information. Were they all in some tacit agreement to maintain the status quo and never talk about it? Had Min Li given up, resigned herself to second fiddle in Father's private life? Had Maria done the same calculations, okay being excised from Father's public life?

It was no wonder he'd had a heart attack. I certainly sped up my heart to think about having to put Bella in one box and another woman in a different box. Although as I had the thought, I realized that's exactly what I'd done with Bella. She'd been the woman I'd lusted after in private, while keeping Liling on my arm in public.

If I hadn't been resolved years, months, or even hours ago, I was now one hundred percent sure I would do anything in my power not to repeat my father's misdeeds by disrespecting all the women around me.

"Starting on Monday, I'll report to your office in Toms River. I'll make sure there is someone assigned to head up manufacturing and marketing here, the same in China, and also find someone take over my responsibilities with CBT."

"That's my boy. I knew that you'd step into my shoes one day. That day has come a little sooner than I thought it would, but now I can rest assured that everything is being taken care of by someone in the family who has skin in the game."

"You get six weeks. Eight tops." I was happy to set a firm boundary. Draw a line underneath my own obligation.

"What? What are you talking about? I may need another month."

"I promise to put the right people in place who can handle it. It's eight weeks max. Take it or leave it."

"Where are you going after that? Running back to Los Angeles and that girl?"

"I don't think so. I'm going to step down from Woo."

This wasn't at all the way I'd planned to tell him, but it was probably better to manage his expectations now, rather than have him be disappointed later.

"Did you have some kind of attack too? Do I need to get you a bed in this place?"

"I've put my life on hold for far too long."

"On hold? What are you talking about? You make no sense."

"My life with Isabella."

"Wu Jian..." I could see that his exasperation was starting to outweigh his exhaustion.

"This is not up for discussion. Every argument you have against this? I've already had with myself. I want to focus on something other than the love of the almighty yuan or dollar."

"Don't look down your nose at the money that has supported you for all the years of your life."

"I'm not going to get into a discussion about how I'm supposed to be grateful for you putting food on the table or sending me to school. That's the least responsibility any parent has. Your obligation, however, has ended. I'm taking over from here."

I don't know if Father's look was one of grudging admiration or drug-induced calm, but either way, I took it.

"I've driven a long way today. I'm going home to call... Mother...then get some sleep. I'll visit tomorrow and on Monday I'll be at Woo."

I didn't ask if he had any questions. I didn't let him serve up a plate full of objections. As a man, I was doing what I needed to do to protect my future, and I wasn't going to let a single thing jeopardize that.

Emotionally and physically exhausted myself, even though I wasn't the one in the hospital bed, I took the rental car to the house. After I got the *other* housekeeper to make the necessary arrangements for me to work in Father's place, I followed Father's instructions and found my way to the Aconi apartment. When I knocked, Bella, looking as exhausted as I felt, answered the door.

"Did you call her?" Isabella asked without preamble.

"Yes. Ten minutes ago from the house. I wanted to wait until it was morning there."

"Did she know?"

I shook my head. "She's going to get on a plane from Shanghai as soon as she can swing it. She'll be here tomorrow or day after at the latest. She's his next of kin. She's also a majority shareholder. Father's medical treatment, how to run the businesses going forward. These are her decisions to make."

"So does that mean you're not going to take over?"

I could see that she'd been bracing herself for that kind of decision. That I'd go back on my promise to her and us and get sucked right into Woo. I looked her directly in the eye.

"I made a deal with them. I'll take over for Father for the next eight weeks. The doctors say we'll know pretty quickly if he can return to work or if a longer recovery is necessary. I'm thinking retirement is probably the best bet. So I'm going to work on a succession plan."

"Aren't *you* the plan?"

I wonder how long she'd warred with herself, thinking she'd have to choose a life like her mother's or give me up. I was happy to clear up her misconceptions that we'd be a carbon copy of our parents.

"No, Bella. I'm not the plan. I don't want this. I don't want to be Father in thirty-plus years, sitting in a hospital bed, the only thing of importance in my life a job and a woman I can't publicly acknowledge. I have something completely different in mind."

"What?" The weight of our future was held in that single-word question.

"Hear me out before you say anything, okay?"

"Okay."

"Nothing about us has ever been conventional. I don't know how it would work, us in New York. Us in Los Angeles. Us in Shanghai. But I do know a single thing. Us...you and me...we *can* work."

"I think so, too. I was unsure for a long time, but I'm starting to think so."

"In order for us to work, we need time. I can't be at Woo Industries or at CBT and dedicate the time we need. On my death bed, or my hospital bed, I can't imagine thinking, 'I wish I'd sold more portable air conditioners, or more cars, or more commercial time.'"

"Okay."

"Can you give us a year?"

"A year?"

"Together. None of the places we've lived have ever really felt like home. I want to travel the world. Find out who we are together. Find *our* home."

"Like nineteen-year-olds backpacking through Europe?"

"No. Not like that. Let's rent a place. Maybe London or Paris or something like...Scandinavia... Copenhagen, maybe. We'll settle somewhere and then figure out the rest. I think we need a change of scenery to really make a go of—"

"Yes!" Bella exclaimed, interrupting my poorly rehearsed speech. "I'll do it."

"Seriously? I thought I'd need to do a lot more convincing."

"Take yes for an answer. Don't talk after the close. All of that."

"Okay." I couldn't help the smile that probably split my face. She was saying yes to us. After all these years, we were finally going to have a chance. My body was so light, I felt like I could float away if I didn't keep both feet on the ground.

"While you're here, I'm going back to New York. I need

to find a replacement for me at Julie House. Also, I want to buy the Philly house."

"The one your Dad left both of you."

"That one. I want to make sure that my mom has a place to go. I know that she didn't do that for me. But I want to do this one thing for her. Make sure that she has a place to land. But I'll need a favor from you."

"Anything," I said, and meant it.

"But I haven't even asked."

"Bella, I've known you more than half my life. You've never been unreasonable." Except about us, but that one was both our faults and wasn't worth mentioning.

"My mom has all her money tied up in Woo. I'm not sure how many shares she owns of what entity, exactly, or how it happened, but if you could unsnarl it and get it into an account for her with only her name on it, I'd appreciate it. If she has a house, and she has that nest egg, I won't have to worry about her and your father. She's sure he'll take care of her. Maybe she's right. But I want her to have a backup if she's not.

"Shares in Woo. Why would she..." I tried to make some sense out of Father taking her money, but couldn't find an answer that didn't involve the words manipulation and control.

"I have no idea. Didn't make much sense to me. But I'm not going to probe that. I want her to be safe is all. This is not any kind of indictment of your father."

"Maybe he *should* be indicted."

"Let's just say that Mama's vulnerable, and I want to protect her in the way she didn't protect me growing up. All that I ask is that you don't share this with her. Okay? She'd tell your father, and it would all probably go to shit. If and when the time comes, *I'll* share it with her. Until then..."

She didn't need to continue. Even if I had to cover the cost of the shares myself, I'd do what she asked.

"Consider it done."

EIGHT WEEKS LATER...

I RAN my hand first across the honeyed wood dining room table, surrounded by royal blue upholstered chairs. Then walked to the counter and smoothed my hands along wood cabinets that were similar in color to the table and chair legs. It was like walking into an upscale version of Ikea.

"Danish modern is a real thing."

"Not just for the odd furniture shop in Soho," Jake agreed. He'd lugged our bags up to the apartment from the cab, and was standing a few feet from me, glass of tap water in hand.

"A real thing," I continued awkwardly.

This was it. We were where we'd talked about being in August. Only now it was October. I'd sublet my Brooklyn apartment and taken a leave of absence from Julie House. Jake had done exactly what he'd said—done an eight-week stint at Woo.

Mr. Wu was recovering and working part time. Min Li had surprisingly stepped in and was doing everything Mr.

Wu couldn't. She'd probably learned a lot at her father's knee. I had to wonder how frustrated she'd been to be sidelined from both intimacy with her husband and putting her considerable knowledge and business acumen to work. Having to subvert her ambitions into shopping, turning that into a profession.

It made me sad to think of it. I made a promise to myself that while Jake and I worked on being a couple, I'd also figure out what would bring me professional satisfaction. Like a three-legged stool or a four-legged table, I needed those other wooden posts to assure I was completely fulfilled.

"Nervous?" Jake asked after I'd been quiet for a few minutes. I *was* nervous, but didn't want him to know that my fear of being emotionally vulnerable with him was paralyzing me.

"Maybe cold?" I lied. "Who moves to Scandinavia in October?"

"We do." His answer spoke the truth in a way that made me shiver with anticipation.

"I'm going to run upstairs and change. Can you see what we can order in for dinner? We can go shopping in the morning, but after the flying and whatnot, I'm a little too tired to do it now."

Back on the other side of the Atlantic Ocean, I'd been ambitiously planning to shop and cook the minute we'd landed. Now exhaustion was starting to wear me down even though I'd tried to sleep on the flight.

"No problem."

I took my time getting freshened up. Lingered in the hot shower. Slathered on my favorite lotion as an armor against the cold, dry weather outside. Then I slipped into some silk thermals. I'd started sleeping in them when I'd been in Amsterdam. The fabric was luxurious against the skin, not itchy like cotton or wool could be. Silk was surprisingly warm. I paired it with a fleece bathrobe and hoped that Jake didn't find me too repellant. A relationship required effort, but jet lag was winning out against my inner diva.

"What's that smell?" I asked once I came down the open stairs into the kitchen/dining room area. It was a heady combo of meat and potatoes and butter that was waking up my appetite.

"*Mørbradbøffer.*" Jake stumbled over the mouthful of foreign-sounding syllables. "That's a mouthful I probably messed up. Anyway, I found an app that promises food from any local restaurant. Picked one and asked what was the best thing on the menu. This is what they sent."

"Language a problem?" I'd spent enough time in Europe to know that many people spoke English, but I wouldn't have been lying to say that I was a tiny bit worried I'd stick out like a big American sore thumb here without the barest minimum of Danish.

"Nope. English works everywhere. That's one thing I'm glad that Min Li forced me to do."

I sat at the dining room table where he'd laid out dishes and cutlery. If there was one thing that had changed about Jake, it was his unflinching honesty. He'd given up on the pretense that everything in his family was perfect.

In one way, it was a huge relief. I was finally getting to know the real him. On the other hand, it threw my own circumspection into sharp relief. Part of me wanted to be open, share everything with him. But even with his reassurances, I feared his judgment. It wasn't like I'd been sitting home crocheting during the years we'd been apart.

When it was possible, I tried to gloss over my past with Daniel. I'd tell stories about trips and experiences, editing Daniel from the picture. When the issue of money had come up, like how we'd pay for this year abroad, I ponied up my share, but didn't disclose how I'd gotten the funds. I'd let him assume it was savings, but that was a white lie that could only go so far. A reckoning between us was coming.

About money.

About love.

About sex.

About us.

I was bracing myself for all of those hard conversations in the next months.

I helped myself to some dinner and poured all the beer from one bottle into the tall glass in front of me.

"There were good things about growing up with them, right?" From the outside it had seemed like a pressure cooker.

"Of course. I never wanted for any material things. I had a top-notch education from some of the finest schools in the world. Like most parents, I suspect, they did the best they could."

"Maybe that's the difference money makes. Your parents smoothed over their indifference or self-indulgence with boarding school. Mama couldn't do that. I just had to suffer up close and personal."

I wondered if jet lag had dampened my filter. Normally I'd have never said any of that out loud. Suffering, I'd always felt, had to be done in silence—alone. But laying this tiny bit of the burden on Jake made me feel so much lighter that I wasn't sure I wouldn't do it again.

"I'm sorry that it was hard for you," Jake said. He grabbed my hand with his and held it for a long time.

When comfort unexpectedly gave way to arousal, I pulled my hand back and took a long sip of beer. "Can we save this for later?"

"I thought you were hungry?"

"Jake. Let's go upstairs." I lowered my voice so there was no question about my meaning.

He was out of the chair before I could get out my last syllable.

"I haven't wanted to push..."

And he hadn't. We'd held hands. Kissed. But until tonight, I hadn't been ready for more even with the crushing guilt that I'd done so much more with other people *and* him.

"You're not pushing. I'm just ready right now for more."

Jake pulled me toward him, wrapping me in a hug, his front to my back. There was no mistaking his interest in the physical side of our relationship.

I pulled away slowly to approach the steps that seemed to float between the open-plan living area and the upstairs hallway. I walked to the first door and pushed it open, exposing a large white bed covered with a smoke-gray duvet. Except for some faint light from the skylights, the room was thrust in shadows.

I knelt on the bed and flicked the switch of two small overhead electric tea lights.

"Is it too dark? Too cold?" My nervousness causing me to be overly concerned with ambience.

"It's perfect, Bella. Anywhere you are is perfect."

Those words, probably meant to soothe me, only wound me up further.

"Oh...okay."

"Come here." He beckoned me toward him as he moved closer to the bed, closing the gap between us. "I don't care about the light or temperature."

I swallowed, tucked my hair behind my ears. Jake knelt on the mattress. It sank a little under the weight of us both. He cupped his hands behind my head and pulled me in for a kiss.

It was electric. Stubble tickled my jaw. A shiver coursed through me. Suddenly, I wanted more. I slipped my hands under his sweater, pulled the tee from his waistband and rubbed my hands over his chest, slipped around toward his back. He skin was so very warm.

I wanted to feel all of him against all of me. This time, I was determined that I wouldn't miss a single thing. I was going to focus on savoring every second that we were together in this way.

When I leaned back slightly, breaking contact, Jake's eyes were just a bit dazed. A surge of desire shot through me. I'd done that to him, made him lose his concentration even for just a moment.

I crossed my hands and grabbed my hem.

"Bella. Let me do that. Let me undress you."

I let go and his hands replaced mine. They grazed my belly, which caused butterflies to flutter everywhere, so much so that I didn't notice my shirt was going up until it was under my arms and neck. Dutifully, I lifted my arms and the silk whooshed over my head.

"No bra," whooshed from Jake's lips.

"No bra."

"Jesus, Bella." Gently, he laid me on the bed and came down next to me.

"Take off your sweater. I want...I want to be close to you. Skin to skin."

He sat up and his layers were gone in an instant. When he lay back down against the pillows, I traced a hand against the side of his neck, between his pecs, toward his belly button to the top of his pants, which bulged with his erection.

I pushed my thumb against the button of his jeans waistband until it popped from the stiff denim. Carefully, I eased down his zipper.

"Let me make this easier for you," Jake said as he lifted himself and shucked his blue jeans.

"Can I?" I motioned towards the boxer briefs that were barely containing him.

"Anything you want."

I propped myself up on my elbow. "I had a dream, while I was on the plane."

"What would make your dreams come true?"

"If I had your cock in my mouth," I admitted. It had been one hell of a sexy dream, which I would have happily finished if it hadn't been interrupted by the flight attendant asking if I wanted a light snack before we landed.

"By all means, I wouldn't want to stop you from living out your dreams."

I took yes for an answer and pulled his briefs down until he sprang free. I fisted my hand long the bottom of his shaft, taking the top half as deep as I could. I'd never been as turned on by any man as I was by Jake at just this moment. His taste and smell were both utterly familiar and utterly arousing at the same time.

"Is this okay?"

"God, Bella, this is more than okay. Okay is not a word I'd use when your mouth is involved."

The laugh that came from my throat surprised me. I couldn't remember sex ever being fun. It had been a job or something serious to prove my feelings, but this time it was pure, unadulterated fun.

Jake sat up and pulled me up. We kissed again, and we rolled around until I was lying under him, his lips doing magical things to my neck, my collarbone, my breasts. I nearly came off the bed when his mouth closed on one of my nipples.

"Jesus, Jake!"

"I want to make you come."

"What about you?"

"Don't worry about me. Your pleasure is important."

"Oh...oh." I couldn't tell what part of him was making me crazy. Whether it was his lips or tongue or fingers or just exactly what it was. Before I could catch my breath, an orgasm completely overtook me.

But Jake didn't stop.

"I can't—"

"You can. Does it still feel good?"

"Yes."

"Then let me."

And he did—two more times.

"I can't...I need a minute to breathe."

"I'll go get a condom," Jake said.

"You don't need it."

"Oh God," he groaned. "Are you sure?"

"I have an IUD, Jake. We got tested at the hospital."

"I didn't know. But I'm happy. Sex is so much more intimate this way."

He took his cock in his hand, working himself.

"I want you inside me, now," I begged. It was the only way I could figure to fulfill the deep need he'd sparked in the last months.

"You feel so good. So amazing. So creamy inside. So much mine."

Those words got me going again. Even in my exhaustion, the next orgasm crept up slowly, then took over, obliterating everything around me but Jake. His face in ecstasy. His golden skin gleaming in the glow of small lights.

Every cell in my body vibrated in time with his slow and deliberate thrusts. His hands gripped my hips, pulling me just that tiny bit closer, my ankles resting on his shoulders. I'd never felt as open and vulnerable as I did right at this moment.

"So good... So good, Jake."

"Yes."

"Harder. Faster!"

Jake accommodated my demands. His eyes closed. I watched his throat as he swallowed in pleasure.

I have no idea how much time passed. Two minutes. Ten.

But with each thrust, with each caress, it felt like my heart was cracking open. I let tears roll down my cheeks.

"You okay?"

"More than okay, Jake. More than okay. I never thought I'd get what I always wanted."

He lost his tempo, and in moments I could feel his warm seed filling me.

"Jake, I've always loved you." I spoke the truth. I spoke from the heart.

"Bella, I will always love you."

We lay in the dark, cooling off. It was perfect. *We* were perfect. I was finally living a life with no regrets...and it was good.

JAKE

ONE YEAR LATER

"WHAT'S THIS CALLED AGAIN?" Isabella asked. She was a few steps ahead of me, looking at the intricate patterns of the sculpted hedges I'd always associated with the British or Japanese. Scandinavians also liked a formal garden, it seemed.

"Frederiksborg Castle. It was built in the sixteen hundreds." I'd done a lot of research before choosing this location.

She shaded her hands over her eyes and turned toward the tall and imposing building at the end of the path.

"Old then. Well, old for America. Not too old for Europe or China, right?"

"Not too old," I answered, trying to hide my nerves. I was taking a really big risk with my plan, but no risk, no reward was a lesson hardwired into me from living with Father. It hadn't been one I'd worked to shake. I was glad of that. It was risking my heart and rejection that had gotten me to where I was today with Bella. I was glad I'd had the guts to take that first leap. Now it was time for a second.

"How many hours a week do you think it takes to keep all these hedges clipped?" she asked breezily.

I'd wanted to be casual, but I couldn't keep up with her walking or her conversation until I got everything out in the open. Until our future was cemented.

"Bella, I need to talk to you about something."

"Okay." She stopped in her tracks. Pivoted. Waited until I'd caught up to her. "I'm not sure I like the sound of that."

"Your mom is moving to Philadelphia. I put your proposal to her." Sadly, I knew that if the suggestion had come from a Wu man, Maria would take it more seriously. I hadn't been wrong.

"What?" I watched all sorts of emotions flit across her face. Last year, she'd have hidden her feelings, but not anymore. And in this year, I'd learned to read her feelings as well.

"Father's going back to China."

"After all these years?"

"His heart is acting up again. He needs to lower his stress. So, he's going back."

"Oh, Mama." Anguish filled Bella's voice. I understood it, because I'd seen Maria's devastation behind her mask of cool civility that she'd always worn with me.

"I put the money aside like you asked," I offered. "It's one million."

I hadn't had the time or inclination to untangle Father's Maria money web. Instead, I'd done a rough and dirty calculation of what she should have earned all these years and put that amount of stock into a money market account.

I'd advised her to buy an annuity to live the rest of her time in relative comfort. But I'd left the ultimate decision up to her. She'd had enough paternalistic care over the years.

"Dollars?"

"If she's prudent, it should provide for the next twenty-plus years."

"Thank you for helping her out. How...how is she?"

Bella had forgiven her mother...from a distance. I understood how hard it was to forgive a parent who'd betrayed you for years, so I'd decided to give her and her mother's relationship wide berth, only dispensing advice when she asked, which had been never until this moment.

"Maybe you should reach out." I spoke softly. "She's alone."

"She never made any friends?" Bella asked, though I knew she already had an answer. Father had been her sole companion. She shook her head in frustration. "He was the center of everyone's universe, and now he's taking his toys and going home. Is your mother...Is Min Li...how does she feel?"

"She's staying in Nanjing."

"So all three of them are alone?"

"I don't think so. Min Li has a boyfriend no one's allowed to talk about."

"She'd kill you if she heard you use that word."

"Probably. That's not the only thing I want to talk about," I said, trying to control my heart rate and breathing, both of which were increasing so rapidly I was getting light-headed. Despite that, I plowed on. "I need to show you something."

I took Bella's hand, still amazed that she was willing to be mine. But I was ready to end the uncertainty. I was ready to change our story's trajectory. I pulled her inside the castle, which had been converted into a natural history museum.

"Wow. This is a lot," she said while craning her neck to see the gilded, coffered ceilings.

"Let me show you the chapel." I pulled her along, quickening her slow pace because if I didn't get to the chapel in a few seconds, I was going to burst.

"The chapel? I left the Catholic church behind..."

"It's historical. We're not going to attend mass or anything."

I pulled her into the massive hall, more gilded ceilings over our heads, these with religious paintings to accompany the decorations. She took in her surroundings swiftly, not paying much attention to detail, for which I was grateful.

While she looked away, I retrieved a box from my pocket and put a single knee on the marble floor.

When she turned back, she frowned a bit.

"Why are you on one knee?" I could see when it dawned on her. "Oh, God, Jake. We're not...you don't have to..."

For the last year, she'd insisted that we didn't have to get married, have two-point-two children, get a house with a white picket fence. I'd agreed on the last one, at least. But I hadn't thrown all things traditional out the window just because our lives and courtship had been anything but.

"But I do. I know we're not conventional. We never have been. There comes a time, though, when I think we have to put away our past. I want to build a future with you. Where our kids are born into a stable family relationship. Where their parents are happily married. So, I have to ask you. Bella...Isabella Maria Aconi, will you marry me?"

I could see her hesitation, then the single moment when she decided that she, that *we*, were worthy of a beautiful future together.

"Oh my God, yes. Of course!" She smiled when I slipped the simple diamond band on her finger.

Then the room broke out in applause.

"Turn around," I implored.

At that point, people rose from the red velvet pews.

Her mother stood, then Julie, then Mother and Father, and even several of my friends, including Cole, who'd been there at the start of our journey together.

"What's happening?" Bella's voice was full of confusion.

"If you'll have me, we can get married today," I answered. After lots of internal debate on my part, I knew in my bones this was the best way to do it. Neither one of us was the kind of person who'd have thrived on planning a big party over months or years. So I'd hired a planner who'd put this together. Now the only obstacle to our future was getting Bella on board.

"Today?"

"There's a room that I've prepped. Three dresses. Hair and makeup. In one hour, I'll be waiting here for you. Are you game?" I stood, brought her close to me for a hug. Whispered in her ear, "I'll always love you, Bella. This is not only for us, but for everyone else to know that we've chosen each other. If you say no, my love for you will never change."

"Yes...yes..." she whispered back in mine.

"Then let's do this."

It was the biggest chance I'd ever taken, and I had no regrets.

The wedding wasn't perfect. Especially with our parents there, faces full of tension. Maybe even having Cole there was a mistake. But it was the life we'd had, the life we'd learned to accept, and the life we were going to share in the future.

As I stood and said, "I do," I couldn't wait for what was to come.

♥

Thank you for reading **WHAT WAS TRUE.**

I loved this trilogy so much. Isabella is my heart. If you love crazy, beautiful, love stories like I do, then you'll want one-click TAMING THE BAD BOY now!

Sometimes good girls do bad things... Can Ivy League Daisy tame bad boy comedian Raphael? Or is Ivy League out of his league?

"Read it. Loved it. The depth of characterization is beautiful. The story feels rich and real. Two flawed individuals that fall in love and must overcome their own personal challenges and resistance to love."

—*USA TODAY* BESTSELLING AUTHOR
MAGGIE MARR

ABOUT THE AUTHOR

I write crazy, beautiful love stories because I believe story-telling is magic. I love complicated heroines with secrets, strong heroes who fall hard, and a long winding road to happily ever after. When I'm not writing, I love to travel to witness the diverse tapestry of humanity, photograph the beauty of the world, visit museums, and watch live theater. I live in West Hollywood, California ten miles from the nearest airport.

xo Jolie Moore

♥

I haven't found my own happily ever after, but I'm not done trying. This year I'm going to go on fifty first dates. Join me as I try to find my Mr. Right or maybe Mr. Right Now. #50first-dates #joliemoore #crazybeautifullove

Sign up here to get weekly date updates as well as new release notifications.

joliemoore.com/50firstdates